SIDEWAYS 3 CHILE

First Edition Design Publishing

Sarasota, Florida

Sideways 3 Chile
Copyright ©2015 Rex Pickett

ISBN 978-1622-878-45-1 PRINT
ISBN 978-1622-877-63-8 EBOOK

LCCN 2015932583

February 2015

Published and Distributed by
First Edition Design Publishing, Inc.
P.O. Box 20217, Sarasota, FL 34276-3217
www.firsteditiondesignpublishing.com

Cover Design: Darryl Glass / Solution 111 Design
Author Photograph: Azul DelGrasso

SIDEWAYS 3 CHILE

A NOVEL

BY

REX PICKETT

PART I

Prologue

At a certain point in my life I reached the ineluctable conclusion that the only truth I believed in was the immortality of my despair.

I have been called every name on the planet: intense, troubled, a *flâneur* (their word was probably *layabout*, but I like *flâneur*), driven, dipsomaniacal, mendacious and a mendicant, taker not a giver, an artist, a loser, the worst writer on the planet (by nasty, underpaid senior editors at publishing houses), "gifted," "raw talent," "a great lover," a "terrible boyfriend," accused of writing from too personal a place ... I've heard it all. Still, I persevere.

I, on the other hand, naturally, see myself differently. I'm generous to a fault. I let others take advantage of me—also to a fault. Yes, I sometimes ruefully believe that I've been persecuted, ripped off, driven to the St. Vitus's Dance at what others have done to my work, or how they've taken credit for things they shouldn't have, the litany of complaints go on. Because writers are at the front line of the creation, the ones who roll up their sleeves when there is nothing, a blank page staring them obstinately in the face, write against seemingly insuperable obstacles, of course they often feel abused.

My name is Miles Raymond. I'm the writer behind a character in a novel that was made into a cult movie that's set in wine country somewhere north of Santa Barbara. A plethora of individuals made a lot of money off my creation. I got the short end of the financial stick. I'm not complaining. If I thought about it, I'd go mad. If I chronicled the injustices, it would make me come across as ungrateful. As the director of the movie of my book advised, "Learn to meditate." I'm learning to meditate. To move on. To continue to live my life in a sanctuary of sanity as the vultures wheel in the cobalt blue sky, waiting for my next creation so they can swoop down and pick at my bones with their raptor beaks. One more time.

I long for the beaches of Costa Rica. I long for a woman who will both understand me and lustily engage in the mutual pleasure of uninhibited sex. I don't think this is asking too much, do you?

Women

She just walked out the door. She has wheat-colored blonde hair and Baltic blue eyes, tall, athletic, a former standout soccer player for her college. She kisses and fucks like you wouldn't believe. Her ardor is frightening. Her liberated manners in the bedroom—and other rooms!—are refreshing. Her energy and imagination vie for depths of boundlessness. When she lets go she can be a screamer, but never a faker. She's married.

I've come to the somewhat fatalistic realization that I have a thing for married women. Let's face it, they mate like dolphins. Starved for affection and no longer constrained by the ethos of the

'50s when infidelity was tantamount to sin, they fornicate with abandon. Maybe they're getting back at their philandering hippie fathers and their sex-deprived mothers and reversing history, I don't know. All I know is that they come to me, without commitment, wanting only a little companionship, conversation and cunnilingus, then they slip into the mysterious deep of their complicated marriages—which I never ask about because I don't want to know— only to return after a flurry of salacious emails with a smile on their faces and a willingness in their hearts.

They're attracted to me because I don't want a relationship with them. I don't want them to fall in love with me, and vice versa. They prefer the security of their quotidian married lives. But they love the thrill of these ephemeral trysts. Now and then I fall in love with them, and that's when it's time to leave.

Katherine had that quality about her. To me, she was haloed with sex appeal, bonhomie, haunted beauty, and a full-throated loving attitude—when she was around, which was only a fraction of the week. I knew I was breaking my rule and falling in love with her when I started to miss her. My heart would sink whenever she slipped, usually in a rush, into her Range Rover and silently motored off into the night. No, I guess I didn't want a relationship. I wanted to be able to protect my eremitic writing life. But then love goes where it will; the arrow can only follow!

I vowed not to get involved like this again, but then it just happened. Katherine came along in an almost incandescent daze. At an event I was hosting she strode up to me and introduced herself. Later she would confide that her husband had come to the dinner with her, but, surrounded by fans wanting their books signed, I don't remember seeing him. We exchanged business cards. We started emailing. Then we started seeing each other. I told her I might be heading to Chile to research a novel on the pretext of writing an article as the wine columnist for *Town & Country Magazine*. She wished she could go. Sometimes, lying in bed, her face flushed, she would straighten at the waist and say, "I'm going."

"Katherine, you're not going. It involves too much."

She gave me a sideways look and said with a stressed smile, "I love you, Miles."

"I love you, too, Katherine."

She held open her hands and stared at the emptiness of them, bemoaning her fate. Her husband was a semi-famous film director, worth millions. In my face, the face of her lover, she saw it all slipping through her hands like minnows: the Range Rover, the AMEX black card, the Frank Lloyd Wright in the Hollywood Hills with the turquoise pool, the kids she was debating having that I would never consent to. It was all a fantasy and we both knew it. What she didn't want me to say was that it was over.

Me

I never said I was likable. Personable, comedic, perhaps, but in fact I've always risked being unlikable. If only I could find a starting point for my journey to redemption.

I'm not amoral, but some have accused me of espousing immorality in my writings. To them I say: I think we live in a complicated world where we are forced to fashion our own rules of morality as we trundle along. My goal is not to hurt anyone and not to take credit for anything I didn't do, like some perfidious producers I know. I like to be treated fairly, but know that I won't be. Life is not a meritocracy, as one only has to spend a lifetime, like I have, in the entertainment business, to affirm.

I have no regrets. I get the odd writing job here and there. I still maintain a patina of fame, even if I have to call it to others' attention, since I'm not physiognomically recognizable. But when I do, it can be a dopamine rush all its own. And end with me in bed with someone too young, too sycophantic, with screenplay or novel manuscript thrust out in her hand, my hand clutching my head, nursing a sledgehammer hangover with the memory of an opium addict.

I'm not unhappy, but I am dogged by melancholy, oxymoronic as that may sound. I realize I have fewer years left on this planet than I've already (mis)spent. I'm not one of those types who feels life owes me anything. I feel privileged to have come this far and never worked an honest day in my life. My hands are free of calluses and my face isn't fissured by the sun. The scars to my psyche and my heart may be another book all together, but then no one who is sensitive to the cruelty of life's vagaries goes unaffected. I'm not privileged in that way. I've got stories to write and I've been afforded the opportunities to write them. I've been fortunate that a few times some undefined deity has shone down on me with its refulgent light and put me, however momentarily, in its spotlight.

I was beginning to get lost in the labyrinth of my ruminations, starting to suck the marrow of my own brain. Time to call my friend Jack.

Jack and I

I realized I hadn't gotten off the couch since Katherine left. My cock still ached from her frantic, clock-ticking, riding of it, and I could still feel where her absence hurt. I shook off the salacious image of her hair splashing on my chest, remembered my mantra about not wanting to get involved, then called my friend Jack if for no other reason than to hear a familiar voice.

"Miles, how are you?" Jack boomed, recognizing the number.

"Jack, what's happening?"

"Not much. How's the married chick?"

"Hotter than hot. But I think I crossed the Rubicon."

"No, Miles. No! You can't do that. It's against the rules."

"Yeah, I know, but the woman's hot, and love is that one thing that C. G. never understood."

"C. G. as in Jung?"

"*Absolutment!*"

"Well, be careful, dude. The fucker's a famous film director, and I don't doubt he'd put a tracking device on your car. Or a nanny cam in your bedroom of sin!"

"I'm well aware of the risks. I trust her for some damn stupid reason."

"You trust too many people, Miles. You're naïve, gullible, a romantic. Look what that fucking producer did to you ..."

"Let's not go there, Jackson. What're you up to?"

"I'm writing a screenplay."

"Oh, no. Say no. Not a fucking screenplay. You're kidding me, right? You're not a writer, Jackson, you're an actor, a director, epigone though you may be."

"All right, Mr. Killjoy, I get it, I'm not a writer, not a hotshot one like you, but I had this idea. And it's not a feature, it's a pilot."

"Well, that cuts your workload in half."

"And you've got all those agents on your end ..."

"Do not go there, Jackson. You use your connections. Last script I read for a friend and wouldn't pass to my agent he started screaming at me on the phone. That was two years ago. Great friend. Haven't heard a peep from him since."

"I'm just asking you to read it and give me your professional advice. I'm not begging you to hand it to anyone that might jeopardize your now precious reputation, forget the fact that it was yours truly who got your book to Mr. Howard CAA whatever ..."

"Whomever," I corrected.

"Fuck you, short horn."

"I'll read it, big guy. But I'm going to tell you exactly what I think."

"And I would expect nothing less."

"Good. Now that that's settled, what else is happening?"

"Not much. The kid is growing."

"That's cool." I didn't feel like asking him about his son because I knew it was a sore point, what with his ex, Babs, dumping him after yet another indiscretion. There were roads we had taken and roads we didn't need to turn down anymore, cul-de-sacs that they had invariably become. And that was our shorthand. "Hey, would you like to come to Chile with me?" I asked out of the blue.

"Chile."

"Yeah. Chile. *Town & Country* is sending me down there to research an article on their wine industry. I have never been south of the equator."

"How're you going to get on a plane, short horn? It's been a few years, hasn't it?"

"I'm doing Biofeedback, exploring meditation. Did you know that 50,000 commercial flights take off and land every day in this country and not"—

"Okay, okay," he said, exasperated. "I get it, you're realizing what the rest of us already know. Flying's safe!"

"Right, sorry. Didn't mean to ramble."

"How much coffee have you had today?"

"Chile. Interested?"

"I don't know, Miles. I've got a lot of shit going on here."

"Oh, like what? Your TV pilot? Shit, man, I could write that with my left pinkie on the flight to Santiago."

"What about that Spanish chick Laura? I thought she was going to tag along?"

"She's coming, too. We'll be a threesome. And if you get me on that flight I'll let you have a crack at her."

"I'm not putting my dick where yours has been."

"How do you know that isn't already a *fait accompli*?"

Jack let out one of his barrel-chested laughs. "I miss you, brother."

"I miss you, too. Think about Chile."

"I'll think about Chile."

"And I'll read your damn TV pilot, even though I know it's going to suck."

"Fuck you. You might be surprised. This writing thing's not that hard."

"Yeah, right. Later."

Waiting for the Bus

I was on my second cup of coffee, waiting for the Mercedes limo that was coming to my door here in Santa Monica to take me and a dozen ridiculously young executives of some hot Internet start-up on a day and a night tour of the Santa Ynez Valley where my novel was set, and which turned my life around. Well, completely around, because when I wrote it circa '99 I was dead broke. Now, once again, I was dead broke. Only this time I was a semi-famous author who was dead broke, which meant I had more opportunities to make money.

Chronicled in many interviews where I wore my heart on my sleeve and spoke too freely, liberated by too much wine, I talked about how fame had gone to my head. Privately, I was on a celebratory party after a decade of deprivation and destitution and all the other great words that begin with D: depression, depravity, despair, darkness, dismay—don't you just love those D words? Yes, it had been a rough decade. My beautiful wife and I had parted company; my mother had suffered a massive stroke, my younger brother had assumed control of her care and, in two years, had fleeced her of all her savings and, with it, my modest little trust fund; my agent died of AIDS; I started having socially crippling panic attacks and had, as a consequence of my affliction, turned into an agoraphobic, as well as an aerophobic and whatever they call the phobia where you think you're going to die of a heart attack every ten minutes. Cardiophobic?

I had hit rock bottom, floored out. It didn't look promising. A few close friends continued to funnel me some money to keep me afloat in my rent-controlled home, but it was tough sledding for a 40-something, and those few close friends were running out of patience. Immured in my poverty, I had nothing to do but write. And write I did. Like a prairie fire in a drought. First, a mystery novel that landed me a prestigious publishing agent. And though we couldn't sell the damn thing it galvanized me to write the book that became the movie that changed my life. I had suddenly gone from the breadline to dancing on the rim of the world, celebratory parties with movie stars—which is where I met Katherine. But I didn't know how to rein in success. A decade of deprivation had transformed me into a libidinous louche who spent lavishly on women I wouldn't remember the next day. I wound up bankrupt, alone and trembling with the jimjams. The climb back was slow and arduous, Sisyphean at first, but every day I started to inch along, make some progress. But I was still stuck on that next novel. I needed all new faces, all new settings, all new colors, all new sounds, all new voices! I needed Chile. But I also needed someone to get on that plane with me.

As I waited for the bus to pick me up I got on the phone and dialed Laura, the Spanish woman I had met on an ill-fated trip to Oregon with my now deceased, but at the time wheelchair-dependent mother. The last time I had spoken with Laura she had gotten angry that I couldn't get on a plane to Barcelona to see her. The plan this time, with a generous advance burning a hole in my secret bank account, was to fly her to L.A. and from there we would go to Chile.

"Hi, Laura, it's Miles."

"Hi Miles."

"So, have you thought any more about Chile?" I knew unemployment was running high in the Euro community, especially after the worldwide economic recession of '08. And I knew that Laura had lost her teaching assistant job in film at the university.

"I don't know, Miles." She paused for effect. "I've been kind of dating someone."

"Oh. I guess I've been out of touch." For some reason her words made me feel like a toilet with no water in the tank trying to flush. "I see."

"So, if that was the understanding, that there would be no, you know, then I might still be interested."

New love interest, huh? Fuck, this was getting complicated. With my left hand I rooted around in the front pocket of my jeans and clasped it around my vial of Xanax, my "placebo-in-waiting." I finger-wrestled open the cap and shook out a 1 mg. tablet into my now free hand with my cell resting between shoulder and ear, crushed it into particles with my teeth and then let it dissolve below my tongue for maximum deployment of advertised calming properties.

"Look, Laura, I don't care if you have a boyfriend. I just need someone to go with me to Chile, a traveling companion. I've never been south of the equator, you speak the language. Frankly, it's less complicated that we wouldn't be a couple. So, do you want to go? I'll get you a ticket to L.A. And then we can fly from here together to Santiago."

I could hear her inhale and exhale. She was probably thinking about what she was going to tell her boyfriend. I knew she needed something a little more to seal the deal. I was desperate. Jack was a flake. He's the kind of guy who might show up at my door with a suitcase ready to go, or just as likely procrastinate until exasperation drove me to the nearest wine bar.

"Look, Laura, I'll pay you to be my assistant. All expenses paid, plus $2,500 a month, tax-free."

"All right, Miles, when do we go?"

My phone beeped and I noticed a text message. It was the Internet crowd and their waiting limo. "Two weeks, Laura. I've got to run. We're going to have fun. I'll email you your ticket. Tell your boyfriend I have no interest in licking your pussy."

She laughed.

"Goodbye."

Self-Destruction

I'd been meaning to get a handgun in the event my circumstances turned dire again and I had no recourse but to take my own life. Bridge jumping didn't appeal to me. The planning would give me panic anxiety and the five seconds of the fall would only compound my sense of indecision, knowing that there would be no going back. And, what bridge? The Golden Gate would make me a cliché, or give others an opportunity to accuse me of grandstanding, seeking sympathy, or worse. Gassing myself was out of the question. That would have to involve drugs, unventilated spaces, and what if I got an important email notification while I was waiting for said terminal sedative to kick in? I doubt that that would happen, but it would surely have me lumbering into the kitchen slamming closed the oven door, then rushing around my apartment and opening all the windows and doors. Pill overdoses I deemed boring and sort of a distaff method that usually ended in failure.

No, I decided a .357 magnum was the way to go. To the temple, sayonara. Maybe a note. "To Whomever it May Concern: I don't want people to think I'm crazy or bitter. But there are people out there who tried to take control of my life and I really don't want to live in a world where they reside." Something to that effect.

But there was a 2-week "cooling off" period on the gun. So, I would wait.

Katherine in Extremis

I was packing for the corporate outing with the Internet dozen when my phone rang. My phone rarely rang. Thanks to a great app called Mr. Number, which I think should win the Nobel Prize for something, I could block calls from any prefix, or any specific number. I could even prevent them from leaving a message. God, I loved Mr. Number. My friends rarely called me. We usually communicated through email, sometimes texts. Conversation was reserved for tête-à-têtes in coffee shops. Telephonic relationships were pretty much dead. So when my phone rang it startled me. A Caller ID picture came up on my screen. I must have uploaded it when I'd had a few too many because I recognized the naked, bent-over, proffered-for-a-spanking ass of Katherine.

"Katherine?"

"Miles," she said in what I detected to be a panicked voice. Static from a one-bar connection crackling over the line only consternated me further. It was clear something wasn't right. Katherine never called me. She usually emailed me from a special account. "He found out!"

"What?"

"Robert found out."

"Fuck."

"He had someone put some kind of bug on my cell which tracked my movements. They had me pinpointed at your place for two hours." Her voice was breathless now as if she were running. "Someone photographed me coming out of your apartment."

"Jesus, Katherine!" I could already see her slipping away in my imagination.

"I don't know what to tell you, Miles, except: I'm sorry."

"We talked about this, Katherine. We had conversation after conversation about the need for utter secrecy and you let your husband bug your fucking phone?!"

"Miles, I'm sorry. I love you, I really do. Don't leave me."

"Don't leave you? If the fucker can put a tracking device on your phone, you don't think he can't take me out because I FUCKED HIS WIFE?!"

She went silent on the other end. All I heard was the roar of her Range Rover, a car I would never ride in again, like I once did to Palm Desert when her husband was on location in the Czech Republic for three months. God, what a car that was! And for my tripartite motto of the day: What a woman! What a world! What a waste!

"I don't know what you want me to do, Katherine. I'm not going to see you again. You realize that?"

"Don't say that, Miles," she pleaded.

"Look, I've got to go," I said, a sour feeling in my stomach, my brain pullulating fatalistic fantasies of being murdered or beaten up by a multiple Academy Award nominee. He wouldn't be that stupid. More likely I could kiss my Hollywood writing career goodbye. Thank God I put in that order for the gun. The truth is, I was going to miss Katherine. Call it pathetic, but she made me believe again in the power of love, even if it was just in the vein of a torrid affair that now was geysering like a slit carotid artery.

Surfrider Hotel

There are only two reasons you stay in a hotel in your own city: impecunious relatives are in town and want to bivouac at your place, or you're on the run. I was on the run. After Katherine's call I put together a carry-on, gathered up my laptop, and beat it to the Surfrider Motel in Venice. Once I was in my room I felt both a sense of security and anonymity. The TV flickered the numbing monotony of a golf tournament. The remains of a fast food meal littered the dresser. Looking around, I realized this was going to be my life for the near future. I decided then and there that I would give up my apartment, unload my books at a local donation depository box. I would put the rest in Public Storage and become a child of the world.

My cell kept importuning. On the third try, fearing a creditor, I took it. It was Katherine calling from a different number.

"What do you want, Katherine?"

She was crying. "Are you angry with me?"

"No, I'm angry with myself. If I hadn't had fallen in love with you, I wouldn't be feeling this shitty in this characterless Surfrider Hotel with my loneliness and all the rest. This was not the narrative arc I envisioned when we met up at that party at that actress's house in Bel-Air."

"I'm so sorry, Miles."

I hardened into a pachyderm. "So, what's going to happen, Katherine?"

"He says he doesn't want a divorce. But he's pretty angry."

"I can imagine. His wife screwing a has-been writer in a one-bedroom walk-up in Santa Monica. He probably thought you were better than that, Katherine!"

"It's not funny, Miles."

"If I don't laugh, I'll go mad. I still can't believe you let him have access to your phone. Jesus!"

"I'm sorry. I didn't think he was suspicious."

"That's what men do when their wives aren't fucking them. They go for the technology, attach tracking devices to your cars. If they're rich, they hire private investigators to do it for them."

"So, can I come see you?"

"Are you crazy?"

"No, I want to see you."

"No, Katherine. Even if you end up getting divorced I just can't have you in my life anymore. I know that sounds cold, but I have to end it for my protection. Besides, I'm going to Chile with the Spanish chick I told you about. It'll help me take my mind off of you."

"What?!" she practically shrieked.

"Laura, the Spanish chick I met on that long, booze-addled trip to Wisconsin via Oregon's Willamette Valley. We've stayed in touch. Now I've got this offer to go to Chile from *Town & Country*. They have an emerging wine region. I've never been south of the equator and I need a sea change, I need to get out of this rut."

"When did all this happen?"

"Katherine, look. I love you to death. You were never going to leave Robert. It was always an affair. I would have loved it if you had left him for me. We could have built a life together. Oh, sure, there would have been some fallout, I could have handled it, but ... look, here's the deal: we live in a complicated time. You'd get bored of my uncertain and insecure life. It's been fun for you to roll down out of the hill in your Range Rover to my crummy little one-bedroom and get the best sex you've had since, I don't know, you fucked that actor or whatever. But are you really going to throw away a 30,000 square foot home high in the hills of Bel-Air, with a view of the ocean to one side, and all of Hollywood to the East? The red-carpet premieres? The muckety-mucks? The private jet? For me? I don't think so. And is he going to let you go? I don't think so. He'll crucify you, then he'll crucify me with his fucking Hollywood omertà you'll-never-write-another-treatment-in-this-town-again hogwash and I'll end up the next *persona non grata* who doesn't even know exactly what happened to him. All because you left your phone on a kitchen counter and he grabbed it, gave it to his tech guy who downloaded a fucking app in mere seconds that now could track your fucking whereabouts. I'm not blaming you Katherine. It takes two to tango and all that bullshit, but you just royally fucked up my life. Not that I wasn't already, but I'm finished in Hollywood. Miles Raymond is fucking Robert Cross's wife. Great! Just what I needed to be pinging around the fucking Internet."

She remained silent. She was getting the full wrath of reality and none of the cotton candy of fantasy that had been the friable foundation for our unrealistic relationship. It was more than a wake-up call; it was a Norwegian barging out of his sauna and diving headlong into a snow bank!

"Look, Katherine, it's over. Try to minimize the damage the best you can." I hung up on her. What was she going to do? Call the cops?

Dinner and a Dilemma

I shambled down to nearby Shutters Hotel on the beach in Santa Monica, a hotel I couldn't afford. In the downstairs restaurant the Maître d' showed me to a table by the window. The Venice Boardwalk was at shoulder height from where I was sitting in the slightly sunken room. A scattering of tourists dotted here and there among the empty tables constituted my company. But the only company I really had was my own mind. My life was still out of control, but I was seeking peace. I took stock of everything. I didn't have a lot of money, and what little I had in various bank accounts the creditors were after—the cliché is true that artists are poor managers of their money. So poor that if they hand over their finances to professionals, the latter will rip them off, too, if they're unscrupulous, which most of them are in Hollywood. In fact, everyone in the film business is unscrupulous when it comes to money. They're only worse when it comes to taking credit for things they haven't done. I've heard the music business is bad, too. And though the publishing world enjoys this reputation for being a kinder and gentler world, don't believe it. What makes them particularly venal is that they'll back-stab you for pennies, not dollars. Fuck, I was so idealistic when I set out from UCSD for L.A. with dreams of being a writer and a filmmaker ...

The waiter interrupted me. I had been talking out loud! This is what happens when you spend too much time alone. He had to be in his forties, a rarity in L.A. for a waiter, so I suspected he was one of those moths (wannabes) to the flame (Hollywood) for whom it didn't pan out for but who now couldn't leave because returning home to Ohio or Texas or wherever would have been even more depressing, an admission of failure so catastrophic he couldn't bear to face it. He couldn't fake it. I could see the grief of a squandered life chasing a flicker of a dream in his eyes.

"How're you doing? Can I get you something to drink?"

"I'm horrible and, yes, I'd like a bottle of N/A beer, no glass."

I figured he'd let my *horrible* pass, but he didn't. "Why horrible?"

"Well, I was just caught on GPS *en flagrante* with some famous person's wife, I'm whoring out on a corporate outing that I don't want to do, and then I fly to Chile with some chick I only knew for a few days. How's your evening panning out?"

"Sounds like you could use something stiffer than a Bitburger."

"Yeah, but I'm off the sauce these days. Doctor's orders."

"Ah. Are you someone I should know?"

I told him I'd written *Shameless* in a kind of roundabout way that I was wont to do.

"You wrote that?"

"Yeah."

"That's one of my favorite movies of all time."

"Thank you," I said, lowering my head in a gesture of humility. "Are you in the business?"

"Actor," he said.

"Have you had any luck with it?" It was a rhetorical question given his current circumstances, but I thought it gracious to ask.

Since the restaurant was uncrowded it seemed to give him permission to launch into a very believable jeremiad about how he was cast in what turned out to be a long-running sit-com, but at the last moment the producer owed a favor or something, so he lost the gig, and since then he'd just been knocking around.

"That's a bum deal," I said, when he had concluded his sad tale of trite Hollywood woe. "You can be really good, but then at the end of the day it's all about luck and timing." We were poised to trade some war stories, which would only have dragged my mood down even deeper into the ditch, so I turned back to my menu and ordered the salmon.

My mind transited to other real estate. I hadn't written anything since that botched HBO pilot with the production company where the imbecile I was dealing with was the epitome of TV series development ineptitude. The pay, when it did come, sucked. I was paying out the nose for an agent, an entertainment attorney *and* a manager. 25%. Then, the Feds got wind of it and they swooped down to claim another 25%. Chile was looking better and better. The waiter's stem-winder had mildly depressed me. "Life's not fair," was all I could offer in solace. He seemed resigned to his fate.

I ate alone. Long-limbed, bikini-clad women swooshed by on rollerblades, bent at the waist, their legs reaching out in front of them, their arms swimming the air. They, too, would one day be dead, I thought. Or miserable. Or lost in a haze of drugs and other addictions.

Katherine at My Door!

I returned to my apartment as the light was falling and the streets were slipping into shadow. Parking was a bitch, but I poached a doctor's designated spot, making a mental note to get up early and move my car, lest I be towed. I clambered out of my modest Honda Fit—dubbed the "skateboard" by a snickering Katherine—and skulked through the alley and slipped through the back gate. I climbed up the back stairs as though they were booby-trapped. Inside, there was a sepulchral quiet, until I switched on a light. Crumpled on my couch was Katherine, a bedraggled mess.

"Katherine, what are you doing here?"

She held up the back of her left hand to show me where she had taken off her enormous engagement ring and wedding band. Then, she opened her right hand as if to reveal a small animal she had trapped. Instead it held the two rings. She set them on the coffee table. "I left him," she said.

"Or, he kicked you out?"

She picked up a wineglass and held it up as if to say, *C'est la vie.* Her face had the aspect of someone who was drunk. My heart, a moment ago in the doldrums, was suddenly racing. While she was thinking that perhaps I was glad to see her, at last in my apartment for good, ready to spend the night—an anomaly!—I wasn't. I worried that her husband's goons were hot on her trail. She held up a bottle of wine, a rare Burgundy from a glance at its label, she had helped herself to from "Robert's cellar." I shook my head. "Don't you want to celebrate?" she asked.

"No, Katherine, there's nothing to celebrate," I replied harshly.

She tilted her head to one side and threw me a desperate look. "I want to be with you," she said.

"Katherine, I'm going to Chile."

"I know," she said sharply. "With that Laura girl. How old is she?"

"Stop it." I crossed the room and sat next to her on the couch. If you back away from certain women when they're in a state of emotional extremis, they will often fly off the handle and go psychotic on you. I didn't need crazy. I needed a normalization of the moment, if that could be bought! "Look, I love you. I've loved you. But it was obvious you were never going to leave him. Now that he's found out, I don't want you here. The divorce is going to be acrimonious. And I don't want to be a tabloid side feature of it."

"You're not going to be," she said, "you're a writer."

I darkened to the serious: "I don't want you here, Katherine, is what I'm saying."

"Don't be like that, Miles." Tears clouded her eyes, unnerving me. I was afraid she was going to go off the rails.

"Katherine, come on," I said gently, stroking one of her dewy cheeks. "Think about me for one second. I've been carrying on an affair with a married woman whose husband is a rich, famous film director. Not that my career isn't already in jeopardy because of all the bridges I've burned, but this'll be the *coup de grâce*." I made her set her wineglass down because I didn't want her to get drunk on me and really unleash the emotional tsunami that was vibrating in the air like invisible tuning forks. "We've had a great year, Katherine. If you had left him of your own volition, and I wasn't part of this now ugly Pinter-esque configuration, we might've found some happiness together. But this is just all wrong now. You realize you give me no choice but to end this."

"Don't say that, Miles," she pleaded. "Please?"

"I'm scared," I said. I took her hands in mine and clutched them as though they were a pair of songbirds left for dead. They were perspiry and warm like a feverish child's. Mine were no doubt colder than the North Sea. "I'm scared someone's going to show up in the middle of the night and put a knife to my throat. I'm scared that someone's followed you. Jealousy knows no bounds. And I don't trust the rich and powerful. They have fucked me over mightily during the course of my so-called career. And your husband is one of the ones I fear."

"You don't have anything to worry about," she said in a beseeching tone. One of her hands withdrew from mine and migrated to my thigh. Erections were hard to come by these days but I felt a stirring in my lower extremities. Just a hint of lavender misted from her neck as she leaned forward for a kiss. I kissed her lavishly lush mouth reluctantly. But reluctance is only a transshipment staging ground for the bigger dopamine delivery to an introverted and lonely writer like me. And she knew it. She kissed me again, and this time I let her. She had a full mouth that nearly swallowed mine. Her surge sagged and she held her face close to mine. "Can I come to Chile with you?" she asked.

"No," I said. "You have a lot to deal with here. And I think we need some time apart."

"You do?" she said, her hand now cupping my cock, which had sprung to life.

"Yes. And tomorrow I have this corporate outing back to the scene of the crime with a dozen of these new technocrati from here in Silicon Beach. And I got to be up for that."

"Feels to me like you're up for something else," she said with an atavistic smile as she groped for my cock in my jeans.

My resolve was like an a compulsive drinker's at a high-end Burgundy tasting. "I can't see you after this," I said.

I don't know if it's loneliness, the end of the road of a relationship, no matter how clandestine and transgressive, the thrill of sex in a life where only so many encounters will be vouchsafed you and your DNA knows it, or what, but, as if she were an elegant spider and I had tumbled into her perfect silken web, I fell off the wagon.

Goodbye sex is better than hello sex because it's fraught with the desperation of two entangled lovers who no longer have anything to lose. Kisses are more intense, tongues pull each other's faces closer like grappling hooks and weld them together. She'll suck your cock as if were a totemic artifact promising her eternal life. With alacrity, you'll go down on her as if it were the nectar of the gods and bring her to a Frankenstein-coming-to-electric-life climax. The fucking will cover an entire king-sized bed as if it were an emollient, equatorial ocean. Linens will be trashed with your sweat and semen and thrashing bodies. And when it's over, it's as if you'd died and gone to hell. The hell of the emptiness of your already missing her. You feel guilty that you caved, but resigned to the long ten paces to the bathroom and the final shower together.

Katherine got what she thought she wanted: an exclamation point to her surprise visit and the glimmer of hope that once she had taken her husband to the cleaners in the bitter divorce I would hang around for the millions and the house in the jungle hillside overlooking a beach in Costa Rica where we had dubiously planned to make art together for the rest of our lives. As the warm water streamed over me and she hugged my naked body from behind all I could think about: is this what will stay with me in the ICU when they hang the morphine and send me to Davy Jones's Locker because the cancer's too advanced? No, I'm going to think about the novels I've written and the movies I've made, no matter how wretched. I'm going to think about the ones I truly loved, and the ones who cared about me. I hope to God I'm not going to think about the mendacious producers who fucked me over, the horrible decisions I made that cost me money and derailed me from my chosen path. I hope, when the smiling oncologist turns the stopcock on the IV drip and the fluid commences its downward movement, that I leave this earth with no regrets. I hope to God I think about the laughter I brought to people, but not the heartache from the drinking and all the infidelities and horrible lies and inebriated *I love yous*'s. I hope to God I'm laughing at something funny I coined instead of shuffling through a lifetime's experience of turning the majority of women I had slept with into nothing more than physical spittoons.

The New Technocrati

All night long I thrashed around as if afflicted with rheumatic fever, thinking about Laura and the complications of that relationship. The thought of the two of us in Chile had ignited fantasies in me of maybe one day finding passion and romance and a soul-mate—cerebral and aesthetical—all in one package. Was it possible? I had fucked up with Maya, a beautiful woman from my past, because I thought she was the love of my life, but drinking and celebrity had derailed that dream from the tracks when I took a corner at a frightening mph, and now here I was, facing the prospect of spending my final days in a state ward getting hosed down by Filipinos, taking jobs that I didn't want to take—TV pilots with imbecilic producers that went nowhere; speaking engagements where I wore out audiences with my bawdy stories that I knew from heart and spit out with a robot-like banality. My life should have been a picnic, but it was anything but.

4:00 a.m. is a horrible time to pop awake. It's between nowhere and nowhere. It's too early to get out of bed and pretend you're going to make anything useful of the day, and it's often too late to pretend you're going to return to the ostensible peace of sleep. Regrets hounded me like ravening animals. I sucked the marrow of my own brain seeking answers to the perplexity of my wrecked fate and spiraled-out-of-control aspirations.

Somehow I managed to slip back into the cold coffin of my troubled sleep. I struggled to pull the day into any semblance of shape. The limo bus would be arriving with the dozen technocrati who had signed up for the ultimate *Shameless* tour with the author himself, a one-off my business partner had promised me, but I knew he had designs for more.

I spent the day dodging creditors with sophisticated new apps that blocked their vituperative entreaties. I wrote a handful of emails to various people, but I knew it would be hours before they got back to me. I dreaded the arrival of the Mercedes limo party bus that Kevin—30's, single, shameless *Shameless* fan—had rented. The payday was decent: $5,000 for 24 hours of spinning anecdotes and answering questions that I had answered time and time again. My Smith & Wesson wasn't going to be ready for pickup for another week, but there was comfort in knowing I had an out if I couldn't get on that plane to Chile and all else failed. I was already missing Katherine, I was strangely eager to hook up with Laura, but anxious about seeing a woman I hadn't seen for months—damn Internet, we wouldn't have been able to maintain a relationship were it not for this new form of communicating and I would have been on to something else.

The text came for me from Kevin announcing the technocrati's arrival. I picked up my carry-on and trudged down to the alley to meet them. Kevin, bright-eyed, new short haircut, bounced out of the huge black limo bus and pumped my hand enthusiastically.

"How're you doing this morning?"

"Good," I lied, hoping I had raked the dishevelment out of my hair with my hand.

Kevin slid open the colossal side doors. Some of the dozen or so IT people—they all worked for some Internet start-up that had to do with adult beverages—disgorged from the van and fanned out into the alley. There was a Dave and a Jason and even a Morgen (quite cute, and I made a note of it!), and more names that I wouldn't remember. They ranged in age from early twenties to early forties (the COO or CFO, I would keep forgetting), and I shook all of their hands and forced a succession of smiles. They had already started the short vacation with some serious vinous imbibing. Though an introvert by nature, the extrovert, dutifully, broke out in me and I pretended to find them all amusing. I tried to be humble in the tsunami of their encomiums for my work. It's always gratifying, but it does get tiresome at times. Mostly what I was thinking about was how am I going to get through this fucking thing? The $5,000 payday and the need to address some bills and other debts galvanized me to adopt an amiable demeanor. Besides, not a bad gig when all you have to do is be yourself for twenty-four long hours.

We piled into the limo bus. Kevin was at the wheel, which I thought was a little odd. I assumed we would have a driver, but maybe he needed the money, too! Since the collapse of the worldwide economy desperation was omnipresent, except maybe— as I threw a backward glance to the dozen technocrati who had ponied up for this one-off corporate outing—the new *nouveau riche*, the Google guys, the coders, the M.I.T. software engineers who controlled the fate of the world, the startup geniuses, this whole new generation of wealth that was co-opting art and bohemian-born cities like San Francisco and New York and Santa Monica, bringing their wealth, pushing the people who made those cities the cultural centers they once were, and then trying to imagine that they belonged somehow. And all overnight. I had nothing but contempt for this new generation. And here I was, a supposedly—in their eyes!—successful novelist who had written a book in the depths of despair, a despair they would never know or experience as their souls rotted in the hell of 0's and 1's, and somehow had miraculously found its way to a famous film director who turned it into a little gem of a movie that had charmed, apparently, the world. Now, these young aspiring Luddites—yes, Luddites, they loved their Royal manual typewriters as decorative art, their boho facial hair, their artisanal coffee, imagining themselves the new Beatniks— wanted a piece of my soul, not knowing, I hope, that I had fallen on hard times and would not have been on this corporate write-off junket in a million years if I didn't need their filthy lucre. I, the new millennium court jester, turned around and smiled like I imagined a motivational speaker smiled, "How is everyone?"

There erupted a chorus of good cheer from the crepuscular back, their shapes cast in shadow by the tinted windows and drawn curtains. Some raised wineglasses in a toast to this 21st Century version of Ken Kesey's Merry Pranksters bus. To them I was their modern day Jack Kerouac and they were the New Age wake-and-bakers and acid-heads who would go along for the party before settling down with spouses and kids and mortgages and nasty prescription painkiller habits that they would have to detox in $50,000 a month luxury rehab centers in Malibu. Should I disabuse them of their grim futures? I tried to humor myself.

On a flat panel TV suspended just over the front seats they were watching my movie, apparently for the umpteenth time because they were performing a kind of *Rocky Horror Picture Show* shouting out of lines in sync with the actors. Music from the soundtrack made me both nostalgic and nauseated. I had seen the film many times—at red carpet premieres, at film festivals, in theaters after it had opened, then finally, pathetically, on DVD at home with a date who had a dream to fuck a supposed celebrity who provided her running commentary while filling her head with Pinot and saccharine words of endearment that would have no meaning in the morning. Not only no meaning, but often no recall! That was the worst.

We rode down to the Coast Highway and headed north through Malibu.

"I used to come up here," I started my rote narrative, wanting the time to pass, wanting to entertain, the laughter emboldening me, "when, if I could have afforded a gun, I would have shot myself!"

Morgen, one of only two women on the corporate outing, was sitting directly behind me and whispered in my ear, "Was it really that bad?" There was wine on her breath and a dagger brandished dangerously in her heart.

"Oh, you don't know the half of it!" In a rising voice so everyone could hear me, "So, I used to take off in my rattletrap Honda Accord with no window on the passenger side. You see, once I had locked myself out of my car, but I had to get home and I'd had way too much wine, so I just put an elbow to the thing to get inside. But, then, when I woke I realized I didn't have enough money to get the damn thing fixed. But the good news is, I didn't need A/C! Which didn't work anyway!" They were jackknifed over in their luxury lounge seats now. I threw a backward glance and some of them were elbowing one another in the ribs, chortling "Do you believe this guy?"

We were past Malibu now, and I was roaring with the incoming surf. The great Pacific Ocean loomed on our left. Recent rains had drawn a dramatic line between a cold blue sea and milky white sky that made me dream of a time when I used to come up here alone, how beautiful the drive was, and how I longed for that time that I was anonymous, albeit destitute, but truly free. Now, I was a captive of my fame. Life had grown more expensive, the past was weighing on me. The specter of Death loomed on the horizon. I mean, I once believed I could read the world's literature and now, at an average of two books a month, I calculated I had less than a thousand novels I could read, so I'd better pick them wisely. Ditto for movies. The sand was trickling out of the hourglass at an alarming rate.

I affected a beaming smile that belied what was really going on in my dark imagination. "Hey, let's get this party started." Kevin threw me a disconcerted look. He knew I had a penchant for going down the rabbit hole of drink and the hair-raising consequences. "It's okay, man," I said *sotto voce*. "I've got it under control. I'm a professional." I turned to the rear of the Merry Prankster bus: "Someone got a glass of Pinot there? I've got a thirst that needs slaking!"

Cheers rocked the van! The celebrity was letting his hair down! Woo-hoo! A wineglass was passed up front as if by firemen performing the bucket drill. I held it up. "Here's to your fucking Internet start-up, what's it called?" Beat. "Soul-suck dot com?!" Raucous laughter. Heck, I thought, self-deprecation is not a dying art. I took a sip of wine. It had been a few months and I could feel the dopamine jolt and surge to the lonely receptors. I was on a roll now. I raised my wineglass: "This is to you, the new technocrati, the death of all aesthetical pursuits, a future forged in server farms and transfixing LEDs where the soul knows only death." I finished off my wine and handed it back. "Ramp me up, folks, let's get this show on the road, shall we?"

In the tenebrous light of the passenger section I glimpsed expressions of both doubt and humor. They were no doubt wondering whether I was deliberately offending them or if this is how artists behaved in the 21st Century where they are on the brink of superannuation. I decided to quell their collective apprehensions.

"Wine is the blood of Christ. Wine wrote the novel the film was adapted from that you're watching now. Wine will liberate you from the shackles of your quotidian mediocrity. You will find sexual partners you never dreamed of sleeping with. You will go down dark paths. You will explore your creative unconscious. Nothing will stop you from becoming the person you always wanted to become. Wine will lead you to the promised land. A toast?"

There was nervous laughter. Then, everyone raised his wineglass and we clinked all around as promiscuously as we could. Kevin had an uptight look of disapprobation brewing like a thundercloud on his face when I glanced over.

"Don't worry," I reassured him. "They love this stuff." I sipped some more wine, then looked out at the marbling sky. After a moment I felt a tug at my sleeve and turned around. Morgen made a gesture with her hand as if gripping an exercise ball, signaling I should come closer. I leaned in to her. Her hot wine breath emanated from her pretty face, and she whispered something salacious.

My eyes widened. She had to be two decades my junior. I mimicked her hand gesture and she leaned closer. I gave her that little backhand Italian goodbye sign again and she leaned even closer. I whispered into her ear:

"You're too young for me, Morgen. I couldn't keep up with you."

"No, I'm not. You're funny."

"Funny does not a relationship make. And I'm done with flings."

"I'm disappointed," she said wistfully. "I was told you were a very naughty man."

"No, you're confusing me with some other Hollywood hack. But, hey, give me a few more glasses of wine and I might reconsider, all right?"

We clinked glasses. Wine liberating our nascent libidinousness, the party was on. I would hear scenes from the movie and it would spark an anecdote, which I would relate, much to the technocrati's delight. I've always believed you could get away saying almost anything if you could make people laugh.

We drove on through Santa Barbara, retracing a route I had taken many times. I stopped letting the technocrati refill me after two glasses because I didn't want to get depressed, I didn't want to become the drunken monkey who gets his brains cleaved out by a ring of cannibals. And even if I was playing the irreverent court jester to their corporate outing, I felt accountable to fulfill their entertainment needs. In short, I didn't want bad reviews on Yelp or any of those other websites.

"So, what's the schedule, Kevin?"

"We're going to check everyone in, then head over to the Hitching Post because that's where they want to go. Then I thought we'd hit the Clubhouse Bar at the Windmill so they can just walk back to their rooms."

"All right," I said. *Get me through this night halfway sober, oh Lord Almighty*, I intoned to myself.

I wheeled around to the technocrati. "Let me tell you a story about personal suffering and artistic redemption." My booming voice quieted them into a kind of restless solemnity. One of the Internet nerds politely put the film on pause. "Ten years ago. No, more like fifteen, I was nowhere. My father went into the hospital for a triple by-pass, suffered a massive stroke during the operation and was plunged into an irreversible coma. They rolled him into a step-down unit and hung a liquid feeding bag, turned him over a couple times a day to wipe his ass. He was cortically blind. He was never going to breathe on his own again without the assistance of a ventilator. My distraught mother, whom he had cheated on a lot for a man of his *Mad Men* times, visited him every day and spoke to him as if he could hear her beyond the dead. I couldn't bear it. The man had a living will and I was dead set on the hospital's executing it. After two months of this feeding tube bullcrap I summoned the head of social services and called for a meeting of the hospital's medical board. I delivered an impassioned speech begging them to let his corpus go to where his soul had already transited. Finally, reluctantly, much hair pulling, they pulled the feeding tube and, an exhausting three weeks later, he mercifully succumbed. Give me some more wine, will you? This gets depressing before it becomes redemptive."

The bottle was passed to Morgen who refilled my glass. I took a sip, then whispered into her slutty ear, "I *am* too old for you." I raised my head to the technocrati.

"A year later my mother slumped to the floor in her condo, a thrombosis having rocketed up one of her femoral arteries and lodged in her brain." Kevin shot me an alarmed look. He was worried. I hurtled forward: "Her dog barked his head off until the neighbors called 911. They rushed her into ICU and saved her life, but when she emerged three months later she was wheelchair-dependent and had the mind of an infant. My errant and unscrupulous brother brought her back to her seaside condo and, in two years of blatant pilferage, had squandered all her savings. I put my writing career—Career! Ha!—on hold and assumed control of her care. Thus began the worst year of my life." I paused and sipped the Pinot. "Not bad," I said in a jarringly jocular tone compared to the one I had momentarily traded it in for. "I crawled my way back to L.A., like an earthworm on hot asphalt en route to Barstow, and my rent-controlled place, which I had rented to animals like you pizza and beer slobs!"

Surprisingly, they laughed. Their howls of risibility galvanized me!

"Back in L.A., I refused to cave in to the establishment and get a job. I blew off creditors and my credit score went south. But, hey, future romantic partners, you think about credit scores and shit like that, there's an upside to bad credit." I paused for effect and slugged more wine. "You're immune to identity theft!" They bent over, pissed in their tight stove-pipe $300 designer jeans they bought on Abbott Kinney Blvd. "I started sojourning up here to the Santa Ynez Valley, which you will see tomorrow. I came to escape my wretched life! I came to play golf because the courses were uncrowded. The elitism of country clubs in L.A., where I was never invited or wanted, mocked me with their exclusionary policies. I came up here ... to feel free."

Someone in the back shouted, "To feeling free!" And everyone chorused, "Hear, hear!" Wineglasses clinked. I realized they were both laughing and reveling in their *schadenfreude* of my endless tunnel of misfortunes.

"Dead broke," I continued, "unable to get laid, somehow I managed to write a mystery novel. It was good enough to land me a top New York literary agent. I was excited; he was excited. But," I threw up both arms, "it didn't sell. Day after day these rejection letters would come to me from my agent. 'Dear Mitchell'—that was my agent—'I'm sorry to say, though the writing is top notch, this is just not for us.' And so it would go. But, did I stop? No. Did I go fill out job applications? Fuck no!"

They all chorused, "FUCK NO!"

"And where was I going to work anyway? I'd never held a real job in my entire life. I was a writer. I *am* a writer," I corrected. "This is what I do. This is a life. Don't tell me you're a writer just because you've written a couple crappy screenplays. This is a life, a fucking hard life, a life that most of you couldn't bear if you really lived it and stopped fantasizing about it." I realized suddenly there was an uneasy bitterness to my tone, so I attempted to mollify it. "I would rather die in abject misery, a fired gun in my limp hand, than live a life I didn't want to live."

They were rapt now.

"You see," I started up again, "the lower you go, and the more you embrace that bottom, as if it were the alchemist's *prima materia*: mud, excrement, rusted steel—the greater chance you have of spinning it into gold. And that's what I did when I wrote the novel that changed my life. I didn't take a backward step from the abyss of destitution and deprivation and depression and despair and darkness and dismay and desperation and disheartening dreams gone downward into the depths—how's that for alliteration?" "Woo-hoos!" from the technocrati who no doubt thought they had signed up for the insane asylum tour by mistake. "No," I finished, "I took those fucking D's and coveted them, imagined them as the clay of my inspiration, and thus was born *Shameless*, and the reason you're all here in this limo bus tonight. I went to the abyss none of you would have the courage to go, and I came back, rising like a phoenix from the ashes, with an argosy of gold!"

Morgen was beaming as everyone clapped. She flourished her mouth for me to kiss. It was dark in the van and I didn't think anyone could really see, so I touched her lips with mine and an electric shock ignited somewhere deep in the primordial depths of my being. I was getting paid for this?

I raised my eyes over Morgen's head. "So many people harbor the fantasy of wanting to write, but they don't want to do the work. So many fantasize about being a writer, but they wouldn't want to live the life!" I finished off my glass of wine. "Turn the fucking movie back on. That's just the prologue. We have another twenty-two hours to go!"

We lumbered on past Santa Barbara. Kevin gave me a thumb's up. A nearly full moon had transformed the ocean into a crumpled ball of tinfoil struck by a soft light. Oil derricks, with lonely men inhabiting their hulking shapes, beamed and winked red warning lights in the distance. A peace fell over me. I started dreaming of Chile and Laura and the money I would be making and it felt good to know that my life would be taken care of for the next year. A life that had grown out of control: the fame, the wine, the women ... it was such an addictive drug to someone who had suffered a decade of terrifying loneliness. I was rambling in my head. Some in the back had nodded off. Fucking lightweights, I thought. The movie had come to an end. Here and there I could see the flashlights of cellphones lit up in the dark as they text-ed and emailed and surfed the web for God knows what reason, other than to be unplugged for more than thirty minutes would make them feel dispossessed from their universes.

It was still early when we pulled into the Days Inn, aka Windmill Inn, where our party of technocrati would be bivouacked for the night. I had elected to stay at the nearby Marriott because I didn't want them inveigling me to join them in their rooms to guzzle Pinot Noir and spew more anecdotes. I was very adamant to Kevin that I stay on a certain schedule. I was determined not to let myself get pulled down into the undertow of their weekend debauchery.

In my room at the Marriott I switched on my laptop and checked for emails. Jack had written and said, as I figured, in his customarily succinct manner, "I can't make Chile, dude, sorry." Fuck, man, that was my back-up. As I scrolled through some emails that didn't need returning I noticed one from Maya. She was now living on a 100-acre vineyard farm overlooking my favorite golf course, La Purisima. I had stayed there once a year ago, but it had gone badly between us—regrets, accusations, a love affair that never panned out largely owing to my then need for intemperance.

"Hi, Miles," it said. "Heard you were going to be up in the area for a few days. Stop on by if you get a chance. My boyfriend and I would love to have you."

"My boyfriend?"

I checked some golf and NBA scores, absently scanned a few articles that would only fill my head with more trivia than needed to be rattling around up there, then decided to follow my own self-coined adage that the Internet was a dark road to infinity potholed with links, and closed my laptop to the galaxy without end.

Without writing a reply email to Maya.

Maya. The love of my life, I had once believed. She was deep, she had soul, she would listen to me ramble on, as I was wont to do. She was a great lover. She was damn near everything and perfect, but when she asked me to give up drinking for a year, I couldn't do it. She was right, of course; it was destroying me. But there was a part of me that wanted to be destroyed, as if I were searching for new material, as if I needed, as an artist, to continue the transgressive journey into the underworld so that I could mine the darkness. And, in order to mine the darkness, I needed to wallow a bit in the darkness. She didn't understand. She thought sobriety would bring me to a higher apotheosis of my art than any opium den of the imagination ever would. And we would have each other.

My mind was racing again, the curse of an overactive imagination that was prone to fatalistic fantasies. Doom and eschatological scenarios dogged me like slobbering Dobermans. I was both the hunter and the hunted in my bleak mind-stories. Nothing could palliate the darkness. I was drawn to the darkness like a demented mariner to uncharted waters. If it had brought me riches, as I had boasted to the goggle-eyed technocrati—who I'm sure didn't have a clue what I was talking about—it hadn't brought me love.

I realized suddenly that Maya's inopportune email had disinterred these thoughts from necropolises of my brainpan and I needed to expunge them. The answer came when I heard a knock at the door.

"Morgen?" I said, acting surprised, when I found her on the other side of my door, "What brings you here?" She had dolled up: brushed out her long dark hair, applied a coquettish touch of make-up, showered so she smelled of lavender, wafting invitations of imminent cunnilingus.

She thrust out a bottle of wine. "Could you open this for me, please?" she asked in a sultry voice.

"Come on in."

She trailed me inside and lowered herself to the edge of the bed. Using the corkscrew she gave me, I opened the bottle in record time. I looked at the label, "*Ne Plus Ultra.*" Never heard of it.

"They said it was good at the place I stopped at," she shrugged.

"A Pinot from Santa Rita Hills can't be all bad," I said, confabulating nervously, but all the while taking the pulse of her surprise visit and wondering what my next move was. I filled the two wineglasses she had also thoughtfully brought with her and handed one to her. I held out my glass and we clinked them. She smiled, then giggled nervously as if she were a teenager and not the late twenties woman she really was.

I plopped myself in a chair and sipped the wine. I had gone in and out of drinking, but I had learned to pace myself. "So, what do you do at Whatever Dot Com?" I asked.

"I'm a consultant."

I raised my head. It didn't seem like there was anything else to ask that would interest me beyond the fact that she was a consultant at a new start-up that would one day make them all instant millionaires. "So, you, do what then, specifically?"

"I'm a liaison between all the departments. Make sure they're communicating and we're getting what we need."

"I see."

"I really want to be a writer like you." I sensed that that was coming. She tilted forward just a little. Her low-cut blouse revealed quite unambiguously that she wasn't wearing a bra! She was gifting it to me. Fuck! Christ!

I shifted nervously in my chair. "What do you write, Morgen? Screenplays? Prose? ..."

"No, I want to write plays."

"Ah. You know I just wrote one."

"I know. I saw it. The way you move people with your words. I'm so envious."

"Don't be, Morgen. I was serious in the van when I said it's not a life I would wish on anyone."

She grew thoughtful. "Do you have any advice for me?"

"Don't have children. Eschew all responsibilities and normal behaviors. Take extreme risks. Don't show your work to anyone until you're done with it, then expect the worst, and expect them to be wrong. Don't stop writing. It's a life, Morgen, it's not an avocation. If you think it's an avocation that you fantasize is going to make you rich and famous, and that's why you're in it, then you've already sown the seed of failure."

"That's so beautifully put," she said, melting. She came toward me and planted a kiss on my lips that was hard and indomitable.

I gently pushed her a foot away from me. "Do you have a boyfriend?"

"It's over," she said.

"Is he one of the soul-sucking dot com group?"

She hung a guilty expression. "It doesn't matter, Miles. It's over."

"Yeah, but does he know it's over?"

"Yeah, he does," she said unconvincingly.

Her body felt warm next to me. It was exciting. But it was an excitement I didn't need. "Look, you should go."

"Why?"

"You're a beautiful woman. And all you're going to do is hurt me when you leave. And I'm tired of being hurt."

"I'm not going to hurt you, Miles."

"You have a whole life, Morgen, that I've already lived. Plucking a flower from the garden of youth doesn't interest me anymore."

She withdrew with a fake clown frown on her face. "Do you want me to go?"

"I do and I don't, Morgen. But maybe you should before I change my mind and have a sensual apostasy."

"You and your big words."

"Yep, me and my big words."

She straightened to her feet, slugged back the wine remaining in her glass, waved, and then went out the door, entombing me inside.

I was nonplussed at my own sense of reason.

Maya, Part I

I joined the technocrati at the Hitching Post. They were seated at a long table, the twelve of them, a modern-day version of The Last Supper, *sans* spirit, *sans* soul. Bottles of Pinot Noir already littered the table. The noise of the restaurant was now a din. One of the technocrati, a retro boho-looking guy named Brandon, straightened unsteadily from his chair and raised his wineglass in a toast.

"Here's to Miles Raymond, a direct descendant of Mark Twain and Jack Kerouac, a writer who has forged a new direction in the literature of the road." I hung my head, pretending humility. Twain,

Kerouac, give me a break! Bukowski with a car is more like it! But I let him have his moment of glorifying his celebrity guest. He prattled on about the future of their company. "And if we don't take risks like Miles here, if we don't look to the future with a circumspect eye, we will never achieve the success that Mr. Raymond now so enjoys."

Everyone toasted. I toasted them all. I had become the very thing I had despised: a prisoner of my own celebrity, a pathetic court jester reduced to corporate outings to pay the bills so I could persevere with my life's work. I smiled. Why wreck their weekend? Brandon broke my self-deprecating reverie and beckoned me to rise. I suddenly felt like a small fish, a hook in his cheek, reeled to a standing position by those who could afford me.

"Here's to Soul-Suck Dot Com!" I said, raising my glass. They all howled with laughter. In the dim light of the restaurant their faces turned gargoyled, as if I had transited from The Last Supper, crashed through a back door and found myself in a Salvador Dali painting.

I continued to narrate the story of my life. I hurtled forward with a litany of the indignities I had suffered over the years. I don't know whether they believed me or not. My life, once something I had valued as that which I had given up for the sake of my writing, had become almost the butt of a joke. But, there was no turning back. I was making them laugh. They loved hearing about the time I opened my door on Wilshire Boulevard and a car careening down, way too fast and way too close, blew it off. And then didn't stop! Traffic halted. I retrieved my door, put it in the backseat. "But I had no insurance back then. And I was broke. So I drove for several months with no driver's side door!" They roared with eye-watering laughter. On a roll, I continued: "Worse, now my car was an open invitation to the homeless. And, as everyone knows, Santa Monica has one of the largest indigent populations in the country. So, my car became the Motel-6 *du jour* for the homeless." I sipped some more wine, staggered in place: "Get this. I wake up one morning and there's a guy crashed in my car. I knocked on the hood and said, 'Room Service!' Yes, my life had fallen on hard times before I wrote *Shameless*."

As they rocked with laughter, across the restaurant I noticed Maya sitting with someone I recognized as a famous winemaker in the area. Hirsute, ruddy-faced, a local legend. For his wines, for his massive consumption of his wines! She caught my eye and we locked gazes for a brief, but intense, moment. I excused myself to the technocrati and circled around the bar and into the bathroom. When I came out, Maya was waiting for me, as if she thought it had been a signal.

"Hi, Miles," she said.

"Maya. Hi."

"What're you doing up here?"

"Corporate outing. Yes, sadly, it's come to that."

"Oh," she chuckled.

"Not what I want to be doing, obviously, but I need the money. I'm headed to Chile in a few weeks. I half-debated asking you to come, but since you're with someone that probably would have been inappropriate."

She cocked her head to one side and smiled wryly. There still existed the vestiges of a once great love, but I had fucked it up with

my wanton behavior and not knowing—ever knowing, really!—
what I wanted from a woman. Yet, when I looked into her eyes just
then—steely blue, intense, two sapphires lit by a thousand burning
suns behind them—I glimpsed her love and it suffused me with
sudden melancholy. Melancholy for a life I had kept abjuring: love
of a woman. Maya had made me feel it more profoundly than any
other woman.

A drunken man bumped into us as he staggered shambolically
back into the restaurant and broke the moment where the cosmos
existed in the inviolable bubble that was only us at that moment.
We both felt the violation.

"I should probably get back to the dot com guys," I said.

"What are you doing tomorrow?" she asked.

"Uh, well, they're all going to get drunk tonight—I'm not.
Watching my P's and Q's these days!—and then get on their limo
bus and head back to L.A. I'm supposed to take the train out of
Lompoc."

"Why don't you come up to the farm in the morning and I'll take
you to the station?"

"What about your boyfriend?"

"He's flying out early tomorrow to Asia to promote his wines."

"All right," I said. We hugged a little awkwardly.

In a backward glance as she sidled through the crowd toward the
bathroom, "The gate code is the month and day of my birthday.
You remember?"

"Yes," I said, smiling. "Despite all the wine. See you tomorrow."

I regaled the technocrati for another half hour, then we all
climbed back into the limo bus and headed to the Clubhouse Bar.

They were shamelessly looking for a *Shameless* experience and I was the designated, and well paid, guide to said experience. I sank heavily like a sack of corn into a depression.

They all went crazy, like Japanese youth on a Friday night, at the Clubhouse Bar, drinking shots, playing pool, dancing crazily. The locals, mostly blue collar stiffs and other heavy machinery guys, had gotten used to the crowds. Hell, they liked the pretty women who came up to girl-bond and do the *Shameless* tour.

Morgen was forgetting her boyfriend and was draping her arms around me like a besotted octopus, her eyes limpidly out-of-focus from too much wine. I kept whispering in her ear that it was best to behave, but she wouldn't give up.

"Oh, screw him!" she declaimed at one point referring to her boyfriend, so loud everyone could hear.

It was as if my presence were inspiring libidinous behavior. Because my novel wallowed in excess, rhapsodized over the lives of characters who knew no insatiety, and because I had found some measure of success with that subject matter, it seemed to give present company license to behave like them. Of course I knew she would regret it in the morning. Be chagrined and all shame-faced, hoping that no one recalled her silliness and gossiped on email.

At some point I signaled to Kevin that I was going to walk back to the Marriott. He smiled and waved me to go on, he would mop up the technocrati from the floor.

It was chilly outside and I dug my hands into my jeans pockets. In the years of my loneliness I had adopted the habit of talking out loud to myself. Usually, it was to some nemesis of mine—some despicable producer who had ripped me off; some pettifogger who had steered me wrong; an agent sharking me for blood—but tonight I was talking out loud to Maya for some reason, addressing her as if she were accompanying me on this desolate walk. I wanted to chronicle our relationship and attempt to put it into some kind of perspective for tomorrow's visit. As cars roared beneath me on the 101 I had to raise my voice so her wraithlike presence could hear me. Passersby would have thought me a madman.

Even though *Shameless* had radically changed this region forever, I was still in many ways the same person. Oh, it was true, when people met me and found out who I was they automatically changed. Women found me more attractive. Men were either envious or instant fan boys, like the technocrati, and wanted to know what my secret was. (Answer: there are no secrets; it's just that's who you are, and the rest is hard work.) But, to me, I felt the same. Money didn't change me. I pissed it away with drink and women—and women were something I was still battling. I didn't understand them. What they wanted. Why couldn't romance be the same a year in, five years in? Why did it have to change? Why could I fall in love with someone and write them 30 emails a day, then start dating, then dating seriously, then mysteriously lose all interest? Was romance meant to be something, as the biologists and anthropologists are fond of opining, to get us to propagate the species and nothing more once we are saddled with children? I had no children. I had no plans to have any children. It's hard enough to make it as a writer or an artist without throwing children into the mix. And, now, children were more or less out of the question. When I see young couples pushing baby strollers in L.A. I wonder: how the fuck do they do that? Why do they want to saddle themselves with that caterwauling little fleshy blob of Shar Pei cuteness? Nope, not for me! I like kids. I like their independent spirits and their undeveloped, tabula rasa minds, the minds that could one day end up being unique and amazing, but which all too often end up mediocre and scared. Scared of the world, scared to do something truly different.

I kept babbling out loud: My father taught me that. He was a captain in the Air Force. He flew the notorious Hump. Hump Pilots flew transport missions over the Himalayas to support the Chinese and our troops in the war against the Japanese. They lost two-thirds of their pilots. Loaded up with cargo—fuel, munitions, other supplies—they took off into the night in waves, hurtled into monsoon winds, battled turbulence that was so fuselage-shaking it could cause a plane to disintegrate in mid-air. Lose an engine and there was nowhere to crash land. Lose altitude and you were headed into one of the Himalayas. I hated flying, but I was never interested in taking on those kinds of risks. All my life was a risk. Normalcy had no place. I couldn't imagine what it would be like to settle down, have kids, enslave myself to a job. All I knew is that there would be no one to carry on my name.

Another car barreled past and the bridge crossing the 101 rumbled for a moment as if I were in a low Richter Scale earthquake. I was headed to Chile. What the fuck was I going to do down in Chile? Well, it was a job, I kept consoling myself. Maybe it would change me. Maybe the experience would help me see the world in a new light. Maybe it would be my salvation. But, I had doubts about going with a woman I hadn't seen in over a year. She seemed liked the perfect traveling companion on paper, but you never know until you're with someone 24 hours a day.

Thoughts bedeviled me. It was time to begin writing another book. But was anyone reading anymore? Would words be replaced by moving images? Would we one day only read in short bursts? Would the novel become a relic like lacework or spear-making? Where were my talents best utilized? Did I have talent? I raised up against the *whoosh whoosh* of traffic and had an epiphany: I needed a new experience. Chile was that new experience.

I debated going into the depressing bar at the Marriott and having a few more glasses before heading to bed, but I didn't want to show up at Maya's farm with a hangover. I would be querulous, old resentments would have a greater likelihood of rearing their gnatlike presence, and I didn't want to feel, or face, those resentments. I wanted to have a pleasant time with her before I flew off to a country below the equator.

I wrestled with falling to sleep. I read one article after another on the Internet: the polarization of wealth in this country was really starting to upset me. I saw a revolution brewing on the horizon. I wanted to be rich so I could get all the homeless off the street and into shelters, but I would never be that rich. I grew depressed.

Maya, Part II

I dreamt that I was homeless, had terminal cancer and no health insurance and that the world was going to end. Somehow I managed to get back to sleep, but was then assailed by more disquieting dreams. I was wandering a vast desolate landscape that I took to be the Atacama Desert, one of the places I hoped to visit. But I was homeless, I had nothing. In another dream, no doubt inspired by my having donated all my books and papers, I had returned to my apartment and there was nothing: no personal belongings, no furnishings, nothing. It was just an empty room made of marble or ivory or something equally cold and hard. I dug deep into my Jung to interpret its meaning: I was about to be a child of the world, with nothing, no ties to anything, living an uninhibited life of the senses, and occasionally of the mind. Where was I going to land? Did I have to land somewhere? Was this the fate of all people? That we have to land somewhere?

My phone jangled me awake at 9:30 a.m. I saw Kevin's name and photo ID come up on my cellphone. *Oh, fuck*, I thought: here it comes. *Why did you get drunk and flirt with the CEO's wife, Miles?*

"Hello?"

"Miles. Kevin. Everyone had a great time. I left your check at the desk. Have a great time in Chile."

"Thanks, Kevin, for everything. Really appreciate it."

I looked at myself in the mirror and didn't like what was staring back at me. The flesh around the corners of my eyes was wrinkling. Gray, puffy sacks hung below them. My hair fountained on my head and I reminded myself that it was time to get it cut.

Maya's 100-acre vineyard farm was located just off Highway 246 near Lompoc. To get there, the taxi cruised right past my favorite golf course in the world, La Purisima—"the pure one," its irony not lost on this wayward traveler circumnavigating its southern boundary. There was no one on the course. There were no homes on the course. I had a yen to pull in, get out of the taxi, rent some clubs and just play a nostalgic round. But I didn't want to cancel on Maya. I had canceled on Maya my whole damn life.

We turned off on Drum Canyon Road. Since the movie came out, Pinot Noir plantings had skyrocketed tenfold. Once, in the '90s, there were few, if any, vineyards planted west of the 101. Now, there were over 3,000 acres devoted to mostly Pinot, the grape my book and movie rhapsodized over in, at times, bombastically grandiloquent language. What was once considered farmland more suitable for broccoli was now prime Pinot growing acreage. And the stakes were high.

Maya's property was situated on a windswept hilltop ruling over Lompoc to the west, the Santa Rita Hills to the south and, in the far distance, the greater Santa Ynez Valley to the east. It was late fall and the grapes had been sheared from the vines. The leaves, shivering in some recent cold nights, had started to color ochre. Her ten acres of Pinot and Chardonnay were immaculately groomed. Soon, vineyard workers, brandishing clippers, would trim the young, but now unruly and rascally, vines to prepare them for the next vintage. This last year had been a bumper crop and it weighed heavily on Maya because it was the first year she was going to de-stem, crush and ferment on the property. Her cult winemaker boyfriend—famous for his wines, and even more famous for his roistering and philandering on his ex-wife—was her consultant. It was a marriage ostensibly forged in the crucible of heaven.

Maya came out of her house to greet me. Overhead the sky was a startling blue color, the air catacomb quiet. The intervening years had only burnished her beauty. A relatively tall woman, her hair fell over her shoulders in a way she always wore it, and she was dressed in denim and a comfortable top. Sun and hard work on the farm had slightly weathered her features, but she had kept her physique in athletic shape with a workout regimen that daunted me.

We greeted with a hug and an exchange of wry smiles, old lovers who had trouble acknowledging their physical past, but who recognize each other in that deep way with the advantage of history.

The sun was overhead and the wind was coming up. Hawks and turkey vultures had taken wing, as they are wont to do when the wind blows, because they save on energy in their drone-like search for the rodent targets below.

"Many targets," Maya said, leading me to a new building she had had constructed on the property. "I battle gophers all the time. Nothing you can do will stop them," she groused.

"Well, better gophers eating the roots of Pinot vines than drunks groping you back when you were waitressing at the Hitching Post," I joked.

She cracked a smile. "So, you're headed to Chile?" she said.

"Yes. I got an offer to visit their wine country, I decided I'm tired of Santa Monica, I'm sick of the film business, and now's a better time than any."

"And you will write another book?" she asked, as I trudged in her wake up the hill toward the new structure.

"I don't know," I said. "Depends on what I find down there."

We reached the building, which truncated the line of questioning. The view was spectacular. Down below I could glimpse some of the fairways of La Purisima. I gesticulated.

"Did you know that in my will I'm to be buried on the 15<u>th</u> hole? Well, have my ashes spread."

"No, I didn't know that."

"Yes. It's my favorite hole on the course. It's when I first fell in love with this area. On the 15<u>th</u> you come out of the canyons and rise up to an emerald green plateau and there before you is the sky and the ocean and the rest of the course. And if you're by yourself it's so serene, so magical..." I shook my head at the memory.

"I didn't know you were so spiritual."

"I'm learning to let go of the bitterness of the past. It'll eat you alive if you train your mind on it for too long."

"Miles, you've been through a lot. You've used up your nine lives." I chuckled. "It's good that you're learning to move on. I'm happy for you. You look well." Our eyes met and locked for the briefest of moments. It was as if we were looking into each other's personal histories and rediscovering a rich commonality.

She opened a garage door and revealed her winery. It was a 500 square foot building, stacked floor-to-ceiling with French oak barrels.

"Temperatures really spiked in late August and we got a bumper crop. I had to order all these extra barrels. And they're not cheap! But I think it's going to be a great year. The Pinot is just to die for." She rummaged around in all the winemaking equipment and produced a wine thief, unstopped one of the bung holes, dipped the thief into the barrel and drew up, as if blood in a syringe, a glassine of wine. She let go her thumb on the thief and half-filled two tasting glasses that were standing at the ready. She handed one to me. "Here. Cheers, Miles. It's so good to see you."

"Cheers," I said, accepting the glass from her and holding it up. "It's good to see you, too, Maya."

"Remember, this is just now going through malolactic, but I want you to taste the fruit. It's so luscious."

I sampled the wine. Grapes recently crushed and put into barrel don't have, of course, all the complexity the wine will one day possess when the tannins have softened, and the oak has lent age and vanilla and other notes. It's bright and red and grape-y and, if you know what you're looking for, you can taste its promise, as if looking clairvoyantly into the chrysalis of a still fermenting grape juice and see the thrilling Pinot Noir it could one day become. "Nice," was all I could offer. "How long will you leave it in barrel?"

"I'm going to let it sit for a year-and-a-half," she replied, tasting the wine, studying it in her mouth, professionally drawing air through her nose to aid in giving her the full, total palate experience. "So many wines are released too early. Of course, it's inventory for most of these winemakers. They just want to get the stuff out onto the market as quickly as they can so they release them too early."

"You're a perfectionist," I remarked.

She cocked her head to one side and smiled acknowledgement.

"It's great here, Maya. Are you happy?"

She started to answer, but her words were hobbled by her wondering if the truth would be a good idea to confide. She stared off, as if expunging unwanted thoughts and said, "Come on, let me show you the house."

She reached for my hand and swung me toward a door that led from the garage into the main house. Our hands fell apart as she bolted inside. It was a capacious, wood-framed structure with raftered ceilings and a kitchen appointed with high-end appliances. We stood in the kitchen, the amateur chef in me admiring the gleaming professional quality Aga range. The afternoon sun poured through pyramidal skylights and bathed us in a golden light.

"It's beautiful," I said. "I could live here."

She laughed. "Come on."

She gave me a brief tour of the tiled bathrooms and the three bedrooms, two with views of La Purisima. We came to a stop in the master bedroom. I don't know what she was thinking, but I was thinking about throwing her onto the bed and making love to her. "How's Cliff?" I asked, referring to her winemaker boyfriend. "Did he get off okay?"

"He's all right," she said in a strained, and strange, voice, its timbre tinged with uncertainty. "Yes, he got off fine."

In the wine world, there are several certainties and dirty secrets. Alcoholism and adultery are pandemic, for starters.

"Do you have to get back today?" Maya asked.

"No. I don't leave for Chile for a week."

"Why don't you stay. We can go out, or cook dinner. I want you to taste last year's vintage."

"Are you sure?"

"The harvest is in. The wine is in barrel. Life is good"—did I detect sarcasm?—"and you're on your way to Chile."

"Yes," I said.

"Let's take a walk, shall we?" she said. "I want to show you my vineyards."

The sun bent toward the ocean, coloring from yellow to orange. The raptors were now wheeling everywhere in the sky, tracing black ellipsoidal lines. An emaciated coyote threw us a baleful, backward glance, then slunk over one of the browned-out hills. A fog mounted like a threatening tsunami on the horizon, but it just hung there in suspended motion, awaiting its greenlight to consume Lompoc and then the valley. The fog that so gloriously acidified the Pinot and Chardonnay grapes through the transverse valleys of the new appellation, Santa Rita Hills. As the sun sank heavily into it, it blurred its burning disc as if a light bulb plunged into black water.

We came to a stop at the zenith of her glorious property. Below us, her modest ten-acre planting of Pinot and Chardonnay rolled in a gentle, immutable wave below us. My heart threw itself up into my throat thinking how happy I could be here, writing, being in love with this woman, this woman who had worked her whole life and scraped and saved every penny, found investors for the property, and then, with a sizable inheritance from her father who had died suddenly of an exploding brain aneurysm, pulled the trigger and bought the 100-acre farm. I was shocked at how little it had cost her given its promise.

"Of course, there was nothing on it when I bought it," she said. "Well, there were rusted-out cars and heavy machinery. It was a dump!" She laughed sardonically at the memory. "It was a lot of work," she said wearily, nodding up and down. "But when those vines went down into the ground I was the happiest woman in the world."

"I can imagine," I said.

"And when the wine flowed four years later, it was as if the ground were giving back the blood I had poured into it."

"You're becoming a poet," I joked.

She smiled without looking at me. "Look at this view."

"Splendiferous."

"Sometimes all I can hear is the wind."

I nodded, not knowing what to say.

The sun was now being pulled into the fog and the fog, itself, was starting to encroach on the land, a ghostly army hiding in its fold if you let your imagination pullulate such things.

"What would you like to eat?" she asked, pinpricking the mood.

"Whatever you have."

"And you can stay here tonight."

"I look forward to a night of sleep."

She turned to go back toward the house. "No Internet connection, though."

I held up my cellphone. "Mobile hot spot."

She laughed.

I prepared the chicken while she put on Lucinda Williams's *World Without Tears*. I rubbed the inside cavity with lemon, then salted and peppered it, stuffed it with fresh thyme and lemon and then trussed it. Maya opened a bottle of her 2012 Pinot and her 2011 Chardonnay. She made her wines in a style that was relatively low in alcohol and with a bright acidity without compromising on the fruit concentration. The soundtrack on her description of the various clones that went into her Pinot lowered to barely a whisper, as if her voice were now music at the edge, and, in that softening moment, she grew lovelier and lovelier.

"The Chardonnay is beautifully complex," I said.

"It is, isn't it?"

I switched wineglasses. "And the Pinot is so Burgundian. I love that."

"I'm glad you noticed. That's what Cliff and I are going for; a more Burgundian wine."

"How is it with you and Cliff? I know he has quite the reputation."

She flattened her hand at chest level and wobbled it like a canoe with a maladroit person standing in it.

"Does he cheat on you?" I ventured. We had had a little wine and it had lowered both our inhibitions.

"I don't want to go there," she said. Her voice rose. "So, who is this woman you're going to Chile with?"

"Oh, Laura. I haven't seen her in over a year."

"What?"

"Well, we met on that crazy road trip to get my mother back to Wisconsin, and it was only a weekend. Then, I was going to fly to Spain, she had a boyfriend, then she didn't have a boyfriend, then this Chile opportunity came up, I wanted someone to go with me because, you know, I have these flying issues, plus I'm tired of talking out loud to myself all the time."

"You don't really know her is what you're saying?"

"I would have asked you, Maya, if you didn't have a man in your life, if you didn't have this farm to run."

"Really?"

"Yes, you know me better than anyone." I poured some more wine. "And what you don't know, and what you probably don't want to know is ..." I sipped some wine.

"What?" she asked, telescoping her head forward.

"I'm still in love with you."

"Oh, Miles, that's the wine talking."

"No, Maya, that's my heart talking."

There was a silence. I could hear the fat from the chicken spattering on the roasting pan. Frogs croaked invisibly from outside. Crickets chirred as if we were in a forest where all the creatures were drawn out of mythology. Then, there was an ellipses, a lacuna of mere seconds, as if the present had stopped and we had leaped forward those few prolonged seconds and our mouths were pressed together like movie star lovers. Hungry. Desperate. Mouths fixed on each other's as if we were trying to disintegrate our skulls and transmogrify a new one.

"Why didn't we work out?" she whispered, the perfumed scent of Pinot enveloping her words.

"Because I'm a fucking asshole," I said. "And I let you go." Tears watered my eyes and they went out of focus. She reached her arms around me and hugged me tightly.

"I never wanted to be with anyone except you, Miles." She withdrew a few inches, steadied my head with both hands and made me stare into her honey-brown eyes. "Never."

"I know. I'm sorry."

"And now you're going to Chile."

"And now I'm going to Chile."

"You get in trouble down there, you call me, okay?"

"I will. I promise."

"I'm serious. I'll come get you."

She came to me, wraithlike, in the middle of the night and wordlessly made love to me. At one point she closed her hand over my throat and gently choked off my windpipe. My cock seemed to grow harder. No woman had ever done that to me before. As my eyes adjusted I could make out a ferocity in her expression and feral narrowing of her eyes.

"You'll always be mine, Miles," she whispered. "No matter what happens. Do you understand?" She gripped my throat tighter. I thought I was going to pass out. My cock grew even harder inside her. She climaxed, and then I came ... the Milky Way.

Then she left just as quickly, as if being cast out into the rain.

The next morning dawned outer space blue. Dew clung to the shrubbery and glistened in the sun as if the ground were scattered with diamonds. My train didn't leave until 1:00 p.m., so we made a stop at the Lompoc Wine Ghetto, the new hot spot for wine in the valley. We ignored the assignation of the previous night as if we were to be dispossessed of it much like morning evanesces dreams. But it was no dream. I could still feel where her strong hand had gripped my throat, where her kiss had branded my heart. Her words reverberated in my brain. My cock bore the sweet soreness from her ravishing me without warning.

Maya parked in an industrial section just east of the town and we entered a high-ceiling-ed building with exposed ventilation ducts and walls stripped bare. Inside, it was balkanized into small production wineries, if you want to call them that, with barrels stacked haphazardly, destemmers in various states of use, rectangular plastic fermentation vats, conveyor belts for sorting the grapes, and other winemaking equipment and supplies. A few men of Hispanic origin were cleaning the large space, hosing down the floor and scrubbing the machinery.

"I'd have to say that you're responsible for this," Maya exclaimed to me, throwing out her arms. "It's almost all Pinot Noir."

"It's manifest destiny," I joked, throwing my arms histrionically in the air. "It's all moving west. To the ocean. Burgundy is coming to California."

A silence fell. Water from a hose hitting the cement floor occupied the void like people who didn't belong at a gathering.

"You know Cliff's cheating on me," she said matter-of-factly, in an unaffected voice, as if she were resigned to his philandering ways.

I nodded, not knowing what to say.

"He has a girlfriend in New York. They *rendezvous* at these big wine events"—she raised both hands and fashioned play quotes—"and who knows what they do."

"Is he in love with her?" I asked.

"I don't know," she said sharply. "I wish I were going to Chile with you, Miles. I heard the wine there is amazing, but we see so little of it here for some reason."

"I wish you were, too," I said. I touched a hand to her shoulder and caressed it. It was cold in the cavernous warehouse. It was maintained that way for the preservation of the wine.

"Have you gotten it all out of your system, Miles?" she asked in a bold *non sequitur*, turning to look at me.

"I want to believe I have. I'm tired of all the post-celebrity libidinousness if you want to know the truth."

"Are you really?"

"I'd like to be with somebody who knows me. On our death bed, are we really going to flip through a deck of cards of our lovers and remember what they were like? No, we're going to think about what we've accomplished, what we made of ourselves, who we truly loved. And hopefully not think about who wronged us. Because," I paused, turning to look at her, "if I did that I'd have one long, lonely, angry walk to wherever I was going, all the people who have ripped me off!"

She chuckled.

"What made you come to me last night?" I asked. "I didn't come on to you or anything, did I? Was it Cliff in Hong Kong with his lover?"

Sadness flooded her sardonic smile. "No, Miles, like I said last night, I've always loved you. And I've always waited for you. Sure, there have been others, but I needed to know that you felt the same thing for me. And last night when you told me I was your most powerful love ever, I thought maybe this time he isn't drunk and he means it."

"I wasn't drunk. And I did mean it."

"So, what's going to happen with Laura?"

"I don't know. Like I said, I needed someone to go with me. I hadn't heard from you in a while, and then when I learned you were dating Cliff I thought that that fantasy had disintegrated. I didn't realize there were problems. And you're married to your farm,

Maya. I'm a child of the world right now. All my books were given away, my papers are at my *alma mater* now ..."

"That is so wonderful," she said, chopping me off.

"Thank you," I replied. "My work rests next to Dr. Seuss's."

"Horton hears an F word," she quipped.

She made me laugh. "Yes, it's a huge honor." I lowered my head. "So, we're just at different places in our lives."

"My offer's still good. If things don't work out in Chile, call me and I'll come get you."

"Okay, Maya," I said.

The Amtrak station in Lompoc wasn't really a station at all. It was a planked platform west of the city hugging the ocean. The wind had come up and the surface of the sea was jagged with whitecaps. A ragtag group of passengers was milling about, luggage parked at their sides, waiting for the train, which only made this stop once a day. Maya and I waited in her car.

"I'm glad to see you're doing so much better, Miles," she said. "Try to keep it under a bottle down there," she cracked.

"That's my limit," I said. "Those days are over."

"Good." She pressed her face against mine and we held our mouths together. Suddenly, as if in a movie, we both heard the whistle of the approaching train, broke free of each other and laughed.

"I guess that's my cue," I said.

"I'm sad to see you go," she said wistfully.

"I'm sad *to* go," I said. And I meant it.

We kissed one last time, just as forcefully as before, but more briefly.

"Email me."

"I will," I said.

I fetched my carry-on out of the back and closed the door to her red-and-black Mini Cooper. We exchanged goodbye waves and then I was on the platform all alone, missing her already. Missing her badly!

The train braked to a squealing stop and stood still, rumbling and hissing like an exhausted bison, waiting for the smattering of passengers to board. Inside, I climbed to the upper deck to my business class seat, still feeling the force and sweetness of Maya's kiss on my lips. I found an ocean-facing window seat all by myself and eased into it. I loved trains. Unlike airplanes, which caused me anxiety, trains made me think, got me to meditating, the traveling landscape like the thoughts and images unspooling from a film projector in my head. There was something about terrestrial travel where you don't have to do the driving that induces reflection.

As the train lurched to a start, the ocean wheeled into view. The water was the color of the deepest indigo like some volcanic lake, the sky a mild milky blue. A fine mist blurred the horizon as if a person scanning it had forgotten his glasses. I started reflecting:

Mostly what I remembered were the hard times. I had not chosen to be a writer, I thought to myself; writing had chosen me. Having been raised in a family where the mother didn't want kids, I had a need, as I tried to explain to the inebriated technocrati, for expression. I tried music, but quickly realized I had no aptitude for it. Ditto for painting. Writing did not come easily to me. I had to work for it, scratch and claw for every sentence, but I fell in love with words in a way I didn't with chords or nude sketches. Words led me to books, great literature, then great films—where words once mattered!—then deep into my unconscious, and then, eventually, as the journey just unfolded of its own invention, to my own writing.

The train clacked noisily over the tracks. We rumbled past Jalama Beach. I couldn't believe how the train had been routed so close to the ocean, the tracks on a bluff that shelved off to the sea. Below us was the camp site and RV park. A novel I couldn't get published began here with my first-person character drinking himself to death in a tent. That was then. Now, I was trampling over those dark memories in this great iron beast, but the memories still seared, rose up from miasmic depths and enveloped me in their pain. I almost *was* that guy in that tent. And then I wrote the next one, which changed my life.

Memories fractured in the prismatic glass of my brain and seemed to stab at the past with myriad swords of piercing light. I kept returning to Maya's kiss. Why do we love those whom we know we can't be with for very long, but push away, or not make room, for those we could potentially love forever? Or, maybe that's just me, I spoke out loud to myself, somewhat ruefully.

The middle-aged woman sitting across the aisle from me stole a glance. I realized that my talking out loud had disconcerted her. Maybe I was a homeless person, or a just-released felon with twenty dollars to his name heading to Los Angeles like so many people did in the early 1900's, disembarked at the great train station and then ... never made it out of downtown Los Angeles, drank themselves into an alley and died of cirrhosis. That could have been me!

I threw a backward glance out the window. I could still picture Maya at the train station kissing me into a stupor. Her strong, athletic body on top of me—those hard-muscled loins and limbs of hers, her mouth like a dream, her pussy like a warm sea anemone—I wanted to go back. I wanted to claim her and take her with me to Chile. If only I had known that things weren't working out with Cliff. All my life it's been regrets. The past has always haunted me with the poor decisions I've made. And here was another one to add to the list.

I turned back in the direction the train was growling: L.A., a city I once needed, now loathed, and, thank God, was about to leave.

PART II

LAX

LAX is dispiriting. It can destroy your soul. Sitting there all alone, my 50 lbs. of luggage hopefully headed to the belly of an Airbus 340, I was waiting on my LAN Airlines flight to Santiago, Chile. Laura had emailed me that she would be arriving the day after as her flight was delayed for some reason that sounded fishy, but I didn't want to begin catastrophically obsessing, as I was wont to do. Perhaps she, too, had someone else she was *saying goodbye to*. It seemed like everyone was partnering up, jumping into bed with someone else, grabbing whatever opportunity was out there and then leaping on yet another person. I was acutely aware that Laura had lost her job at the TV station she worked at, that Spain was mired in a horrible fiscal crisis, and that maybe three months in Chile with free room and board might have outweighed the deterrent effect of a boyfriend.

Musings. I always went to the fatalistic. It could never be the felicitous. I wondered if this was a genetic defect in me, or if my mother's drinking while she was pregnant with me had inked a few dark spots on my developing brain! Or if in the fatalistic I found the comfort of a world that made sense to me, that nurtured my art.

I had never been south of the equator. Hell, I had never even been south of Mazatlan, Mexico. Once I had to be de-planed from a 50-seat Bombardier out of Rapid City, South Dakota because I had had a crippling, near psychotic, panic attack. It was not a fun 2,000 mile drive home to L.A. all by myself. So, yes, I worried about boarding the flight to Santiago. I had been back on a plane since: once to San Francisco and once coming back from Nashville, of all places, and twice to New York. I felt confident I could get on the plane. I had to. An advance had been wired into my account, and Chilean vintners were excited to have the *Shameless* guy jet down and tour their wine country, maybe even write a book if he felt so inspired.

I kept thinking about Maya and what had happened in the Santa Ynez Valley. I thought about Katherine—thank God I was leaving that complicated love relationship behind! And then Laura. I was excited to see her, but more than that, I needed her with me in Chile. I feared being alone.

A bilingual announcement blared over the loudspeakers that my flight was boarding. Weary of rumination, weary of body, I dragged my carry-on across the lounge and stood in line with an international cast. Many were conversing in Spanish, but it was a Spanish I had trouble understanding. I had been warned that Chilean Spanish was different than other dialects, but this sounded incomprehensibly different. Worse, as my penchant for aerophobia panic arose, I noticed a lot of children. I worried that caterwauling babies were going to have me reaching for my Xanax, which I had prudently fortified with a triple prescription on my last medical visit.

I found my Business Class seat on the plane and settled in. There was no one seated next to me. Yet. As obese passengers waddled down the aisle I dreaded my traveling companion. It was a punishingly long flight to Santiago, with a stop in Lima, Peru, and I was starting to grow anxious. Fantasies of disembarkation before takeoff started to bleed in my already fearful brain. I don't know why I hated flying so much. Most people saw it as an adventure. Maybe it was because my father was a captain in the Air Force and once, when my two brothers and I were young, he took us for a ride in a single-engine Cessna. I'll never forget my mother standing at the door, weeping. She had flown with my father many times—in fact, she, herself, had a single-engine pilot's license—and knew what a rascal and daredevil he could be once airborne in the deep blue of the southern California sky. After flying dangerous C-47 transport missions over the Himalayas in the dead of night, battling barbarous monsoon winds, a single-engine over temperate San Diego was probably like Ayrton Senna in his prime performing hairpin turns in a Go-Kart at the village fair with a confident grin creasing his youthful face.

All I remember from that flight is that my hotshot, Dennis-Quaid-in-*The-Right-Stuff*, dad showed off every aerial stunt in the book. He gunned the plane and aimed it at the infinitude of the sky until it went into a stall. We plummeted through space, corkscrewing downward like some plane in WWII stock footage, the three of us kids shrieking in mortal terror. After that stunt, he performed a gut-wrenching series of figure-eights. My brothers vomited into their laps. My dad cackled like a madman. He wanted to show off for his sons, and he didn't care if he risked killing us all, widowing his wife and making her childless in a matter of seconds.

As the LAN Airlines flight filled up, I was now suffused with dread. I got up to go to the bathroom, had trouble peeing in the upright coffin of a rest room. I was headed to Chile to research a novel, was going to travel the length and breadth of this sapling of a country that stretched north and south for nearly 3,000 miles, but never more than 100 west to east, to explore their wines for the *Town & Country* piece. All I knew about Chile was that they had 12 very distinct wine regions and that our CIA had assassinated Salvador Allende and installed a military dictatorship to govern with an iron fist back in '73. And I only had a smattering of Spanish. On top of everything, Laura was acting strange, as if she didn't want to come. I took a milligram of Xanax, crushed it with my teeth, then let the powder dissolve underneath my tongue. My pee was not forthcoming. Maybe I didn't need to go. I braced my hand on the inside of the fuselage and banged on it, hoping for a stream. A passenger pounded impatiently on the door. Had I been in there *that* long?

I tried to wash up as the importuning pounding continued thundering. My beleaguered brain was locked in combat between *I've got to get off this fucking plane to Chile* and *I can't get off this fucking plane to Chile because I need the writing gig and I'd be disappointing an entire nation*!

I finished up inside and unlocked the bathroom door. My image of the person knocking was of a man over six feet tall with the girth of an interior lineman. Much to my surprise it was a tiny Asian woman who had a scowl on her face as if she were about to fly for half a day to a place she didn't want to go.

"Sorry, Ma'am. I forgot my Avodart."

She didn't get the joke and scrambled inside to do whatever she needed to do to prepare for a long equatorial-crossing flight.

I walked back to my seat, like a woman in high heels who had been fucked all night long, steadying myself with sweaty hands on the headrests of the First Class passengers, as if the narrow aisle were booby-trapped with land mines. I tried to find that Zen space that Maya had implored me to focus on, but I was thinking Zin, not Zen, at that moment. God, I could use a drink to take the edge off!

When I returned to my aisle seat—no way was I going to be stationed at the window, 35,000 feet in the empyrean—I could see that the seat next to me was taken. The woman was turned away from me and staring out the window and I couldn't get a good look at her. As I sat down she turned to me. I was so anxiety-riddled at that moment, my brain a bag of Mexican jumping beans, I was afraid it was going to be someone I couldn't relate to, that we would sit in silence for hours like cellmates and go about our electronic device business. Instead, to my amusement, it was a woman, late 30's/early 40's I hazarded, with a face painted by Botticelli. Or was I hallucinating?

"Hi, my name is Ariadne," she said, offering me her hand over the armrest.

I took it and held it probably a little too tightly. "Miles," I said. "Miles Raymond."

"Nice to meet you," she said.

"Ariadne. Lover of Theseus. Led him through the labyrinth," I said nervously, stupidly probably.

"Yes." She smiled warmly. The Xanax was kicking in and I could feel Ariadne's presence as an anodyne to my anxiety.

"And, later, she became the lover of the god Dionysus."

"I didn't know that," she said with genuine surprise.

"What's your nationality, Ariadne—I love that name for some reason—at the risk of impudence and impropriety and probably some other IM- words I'm blanking on." I was nervous, and when nervous I grow loquacious. She had wavy, honey-colored hair that flowed over shoulders. Her eyes were the color of the Mediterranean on a hot summer day: aquamarine and mythically translucent. Her head rode atop a slender, but not anorexic, figure, and she appeared to be close to my height of 6'1", though that would prove to be a miscalculation when, later, she excused herself to go to the bathroom.

"I'm Greek," she said.

"Greek? Wow," I said. "I don't think I've ever met a Greek woman before."

"I was born in the U.S."

"You don't speak the native tongue?"

"No, I do," she said. "I work for the Greek Embassy."

"What do you do?"

"Educational development."

"And you're going to Chile to ...?"

"They've hired me to come down and help with their educational system. They're a developing country and they're famous for bringing in experts from all over the globe. Have you been before?"

"No. First time."

"Vacation?"

"I've spent my whole life on vacation!"

She chuckled. One of the flight attendants closed the door and locked it shut. I sucked in my breath. Anxiety suffused me again like an electric current to a condemned murderer. I gripped the armrests.

"I don't like flying," I said. "I once had to be de-planed. But, don't worry, I think I've gotten over my fear. I mean, did you know that 50,000 planes take off and land every day in the U.S. alone and, when was the last jetliner crash? Huh?"

"You'll be fine," she said.

Sharp cockpit announcements took us out of the conversation, then quieted as the flight attendants threaded down the aisle checking to make sure our seats were in their upright positions.

"How do you know so much about Greek mythology, Miles?" Ariadne asked in a mellifluous voice.

"Well, when I was nineteen years old I took a break from college and read the entire *Collected Works* of C. G. Jung. Yep, all twenty, big black volumes."

"That's impressive."

"It was a very eremitic time in my life."

She crinkled her nose at my use of *eremitic*. The plane started to taxi out to the tarmac, the engines rumbling thunderously.

"Takeoffs are the most dangerous," I started, in a state of controlled agitation. "My dad, who was a captain in the Air Force, once told me it's the most dangerous part of flying because the plane is loaded with fuel and is the heaviest it'll ever be during the flight and if something goes wrong ..."

She touched my hand with hers and the feeling was electrifying. "It's going to be fine," she said reassuringly.

"I'm terrified of flying," I confided.

"It's going to be okay," she said, after she let me go on with my litany of fears, my aerophobia anecdotes, and all the rest. As the plane came to a staggered, vibrating halt at the edge of the runway and revved its engine for takeoff, Ariadne asked, "And what are you going to Chile for, Miles?"

"Well," I began, my voice quavering, "I'm a writer. And they've invited me down to research the possibility of writing a novel. You could say I'm sort of an artist-in-residence of an entire country. Plus, I'm contracted to write a wine feature for *Town & Country Magazine.*"

"Are you someone famous?" she asked.

"I wrote a novel a while back that became kind of a cult film set in the wine world."

"What's the title?"

I told her.

She knitted her brow and looked at me, then shook her head.

"Well, it was a big success. A while back, admittedly."

"I'll have to check it out."

"And so what is it exactly you're going to be doing in Chile?"

"Self-educational development in their world of wine."

She smirked at my little dig.

"I'm just teasing," I said. "But, yes, I'll be touring their wine regions and meeting their winemakers."

"All by yourself?"

Her question caught me off balance. Lying came naturally to me. It was an affliction of my heavy drinking days and my years in Hollywood where you never volunteered the truth when it came to your C.V. In fact, you made shit up all the time. Prevarication is sport in the entertainment business; the best producers are pros at it! "Uh, yeah," I said. "I mean, I'm going to be meeting up with various people here and there, but, yeah ..."

The flight attendant materialized with the beverage cart. I turned to Ariadne. "I doubt they're going to have anything drinkable, but can I recommend a wine?"

"I'd love that," she said. She turned toward the window to watch the lights of L.A. flooded out by the clouds we were climbing heroically through and the distance we were putting behind it. The curve that adumbrated the side of her face looked sculpturally perfect, regal; Hellenic? I wanted to lean into her. She turned her head without moving her shoulders and smiled at me.

Our wines came. It was my first of many Chilean wines: Santa Rita. How appropriate. They had contested the Santa Ynez Valley AVA appellation of Santa Rita Hills, and a compromise was struck where the latter would spell its appellation Sta. Rita Hills. It was a Carménère, a sub-noble grape of southern France and elsewhere in the world that I had read Chile was pinning its hopes on much in the way Argentina had hung its fortunes on Malbec and Australia had crashed and burned with Shiraz—its goofy, and now national embarrassment, sobriquet for Syrah.

Anyway, the Carménère wasn't at all bad. Maipo Valley, here I come! We ordered a second round of Santa Rita Winery miniatures. Conversation tumbled out of us as naturally as if we were college alums. She was a gregarious gal. Get a little wine in her and she was positively verbally lubricious. She asked me some questions I had been asked many times: e.g., what the inspiration for my famous novel was? I launched into a lengthy narrative about my failed marriage, my failed feature indie films, my failed writing career ... "And, then," I concluded grandiloquently, "in one great Hail Mary, I wrote *Shameless*, with nothing to lose, didn't care a whit what I wrote, let it all hang out, as it were."

We were getting giddy on the wine as the Airbus hurtled through the sepulchral night. Whatever panic I had been experiencing in the bathroom earlier had vacated me and left me soaring in peace. There was a moment when I let myself go to the concept of Fate. What if I had been sitting next to that impertinent Asian woman? Or some obese cartoon fuck eating a Subway sandwich? Was there indeed someone looking over me, puppeteering my fate? And, if so, why would he care about me? I didn't believe in the spiritual world. Jesus to me was just the name of some underpaid laborer picking Pinot Noir grapes and occasionally getting crop-dusted for his efforts.

"Ariadne," I said, slurring my words a little, "I want you to lead me out of the labyrinth of my fears."

"Just exactly what are your fears, Miles?" she asked me in all seriousness, jolting me to reality.

"I fear not writing this next book. I fear being in a foreign country surrounded by people I don't know. I fear returning to L.A. and having no home. You see, I gave up everything: books, memorabilia, my papers—put it all in storage ..."

"Sounds liberating," she remarked.

I furrowed my brow and stared inward. The miniature of wine lay on the tray table in front of me. "I fear ... I fear not being able to find peace in this world. You see, for a long time I thought it was more important to have all this *Sturm und Drang* in my life, as if that were what I needed to create my art. I wanted conflict. I wanted turmoil. I wanted break-ups and personal destitution. Had I been happy I never would have written *Shameless*. Had I not been in arrears and living the life of a pauper those now iconic scenes would never have come to me. I needed to live in a world that was a maelstrom of personal tragedy so that I could find immortality in my despair. Does that make sense?"

"And you believe if you find peace that you won't be able to write anymore?"

"Exactly!" I said, and wanted to kiss her for the insight. "It'll be as if I had disembarked a placid harbor and headed out to stormy seas, then found myself in some port with calm, turquoise waters and blindingly white sand beaches and nut-brown girls with leis and skirts of grass and ..."—

"There won't be anything left to write about?"

"Exactly." I leaned in to her so that our shoulders were touching. "I have this fear that I'm going to close my eyes and when I open them you're going to be some three-hundred pound sweat hog stuffing your face with airline peanuts and breathing like a dragon with bellows-like lungs."

She laughed. "Then, don't close your eyes."

"I wish you could travel with me, Ariadne. We would have so much fun."

"But then you would have nothing to write about," she jested.

"No, no, no, no. I would write about this guy who had been through everything and now had come to a place of serenity. I would write about peace. But peace would involve finding a woman who could share that peace with me, because there's no peace in being alone." I was getting a little tipsy on the wine mixed with the Xanax. I could sense that I was growing maudlin, mawkish even. Airplanes did that to me. It was as though I were going to die every time I went up in one, so if I found a willing interlocutor I would talk a blue streak, stem-winder after stem-winder—if she would let me! As Ariadne was!—until I had exhausted all my fears, emptied them from my psyche. "What are your fears, Ariadne?"

"That I would get on a plane and be seated next to a guy who couldn't stop talking."

"I'm sorry," I said.

"I was joking," she said. "Where're you staying when you get to Santiago?"

"In Bellavista. At the Aubrey. Supposed to be nice."

She stared ahead without saying anything.

Lima, Peru

We touched down in Lima, Peru sometime after midnight. Ariadne and I had grown close during the flight. There was an announcement that there would be a change of planes. We deplaned on to the tarmac. The air felt different; it smelled different; it even tasted different; it was not the air that I had come to know in Southern California. Lights twinkled in the distance. A shuttle motored us to the terminal to wait for the next plane. I was worried about my baggage, but Ariadne reassured me that LAN was government-owned and that they didn't "fuck up, because they would have the president of the country breathing down their throat."

We followed the others into the LAN terminal. It was equipped a bit like a nightclub and the noise of the passengers assuaged some of my fears.

"Have you ever had a Pisco Sour?" Ariadne said, as we took seats next to each other.

"No," I said. "I've heard of them. What is it? I should know."

"Pisco is a distillate made from the Muscat grape. Highly alcoholic. They mix it with lime juice and a little bit of egg white. Should we try one?"

"Yes," I said.

A shapely cocktail waitress approached us. A thick nest of dark hair rested precariously on her small head and her face bore a monochromatic mask of make-up. Ariadne spoke to her in Spanish and the waitress pivoted in place and walked away.

I powered up my phone, but I couldn't get a connection. Ariadne explained that I would have to get a SIM card and sign up with one of the telecommunications carriers in Chile. An experienced world traveler, she was chockablock with advice. As we fell momentarily into our own universes, I turned on my laptop. It came whirring to life and the screen blasted me with familiar images. I checked my email quickly. There was one from Laura saying that she would be arriving in a few days, and I started to panic that maybe she wasn't going to come. There was one from Maya wishing me "safe travels," without referencing our night together. Maybe she wanted to expunge it—and me!—from her memory. Women do that to guys, too, I learned the hard way.

I looked up and there was Ariadne smiling. Our Pisco Sours came gleaming in their champagne flutes and we tasted them. It was highly acidic from the lime juice, but the beaten egg white imparted a kind of softness, a bit of velvet on the palate.

"Hm," I said, forearming a little moustache of the foamy concoction from my upper lip. "Not bad."

"Don't drink too many," she said. "You'll have a nasty hangover."

"I've learned to pace myself," I said ruefully, not wanting to go into the debauched and louche life I lived for several years after the movie came out.

"So, Ariadne, do you have a boyfriend?"

She leaned forward and fixed her gaze on me. "No."

"Why not? You're an alluring woman. You've got a great job. You're trenchantly insightful, well read ..."

"Do you think that's what men are looking for?"

"Well, I do have a tendency to project what *I'm* looking for onto the world."

Her eyes bore into mine without answering, as if she were attempting to wordlessly mine the truth from my soul. I could sense—or was it the *fata morgana* of the booze?!— that she was debating whether it felt right to be on the verge of letting herself go to a romance, or even a fling. Her eyes glinted like mica in sunlight above her smile. If I had to be honest with myself, I was hoping to fill the two days before Laura came with someone who could be a mirror to my anxieties. But, of course, it had to be someone who understood me. I honestly believed at that moment that someone upstairs had put her, Ariadne, on the plane next to me to protect me, that she was my guardian angel, a ghostly presence who had taken human form like some benign avatar, that there was a precious consanguinity between us that was immutable. And I knew in that moment that I was just feeling lonely, that I was using all my lexicological skills and pulling out all the stops to have her not leave me when we landed in Santiago. I was so afraid suddenly that I was going to go mad. I needed somebody. And here she was. And I had transformed her into the most dangerous of all women: the ultimate anima figure, the woman in dreams who Jung said destroyed men as they quested in their unconscious for the meaning of life.

"I don't know what you're looking for, Miles," she said over the hubbub in the LAN lounge, jarring me again out of this abyss of a reverie I had found myself tumbling down into. "But I can see that you're troubled. That you haven't found what you're looking for. That much I know. It's ironic, isn't it? You write comedy, but your life is anything but a comedy. If I were psychoanalyzing you, I'd say you were looking for a way out of the despair, and that you found it in comedy, but sometimes comedy belies your true emotional needs. Sometimes," she leaned even farther forward, "comedy is the way in which you avoid the emotional truth."

Her words stung me like nettles to the core of my being. She was right, of course. I found myself nodding, staring into my half-drunk Pisco Sour, ruminating on her words. I had Bandaid-ed my world with comedy. I had made fun of every important human emotion and I was left with not having felt anything. In trying to make light of things I had diminished their gravitas, brusquely shoved them aside. Even though I was often a basket case, I was living an emotionless life.

"You're probably right. I've been feeling anxious about this trip. My life has been in flux. I gave up practically all my worldly possessions to travel the world. I had this opportunity to come to Chile and I took it. I don't know where I'm going to land."

"It must be very freeing," she remarked in a rising tone to compete with the loudspeakers announcing that they would be boarding soon. "I, on the other hand, have a real job."

"And that must be very reassuring," I said.

"Reassuring or imprisoning?" she retorted.

I looked at her. We had forged a connection on a very deep level in a very short period of time. I'd be lying if I didn't admit that I was concocting a lie to not have Laura come after all and take off for three months in Chile with this woman who had parachuted to me, literally, out of the sky. But there was so much to figure out. All I knew was that I needed someone to be with me, that I would go mad if I was alone.

"We could have a lot of fun in Chile together," I said, to warm up the possibility on the burner of lunacy—knowing that Laura *was* coming, and that I wouldn't be able to stop her.

"We could," she said definitely. "You know, I think we really could." She leaned back and gazed out over the passengers straightening wearily to their feet. "By the way, I'm staying at the Aubrey, too."

My heart leaped out of my chest and I caught it in my throat before it hurled itself across the table.

We were herded back on to the shuttles that ferried us out to the tarmac. I had crossed the equator for the first time in my life and I was cocooned in trepidation. If it hadn't been for Ariadne, I might have had a meltdown. Maybe she was right. Maybe not having a mother who had wanted us three boys had left me with no foundation. Maybe I had grasped hold of writing as a substitute foundation for a fragile psyche that was prone to all manner of neuroses. I needed someone like Ariadne who understood me. But she was based out of Switzerland. I didn't want to move to Switzerland! Or Greece! The whole world was opening up to me like the earth fissuring apart as if in some science fiction movie where an overpaid celebrity saved the planet from the eschatological catastrophe that I always imagined was on the deadly horizon.

We re-boarded the fresh jetliner. "I hope our luggage made it," I chuckled nervously. I tried not to talk so much as the pilots warmed up the jet engines and issued announcements in Spanish which Ariadne translated for me. "Lima, Peru. Have you ever been to Lima?"

"Yes," she said. "They have great restaurants. It's the culinary capital of the world."

"So, you're staying at the Aubrey?" I finally acknowledged.

"Yes."

"Would you like to have dinner together?"

"That would be lovely, yes," she said.

Santiago

We landed in Santiago, Chile in the early morning hours. Out the window of the plane, when I hazarded a view, I could see the Andes to the east, towering jagged, peaky, arêtes, mountains like I had never seen before. The sky was an autumn blue, but, below, a blanket of smog covered the city in a brownish gloom. I still couldn't believe I was in South America. I still couldn't quite believe I had ventured below the equator.

Ariadne and I were both being met by people; she by her boss, and me by Silvio, a kind of uber-culture rep whose idea it was to invite me to come down and research the possibility of writing a novel about Chile's emerging wine region. I had only met Silvio once. He was short, European Spanish with little trace of the indigenous population. We had Skype-d many times. I was very clear in my exhortations that this three-month excursion not be about influence-peddling, but different cultures have different ideas about what's said and what's advanced as the truth. You'd think with all my years in Hollywood I would know the difference between speciousness and honesty.

My bags arrived and I said goodbye to Ariadne, who was still waiting for hers. We agreed to hook up later at the Aubrey. We hugged and waved, turned and waved a second time, and then she was swallowed up in a sea of arriving passengers.

I passed through Customs without a glitch. I was glad I had made a friend in Ariadne, someone who spoke fluent English and whom I could lean on if I started to feel panicky.

Weariness settled in on me. I needed to get somewhere to sleep. Silvio came bounding up to me. He was a little bulldog of a man with thinning hair and darting eyes. He had a thousand things he wanted to tell me, but I wasn't listening.

"How was your flight?"

"I made it," I attempted a joke.

"We can take you to your hotel," he said, solicitously taking my largest piece of luggage and manhandling it through the parking lot to his waiting SUV. "But they don't check in until 1:00 p.m. There's something we have to do first."

"What's that?"

"Interview."

"You didn't tell me about any interviews!"

Suddenly, the suave, urbane Silvio whom I had met in Hollywood several months ago turned into the PR flak with an agenda I was more acquainted with. "Yes. The interview. Remember?"

"No, I don't remember, Silvio. I'm tired. I need to get some food, anything."

"Food. We can get you food."

We pulled into traffic, and it was insane. Chileans drive like motorists in Italy: crazy, darting this way and that, with little regard for lane changes. Worse, the affable Silvio thought he was in a Formula One car, finding gaps and darting into them like a honey badger through a fence hole.

"Could you slow down, Silvio? Nerves are a little frayed."

"Yes, sure, of course, I can slow down."

He downshifted into third and my head jerked back like a crash dummy. The traffic was unnerving me. "Smoggy here, Jesus," I remarked.

"Yes, this time of year, the Andes are like a basin, there are too many cars in Santiago, way too many cars."

Santiago opened up like any major metropolis. It was no worse, no better than Los Angeles or what I imagined Mexico City to be like. I might have had a better first impression if I hadn't been so exhausted. Maybe I'd have felt less unsettled had I, or someone else, and not this nervous man, been driving. I knew there was going to be some culture shock, but I hadn't prepared for it. There was no way *to* prepare for it. Nightfall was my friend, but it was hours away. I imagined Ariadne and me at dinner, but the day was long before us.

Silvio found a place to park in the Beverly Hills-like Las Condes district. It appeared to be one of the more affluent neighborhoods in Santiago. He led me to a nice restaurant which was situated inside a delicatessen. I was feeling querulous, out of sorts, uncertain of why I had come, what I was doing in Chile; in short, plagued by doubts.

I ordered some eggs and coffee. The coffee tasted bitter, horrible. "What is this?" I said to the waitress. "*¿Que es eso?*"

She eyed me strangely. "*Café.*" She turned to leave.

Silvio explained: "Coffee is very bad in Chile. It's all Nescafé. But we will try to find you some good coffee."

In L.A. I had gotten into my single origin pour-over coffees, roasted within days of using, ground just before brewing, brewed at exactly the precise temperature, coffee so sublime it rivaled great wine, coffee, as far as I was concerned, as it was meant to be drunk. "Nescafé, Jesus." I shook my head.

Silvio didn't order anything. "And then after the interview we will go to the Vintners Association of Chile and meet everyone."

"Silvio, I'm tired. I've been flying for half a day. Can't we do this tomorrow?"

"No. They want to meet you. I told you all about this."

"No, you didn't tell me all about this. And, no, I don't remember," I said testily.

Silvio appeared to be put out, but he wanted to mollify me. I was about ready to accuse him of a bait-and-switch, but realized I was tired and maybe over-reacting. "We will just do this one interview and then meet everyone at the Vintners Association, okay?"

"You had more interviews lined up?" I asked incredulously.

I drank four cups of the watery, industrial waste-tasting instant coffee in a desperate effort to get a caffeine jolt, but I wasn't getting the buzz I needed to get up for the interview, the interview I hadn't been warned about. Jet lag was setting in. Living out of a suitcase now, I felt like a child of the wind, the pure *puer aeternus*, but now, suddenly, I felt too cut adrift, a prisoner, paradoxically, of my own outlandish freedom.

In hot November sunlight—I was reminded that November was May in Chile and summer was around the corner—Silvio drove me in a clock-ticking silence to a large industrial complex through a maze of traffic that he negotiated with practiced, if manic, ease. Solicitously, he led me into the foyer where we had to sign in through security. Then to an elevator that rode to the fourth floor. My first impression of Chile, of Santiago at least, was that it was a very modern city. I was still on tenterhooks from the long flight and I wanted this interview to be over with.

The moment we got off the elevator the building started to tremble. *What the fuck?* Employees of the TV station we had stopped at leaped out of their chairs and dived helter-skelter underneath their desks. Silvio grabbed me around the waist and took me to the ground like some high school wrestler. "Put your hands over your head," he instructed.

A native Californian, I had been in many earthquakes before, but never in unfamiliar buildings, and never after a 12-hour flight, my nerves raw from hurtling through the night's oblivion.

"Just an after-shock," Silvio excused the earth's geologic outburst. He dusted himself off and clambered to his feet. He could see that I was shaken. "We have a lot of earthquakes down here in Chile," he said. "Nothing to worry about."

"What about that 9.2 in where the fuck was it?"

"Concepción. And it wasn't 9.2. It was a 7." Actually, it was an 8.8. and some believe it might have been more powerful than that because the old Richter Scales they had hadn't been recalibrated.

I glanced around. No one seemed too disconcerted by the "after-shock." They scrambled back into their desk chairs, wiped up spilled coffee, rebooted their computers and went back to work like nothing had happened, like it had been a Chilean fire drill. In L.A., of course, the buildings would have been evacuated. The employees would have been given the day off. People afflicted with anxieties— half of the greater L.A. area!—would have speed-dialed 911 and been transported to area hospitals where the ERs would have been flooded with people believing they were having a cardiac event, when in fact they were having a panic attack. The whole fucking city would have shut down. Not in Chile, apparently. These stalwart souls proudly, and defiantly, took their earthquakes in stride.

Silvio ushered me into a waiting room. My nerves were still vibrating like taut piano wires. I wasn't sure I wanted to be on the fourth floor of a building just then. A glass of wine might have calmed my nerves, but I didn't dare ask—it was only 11:00 a.m.!—as I had developed a reputation as someone who could put it away, even if those days were long in the past; though the Internet made the past all too present.

In a waiting room, Silvio coached me, "They're just going to ask you what you're doing down here. Say nice things. Don't mention the earthquake."

"Don't mention the earthquake?!" I exclaimed. "I say what's on my mind, Silvio. If this were L.A., *everyone* would be talking about the fucking earthquake."

"I know, I know, I know," he said in his rapid-fire manner of speech. "But, here in Chile, we don't want to scare away the tourists."

"Ah, so I'm the PR flak for an entire country, is that it?" I said peevishly.

"No, no, no," he said. "It's not like that."

"I want to like Chile," I said. "I don't want to believe I'm being used."

Silvio went silent. He had his own little immurement of petulance in his being. We were not off to a particularly propitious start.

Carmen, a Chilean production assistant in a short skirt, came out to get us. She wore little make-up and her hair was the color of a raven's. She bent from the waist to greet me. "You are Miles Raymond?"

"Yes. I mean *si*."

For some reason this made Silvio laugh. Then Carmen laughed. "Come with me," she said.

I rose on shaky legs—the long trans-equatorial flight, the no sleep, the Go-Kart drive through a foreign city of seven million polluted by smog and the din of honking horns, and then an earthquake!

Carmen led me into a large room. Everywhere I looked there were TV cameras on movable, wheeled platforms. Large monitors protruded from wall mounts for the techs to adjust and tweak.

I turned to Silvio. "Silvio!" I said in a rebelling tone, "this is a fucking live TV show!"

"You'll be fine," he said, reassuringly. "Just five minutes. We want you to say hello to the country of Chile."

"Hello to the country of Chile? Are your empanadas spiked with LSD?" I quipped. Silvio chuckled, oddly. "I did not agree to go on fucking live TV. I came down here to visit wine regions, meet the locals, research a book," I protested.

"And tomorrow we get your car," he said, as if that contractual stipulation fulfillment would mollify me.

I took a deep breath and exhaled. My mind raced. It was as if I had no one to talk to except myself, and that's a dangerous dominion for a writer to reside!

I was directed by a gesticulating Carmen to a swivel chair behind a desk. Across the room a newscaster was finishing up a report in Spanish. I couldn't tell what he was talking about. Another woman scurried over and Carmen introduced her as my make-up person. She was a young woman with a shy smile on her face. Suddenly, I feared that they were going to make me look like a Kabuki actor and I waved her off.

"I don't need any make-up," I said.

The make-up artist looked hurt. She turned to Carmen. Carmen said to me, "You don't want make-up?"

"No. I'm fine. Let them see the real Miles Raymond!"

"We just put a little bit on maybe?"

"No, I'm fine. Really." I tried to be amiable, not peevish, even though my nerves were unraveling like old toaster cords.

Silvio hovered nervously. His gaze darted around everywhere. Worry etched into his manhood and you could see it in the gloom of his countenance. This was not off to a good start. His commission was in jeopardy. The artist wasn't cooperating!

A slim man in his forties, elegantly attired, materialized out of the back. He was introduced as *señor* somebody, but the name arrowed through my tired brain to a hole in oblivion. We shook hands, exchanged pleasantries, then took seats side by side at a crescent-shaped desk facing three cameras. He smiled at the camera. I reached my left hand into my pocket and fingered my vial of Xanax and fished it out. I tried to discreetly uncap it, shake out one of the blue pills. The interviewer threw me a strange look, but proceeded with the introduction as I dissolved the pill and let it sink between my tongue and the bottom of my mouth for maximum delivery of the Alprazolam that I desperately needed. Another earthquake and I would have been hauled off to Santiago's version of the loony bin.

"Welcome to Chile, Miles," he said, after concluding his introductions.

"Thank you. *Gracias*. Happy to be here," I said, forcing a smile.

"And what brings you to Chile, our viewers would like to know?"

I contemplated the question for a second. In my peripheral vision I could see Silvio pacing behind the cameras, hoping this would go well, hoping I wouldn't launch into something that would compromise all he had promised about my coming to Chile. "Well, I'm here to drink, I mean learn about, the fabulous wines of Chile," I said, digging deep for my least specious PR.

"What are you hoping to discover?"

"Well, I don't know a lot about Chilean wines. So, I'm hoping to find that this emerging region is eminently suitable for producing some world class quaff."

The interviewer chuckled. He continued on, asking me mostly inane questions about *Shameless*, and what my new novel would be about.

"I don't know," I said, feigning a bit of exasperation. "All I know is that Chile is a country of vast meso-climatic diversity, that it's the most topographically and geologically varied country in the world, which bodes well for the variety of wines that they produce. I look forward to nights of over-imbibition."

The interview was over. I can't remember all what I said. Silvio escorted me to the elevator and down to the first floor and out into the bright sunlight.

"How'd I do?" I asked.

"Fine," he said. "Fine."

I didn't know if that was code-speak for it not having been fine, or if it really was fine.

We drove to a neighborhood where there was a commercial building. The Xanax had zoned me out. I was tired, but I felt like I was ready for anything, my anxiety having been quashed.

We rode two floors up to another warren of offices. Silvio, moving quickly, as if he had other pressing obligations, brought me to a reception area. Large posters advertised wineries and wine regions. Above the posters was brightly-colored lettering spelling out "Vintners Association of Chile."

After a moment we were ushered into an office. There, two people, a silver-haired man named Carlos and a woman in her thirties who went by Francesca, greeted me warmly. We talked about my itinerary, what I hoped to accomplish in the country. I kept telling them that I just wanted to discover Chile's vastness, that I wanted to be left alone. This announcement seemed to disconcert them and they exchanged dismaying glances.

"Yes, Miles will do some interviews and then we will let him discover the country."

Even in my befogged brain I could sense there were competing agendas here. Whenever I smell discontent I know what lies behind it: money. A private investigator, whom I interviewed for research for a novel I was writing, said to me: "They come to me for two reasons, Miles. Love or money. And it's usually the latter." I always remembered that.

Back in the car, I said to Silvio, "Take me to the hotel."

"We just have one more interview, Miles."

"Silvio! I didn't come down here to do fucking interviews. It looks like influence-peddling. I came down here to explore your great country and hopefully return with enough material to write a novel."

He angrily downshifted into second and bulled past a dilatory car, honking his horn as if he were ready to kill him. Or me.

"This is not what we agreed to," I said.

"Just one more interview," he cajoled.

"Please," I expostulated. "I'm tired. I just got off a long flight. I need a shower. I need a glass of wine. I need something. But not another interview!"

He looked alternately wounded and exasperated. I sucked in my breath. "Okay, one more interview."

His hard-bitten expression was suddenly flooded with emotion, as if his daughter had just recited *I do* in front of 500 people.

At the next interview, which we were late for, there was a professional photographer. I wasn't ready to be photographed, but here he came after me, like some deranged paparazzi. He ordered me around in Spanish and, too tired to complain, I just resigned myself to complying. Half of me kept thinking: I can get on a plane and just fly the fuck out of here.

The interview was with a young man who asked intelligent questions about my coming to Chile for a major newspaper, *El Mercurio*, that I later learned had supported the Pinochet coup d'état. *Miles*, I thought to myself, *what have you gotten yourself into?*

Ariadne

The Hotel Aubrey was shelved into a hill overlooking the barrio known as Bellavista. It's a small hotel with only a dozen or so rooms, a restaurant on the premises, and a relaxing pool whose cooling waters beckoned.

I checked in. The room was average sized, but well-appointed. I threw down my luggage and collapsed onto the bed. I laid there thinking about my life.

At age 25, hopes and dreams bursting in my wretched heart, I moved to L.A. to attend film school. That didn't work out. I married the woman of, then, my dreams and, with her parents' support, wrote and directed two independent feature films. The second one floundered at the box office and left our marriage in tatters. Our lives, and sensibilities, bifurcated. As she went off to become an Oscar-winning filmmaker, I fell into impecuniousness. At wit's ends, having given up my dream to write and direct movies, I wrote a novel. Through sheer luck it found its way to a prominent, up-and-coming, director. Nothing could prepare me for the mess I would make of my life after all the acclaim. It was as if I were in a whirlwind of expectations with everyone now venally wanting something from me. When you're a loser you meet only honest people. They'll tell you: "You're a loser, Miles!" When you're a success in Hollywood the mountebanks and the con artists and the mendacious agents and managers fan out like cockroaches to feast on the carcass of a freshly roasted chicken left overnight in an apartment in the East Village. They will lie to your face to close a deal. They will get you to sign contracts whose fine print will one day sodomize you. You learn that so many people made money off of something and you made next to nothing. You wonder how this could have happened to you. Weren't my agents and lawyers looking out for me?

The images and emotions of my life were unspooling at me in a kaleidoscope of scenes and voices and distorted fun-house faces as I stared at the ceiling fan, turning slowly, as if stirring up these resentments in the murky basement of my beleaguered psyche. I should have been a millionaire, I tried to calm myself with a sardonic joke, a joke that only I laughed at. Of course it's a cliché that fame and fortune is fleeting. Of course others are going to swoop down and rip you off, Miles. What'd you expect? You're not stupid. You saw *Sunset Blvd.* a hundred times. You saw *The Player*. You know better than anyone else that it's a mercenary world and that the players are all schmaltz and smarm and schmooze when you've got the goods. And then they're off to their hideaways, no longer even replying to emails when your well has run dry. You know there are dark and perfidious forces lurking everywhere you go. I guessed, I continued talking out loud to myself for fear I would go mad, not that people would treat me with respect, but that they wouldn't so blatantly rip me off. Worse, they ripped me off without a conscience! It's as if it were business as usual. *You're gullible*, I kept intoning to myself. *So fucking gullible* ... I believe almost anything anyone says to me until the lie becomes so monstrously obvious.

I couldn't believe how extravagantly the players in Hollywood could so openly lie. Because I refused to lie, because I refused to sell out, because I felt the need, after a decade of loneliness that followed in the wake of divorce and the tragic death of two parents and my steep fall into obscurity and suicidal despair, to celebrate. But celebration can lead down dark roads, can lead to rabbit holes and cul-de-sacs, and there I found myself one day, curled up in a fetal position wondering what had become of me.

I pulled myself together, examined the carnage, much like the last surviving soldier on a battlefield whose enormity had ended many young lives, and saw that the devastation was worse than I first feared. The climb back did not, unfortunately, provide me a side exit back to the life I had when I was attending the Academy Awards and the Golden Globes and being fêted by wineries and wine festivals and all the rest of the hoopla that had now subsided. No, the climb back was a 180-degree turn and slow ascent over the oleaginous-slippery path I had gone down. There was no other way of ascent than traversing back over my own shit.

Enantiodromia: "The super abundance of any force inevitably produces its opposite." A Jungian principle. I should have known, more than anyone else, that I would pay a price for my not knowing the limits of satiety during that heady time. And to blame anyone other than myself is just pure naïveté. I should have known from my Darwin that if you've got a cache of food—in Hollywood terms, a hot property that everyone wants—then the carnivores are going to converge, the vultures are going to wheel in the sky in blackening swarms. That success, unguarded, is an invitation to rack and ruin.

I thought I had a handle on it all and was hoping sleep would claim me. But I never could sleep during the day. Thank God my phone didn't work. I feared Silvio calling me to implore me to do another interview. Yes, I had come to Chile to escape L.A. 30 years of my life was on that pavement, the most roads of any city in the entire world, and I had probably worn the tread of my soul on half of their miles. I had come to Chile to escape the onus of living my life as an artist. It had not been a fun life so far. True, I never succumbed to the barbarousness of a steady job, the responsibility of kids, and all that that entailed—I couldn't fucking imagine!—but loneliness is a curse all its own. Then it struck me like a wayward meteor plummeting to earth:

I had come to Chile to dispossess myself *of* myself!

Sleep fell upon me in that way that we only know after the fact. A red light was blinking on the phone. I phoned the desk. They spoke perfect English.

"You have a message from someone named Ariadne. She is in room eleven."

Eleven was my lucky number. I'm not into numerology, *per se,* but I've always had talismanic objects or carried lucky coins in my pockets. Maybe it can be traced back to my golfing days where we all carried a special coin—that is, of course, until it didn't work anymore and we had to "get new change." But, as I passed the 40 year mark in my life, as my novel became a movie and turned me into a minor celebrity and finally put some money in my pocket, superstitions started to haunt me. Was I reaching for the numinous? Was I trying to find meaning and understanding in things that had happened? Why had I gone so many years as a writer before finding success? Why was I meeting certain people in my life, all of a sudden? Was there a deeper purpose, a teleology behind it all?

Hot water rained over me as I hung my head in the shower and cogitated on these pinwheeling thoughts. I realized I was spending too much time talking out loud, and that it wasn't healthy. And, too, Chile was panicking me. I had only been here but a day and I felt like I had been massacred on the I-5 and this is where the spirits had sent me instead of heaven.

As I was toweling off, the phone jangled. I lunged for it, thinking it was Ariadne. It was Silvio.

"Are you okay?" he asked nervously.

"Yes, Silvio. I'm fine."

"Did you get some sleep?"

"I took a nap, yes."

"There are some people I'd like you to meet."

"Not tonight, Silvio." I glanced at my watch. On the flight down I had set it for Chilean time. It was 8:11. (My God, there was that 11 again!)

"They had a dinner planned."

"You didn't tell me about it," I said testily. "Reschedule."

"Please. I come get you."

"No, Silvio. I have jet lag. I'm wiped. I'm tired. Please, just leave me in peace for twenty-four hours to gather myself. Please. *Para el amor de dios.*"

For some reason that evoked the biggest laugh from Silvio, a laugh so boisterous that the receiver seemed to rumble in my very hand. Maybe I had assuaged *his* nerves because, by employing my smattering of Spanish to make a point, I had started to accept the fact that I was in Chile. Maybe I was becoming Chilean! That seemed to calm him and he said goodbye and hung up.

I pulled on a black T-shirt and faded jeans and dialed the desk and asked for room 11. There was no answer. I declined to leave a message. For a brief moment a nauseation invaded my stomach like an army of ravening insects. Had she left? Would I be all alone tonight? God, I was feeling so insecure all of a sudden. And with Laura coming in a few days. Was I going out of my mind and didn't know it? I needed a glass of wine.

Sometimes in this life, out of nowhere, the greatest pleasure strikes in the heart and paralyzes you like a curare dart blown at you by some unseen person. In this case it must have been *Amor*. On the patio of the Aubrey, where the restaurant spilled out to, sat Ariadne. A single candle in a yellow cup colored her face golden. When she saw me cross the patio and come toward her she turned and flourished a warm, reassuring smile.

I grabbed the back of the chair across from her. "Do you mind?" I asked.

"No. Please."

I sat down across from her. The table was tiny and our faces were suddenly closer than I had imagined. She looked different now that she had showered and applied a light touch of make-up and, I thought, a bit more lipstick than a woman having a casual dinner all by her lonesome would.

"I didn't know if you'd be here."

"Why? Did you think I would lie to you?"

"The world I live in is full of prevarications."

She laughed. "I'll bet."

"It's good to see you," I said, training my eyes on hers.

"You, too."

A waiter surfaced out of the dark. He spoke in halting English, but Ariadne shifted him quickly over to Spanish, which she appeared to be fluent in. "Would you like a glass of wine?" she asked.

"Should we get a bottle?"

"Yeah, let's," she said. "Let's celebrate being in Chile."

I flipped open the wine list and was greeted with a daunting selection of mostly Chilean wines. "Well, we have to have a wine from Chile. Red or white, Ariadne?"

She threw back her head and her hair tumbled over her shoulders and she gazed up at the stars. "It's so warm out, let's have a white."

"I'm flying blind here," I said, perusing the wine list. "How about the Casa Marin Sauvignon Blanc?"

"Excellent choice," the young waiter replied, smiling, leaving us to the immurement of conversation.

"So, how was your day?" Ariadne asked.

"My day was ... hectic. I had a live TV thing, an interview with *El Mercurio*, a photo shoot ..."

The bottle of wine came. It was ice cold. The waiter uncorked it and poured me a little dollop to taste.

"Mmm, this is interesting," I remarked. "Pour us."

He smiled and poured us two full glasses. I toasted Ariadne. "Here's to my first night in Chile. With a beautiful woman I somehow serendipitously got seated next to on the plane."

"Here's to your next book," she said.

"The one I may or may not write," I said, clinking glasses conspiratorially with her. I nosed the wine and took some into my mouth and slurped it around inside. It wasn't like the Sauvignon Blancs I was used to. The minerality of it alone made it stand apart from any other Sauvignon Blanc I had ever had. "Wow, that's astonishing."

"It's the Andean snowmelt," Ariadne said.

"You think so?" I asked.

"What are grapes but water? Isn't the water and the land everything?"

"And the climate, too, yes," I added, glad to be in the company of someone so wine knowledgeable. "I mean, there are Sancerres, but they've become so fucking prosaic. And the New Zealand ones don't do it for me anymore once I realized how adamant they had become in the commoditization of a flavor profile."

"You think?" she said, swirling the wine in her glass.

"They found a formula and they repeat it, or try to, every year. I'm sure there are still some good ones, but they've lost whatever originality rocketed them to attention in the first place. And the Sauv Blancs from Napa are just too flabby. Big and golden"—I was hitting my stride—"and probably malolactic and barrel ageing and all this fucking manipulation. I mean, Ariadne, look at this wine." I held up the glass. "It looks like water from the purest aquifer on the planet. I'm getting excited." I threw up my one free hand. "Over a Sauv Blanc!"

The waiter returned and asked how the wine was. I re-exclaimed my enthusiasm in no uncertain terms and he was happy that I had found his country's wines so thrilling. "Are you ready to order?"

We ordered. As we were in a hotel that was frequented by Americans and Europeans they didn't really have any authentic dishes on the menu like *congria*, but I needed, for some reason, not to plunge myself so quickly into the culture. I needed baby steps, as it were.

When we were done ordering and had surrendered our menus, Ariadne turned to me and smiled wryly. "So, it was a stressful day," she said.

"Yeah," I said, exhaling a sigh.

"You're the court jester."

"I know. In life there are two people: those who can create and those who want to create. The latter outnumber the former by a thousand to one."

She laughed. "I guess I'm one of the 999."

"What do you do?"

"I paint," she said.

"Something I know nothing about."

"It relaxes me. I would never think to myself that I could be an artist."

"What most people don't realize is that it's not an avocation. It's a life. And it's a life that most of them would not have the stomach to live. But they dream about it. And if they have money they can buy you. And, you see—because this has happened to me so many times—at first they're all excited to be in your company. You can see it in their gleeful faces. I mean, I never thought of myself as anyone special, as a celebrity or anything. In fact, I generally thought of myself as a piece of shit, if you want to know the truth. And, for most of my life, others thought so, too."

I paused as Ariadne laughed at my hyperbole. I took the opportunity to take another sip of the wine. The mineral characteristics of it were just surging through. When we drove into town I noticed that the river that bisected Santiago was a bluish-white color, not achromatic exactly, more of a coastal blue or a snow white dusted with robin's egg blue, and it's that water, water the color I'd never seen before that, Ariadne was right, that was in the grapes in my glass. I had never had a Chilean white wine before and I realized I was tasting the Andes! How could I not be? They were mere miles away. Their abundant snowfall melted and flowed to the twelve wine regions that made up this fascinatingly topographically diverse country. I was exulting in my head.

I attempted to parachute back into the thread of the conversation. "I lost my train of thought. I was thinking about this delicious wine."

"You were talking about artists versus non-artists, I think," she reminded me.

"Well, yes. You know, at first they're all enamored that they've hired you, or whatever, then, as one famous producer once said to me, 'When we hire you we feel like we own you.' And I get it. But I didn't come down here to be puppeteered."

"Tell them."

"Should I threaten to head to Santiago International?"

She laughed. "They would have a heart attack."

"We'll see how it goes."

"Speaking of artists, did you know that one of Pablo Neruda's houses is right next to here?"

"No, I didn't. I haven't read all my brochures yet."

"Well," she said, chuckling, "it is. Though I would doubt that the people you are dealing with would be fans of his."

"What? He's a Nobel Prize-winning poet!"

"He was a communist. In fact, they disinterred his remains recently to see if maybe he was poisoned by the CIA in collusion with Pinochet's henchmen," she said.

"I thought he died of prostate cancer?"

"He died within weeks of the military coup. That was the official statement on Neruda's death. But there's strong evidence that he, like Allende, was assassinated by the CIA. You have to realize, Miles, Neruda had a voice that could reach the world. And you also have to realize that Chile is a very, very complex country." She held up her wineglass. "Just like this wine."

I nodded. No doubt there was truth in her words, but I had yet to discover Chile. "Do you want to go out somewhere?"

"Sure," she said. "I will take you somewhere I know you will like."

I paid the bill, then we walked down out of the Aubrey's hillside compound. On the streets I noticed that the police were all in riot gear and that all the patrol cars' windows were barricaded with steel meshing.

"What's going on there?" I asked Ariadne, as we waited for a cab.

"There were student riots recently. The Socialist Party is still very much a factor in this country," she explained as we hopped into a tiny cab that cramped my legs. She spoke in Spanish to the cabbie. All I could make out was "Lastarria" and the name of a street, "José Victorino."

The cabbie drove us through Bellavista, a section of Santiago that was popular with students. Being their summer, the barrio's streets were lined with outdoor cafés. There was so much life in the streets! And it was loud. Music pumped from every bar and every restaurant.

"And it'll get louder as the night wears on. Chileans like to stay out late. There's the Chile that you see, and then there's the Chile that you don't see," Ariadne explained. "There's this book, *Bizarro Santiago*, that tells you all about this other Chile."

"I have to get this book."

"I'm afraid it's only in Spanish. You would have to get someone to translate it for you."

"Where are we going?"

"We're going to Lastarria," she said. "To a place I think you'll love."

Bocanáriz

The cab lurched to a stop on a busy, narrow street. Within minutes we were on a pedestrian street, José Victorino, in the barrio Lastarria, where cars were not allowed. There were more cafés, one after the other. Ariadne ticked off the ones that were worth visiting and the ones that were tourist traps.

There were also a lot of dogs ambling around. They all seemed to be mixed breed Labradors. They moved in packs. The Chileans ignored them. The dogs were not aggressive. In fact, they were quite passive.

"Ariadne, what's the deal with all the dogs?"

"Ah, *los perros*," she said. I had taken three years of Spanish in junior high school so I had a smattering of their lexicology. "Yes, they are everywhere. It's common in these countries down here. They let their own dogs have litters, then they throw them out because they're too expensive."

"There are so many of them. They're everywhere!"

"I know."

"But they look so timid."

"They're very friendly. They're just hungry. And the Chileans feed them."

"Don't they have Animal Control like in the U.S.? You know what would happen to these animals in the U.S., don't you?"

Ariadne leaned into me sort of conspiratorially. "This is a very Catholic country," she said. "They are very pro-life. No mayor or president could ever campaign on a platform that they would get rid of the dogs. They would lose."

"They co-exist with them."

"Yes."

"But, during Pinochet's regime ..."

"I know," she said, chopping me off. "Like I said, it's a very complicated country. It was just granted developed nation status. Chile has growing pains."

We waded through the throngs of mangy, hungry, but paradoxically, friendly dogs, and young Chileans—Ariadne pointed out that we were surrounded by universities—out on the town.

Two short blocks down José Victorino's version of Barcelona's Ramblas we came to a small café called Bocanáriz with fenestration that flowered out onto the sidewalk. The sky was still colored a deep shade of blue and night hadn't fallen yet. The milieu and the ambiance felt very romantic as we stepped inside. There were tables on the sidewalk, but I preferred to sit inside.

A pretty, young Chilean woman led us to a small table against the wall.

"I love how all the people are out in the streets, walking and talking. You wouldn't find this anywhere in L.A.," I remarked.

"You're not in L.A. anymore, Miles," Ariadne said. "You're halfway around the world vertically."

I smiled and turned my attention to the interior wall. On it was a chalkboard that seemed to stretch to all four corners of the wall. In white paint meant to look like handwritten letters in chalk was a vast selection of wines, none of which I had ever heard of. They were listed by grape variety, leading off with Chile's adopted national grape, Carménère.

"Wow," I said. "Look at that wine list!" I scanned it more closely. "They're all Chilean wines," I said.

"Yes," said Ariadne.

The dark-haired woman re-approached the table, bearing menus. She said something in Spanish I couldn't understand. Ariadne asked her if she spoke English. She did, brokenly. "You would like to do some wine tasting?"

"Yes, we would," I said, excitedly. "And bring us a spit bucket."

She frowned at *spit bucket*. Ariadne didn't know the word for it either. So, she launched into a little charades that our server still didn't comprehend. So, I picked up the candle holder with both hands and pretended to expectorate into it.

She brightened up. "¿Ah, *escupitero*?"

"*Si*," I said, etymologically splicing together part of the word that meant *spit* or *expectorate*.

"*Si*," said Ariadne, "*Escupitero*."

"I can't swallow all the wines that I'm hoping to sample from your amazing wine list," I enthused, gesticulating to the chalk board. She got the message, loud and Chilean.

"Yes, we have many wines."

"And all Chilean?"

"*Si*," she said. "You are American?"

"Yes," I said.

"You are in wine?"

I wasn't sure I wanted to tell her who I was. Ariadne decided it wouldn't hurt, so she confided to her the title of the book I had written. She beamed like a stadium's floodlights suddenly switched on. She snapped her fingers, as if trying to remember something. "You were on the TV today? You come to drink Chilean wines."

"And to write a novel." (Ariadne translated what I said.)

"You will have much to discover," she said. "I am Daniela. Welcome to Bocanáriz."

"Thank you. I'm Miles. This is my new friend, Ariadne."

We shook hands all around.

"I love this place already, Daniela. There is no place like this in Los Angeles. The city of lost angels."

Ariadne laughed, then translated for a furrowed brow Daniela. Then, she, too, laughed.

"Bring us the wines that you like," I said.

"Start with white?" she asked.

"Yes. And the *escupitero*."

She laughed at my pronunciation and then pivoted in the small room and disappeared into the kitchen.

"Thank you for bringing me here," I said to Ariadne.

"They didn't tell you about this place?" she asked, incredulous.

"No, no one's told me anything."

"This is the hub for all wine in Santiago. You will not discover a better place to sample the wines of Chile."

"It's an incredible wine list," I said. "We are going to drink our way through Chile."

"I don't want to sleep with you, Miles," Ariadne said, in a tone meant to get it out of the way.

I nodded. It was as if some ghostly incubus had entered my soul and stolen all its romance and left it bereft, the night empty of excitement. "That's okay, Ariadne," I said, trying to disguise the disappointment in my voice. "I'm just glad we met and you were able to help me acclimatize to this new land, as it were. I'm terrified, I guess, of being alone."

"I know. But you have someone coming tomorrow, don't you?"

I sat back in my chair and studied her face. She gave me a look, as if, *Are you going to deny it?* "How do you know that?"

"You fell asleep on the plane and left your computer on. I saw an email with a photo. She's very pretty, this Laura."

"Ah, yes, Laura. We haven't seen each other in a year. We only had a weekend together. I wanted someone to travel with. If I had known I was going to meet you I would have made different arrangements. This is some cruel twist of fate from a god who knows no mercy," I said in my occasionally magniloquent manner in an effort to disguise a rising emotion.

112

Ariadne chuckled a little.

"Let's just have fun tonight, okay?" I said, reaching a hand across the table and resting it gently on top of hers. "Let's pretend there's no one in my future and no one in yours, that tonight we only have each other, and that it's the only night we have to be together, and make every moment rhapsodic with the promise of what it might have been had we met under different circumstances. Okay?"

Her head lolled to one side and her eyes grew a little starry, I thought, for a moment. "Okay, Miles. I love how you talk."

I squeezed her hand. "It doesn't always have to be about lovemaking. Just to be in the presence of a beautiful woman like you, connect on a cerebral level, sometimes that's just as euphoric. Sometimes more so."

Daniela returned and ended the moment. She set down six tasting glasses, each holding a small amount of white wine. Below the wineglasses were cut-out pieces of paper with the descriptions of the wines.

"Sauvignon Blancs from Casablanca and Leyda Valleys," she said. A young waiter appeared behind her and handed her what looked like a small flower vase. "And your *escupitero!*"

Everyone laughed. Daniela ceremoniously passed me the spit bucket. I set it next to me on the small table. We declined appetizers, explaining that we had already eaten, but we welcomed bread and olive oil and cheeses.

The wines helped Ariadne and me shift the focus of our conversation from our inchoate romance—if that's what it was—to the romance of wine, where a different kind of danger lurked, one I hoped the *escupitero* would rescue me from.

We started with an '11 Casas del Bosque. In the glass the wine was pale yellow. It had a pure color like the Casa Marin we had shared over dinner. "I'm so used to Sauvignon Blancs being golden in color. These wines look so pure to me," I said, holding my wineglass up to the light and studying it.

We sipped, slurped the wine around in our mouths, then I spit. Ariadne didn't. That was a promising sign, I noted to myself, if I had any chance of getting her to change her mind about wanting me in that way that brings people to the apotheosis of oblivion. In truth, I didn't even want sex; all I wanted was the gentle comfort of her strong arms. There was something so calming and reassuring about her demeanor. I felt safe in her presence. And, unquestionably, I was having my doubts about the tempestuous Laura. You know very quickly when you travel with someone if you want to be with her for the rest of your life. Very quickly. Consternation was never far from the penumbra of my consciousness when I thought about Laura's arrival.

"If I'd known I was going to meet this beautiful woman," I found myself poeticizing over the noise of the café, "whom I feel a connection with on such a deep level, I would have told Laura to cancel her plans. I'm serious, Ariadne."

"What do you think of this wine?" she asked, bucking me from the subject. She flung her head across the table and met my eyes with her piercing blue ones. "You're just lonely, Miles. You've been lonely all your life."

Her words halted me dead in my tracks. Had I been hopscotching from one woman to the next to fill this emotional void? Now that I was no longer drinking as heavily as I once had, the emotions were so much rawer, so much more omnipresent, not entombed by over-imbibition, only to rear themselves, Hydra-headed and cause even worse havoc under the piercing, throbbing sun of a hangover?

I turned back to the low common denominator of my wine. I stared into the miniature oceans of her Mediterranean blue eyes, fixing my gaze on hers. I was falling in love and it was impossible for her not to feel it. "You can taste the sea in this wine. What do you think?"

"Yes, I think you're right."

Daniela was standing over us again, smiling at our reactions. Ariadne translated what I had said. She spoke in Spanish to Ariadne, but kept turning to me, hoping I would understand.

Ariadne translated: "She says that this winery is in Casablanca Valley, just west of here. That the ocean is very near. And very cold."

"Yes, I know," I said. I read that the water never gets above 60 degrees and, in the winter, plummets into the insanely cold 40's. How do they get grapes to ripen?"

Ariadne turned to Daniela who explained to her in Spanish that the inland weather can be hot in the summer, but that they have had challenging years. The soils, she said, are also different than anywhere in the world. They are alluvial and interlarded with volcanic and granite rock. The taproots of the vines spiderweb deep to find moisture. They twist and turn around granite until they find the source of their nourishment and the slow, dripping distillation of horticultural hydration. And then they bring that to the *cepas* (the grapes).

The second white was from Kingston, another Sauvignon Blanc. I looked at it in the glass with what I thought, if I had a mirror, was an expression of astonishment. It was as pure as water, not even a splash of gold or straw. It looked like a translucent silver.

"Sauvignon Blanc," said Daniela.

Ariadne and I tasted it and cogitated. It was a delicate wine. There was no wood in its fermentation or ageing. It was as pure an expression of the Sauvignon Blanc grape as I had ever experienced. Totally unmanipulated, unadulterated.

I said to Ariadne to translate to Daniela: "Why is Chile so intent upon pushing Carménère on the world as its national grape when these Sauvignon Blancs are world class?"

Daniela shrugged. One got the sense that whatever the reason, the force of this marketing idiocy was out of her control.

We pressed on with the third white. It was a winery named Matetic. Daniela explained that it was a Chardonnay, but that it was totally fermented in a "cement egg."

"A cement egg?"

Daniela tried to pantomime the object. "They are looking for purity," she explained.

The wine didn't taste like any Chardonnay I had except maybe a few from Chablis. The wines were all high in bright acidity, but they possessed an almost mysterious element of minerality.

"I taste the Andes in these wines," I exulted.

Daniela smiled. "Would you like try to some reds?"

"Yes. Bring your most unusual. Bring the ones that you would bring to a party."

Daniela disappeared. Ariadne turned to me. "They love your *pasión*. Passion."

"You know, I'm not a wine critic. People sometimes think I'm a snob, but I'm not. Snobbery is when you brandish your wallet over others and hoard wines that no one can possibly afford and then lord your experience of those rarefied gems over others. I am *not* that person. And if I don't like a wine, I'm not interested in saying anything bad about it. It's not like a movie or a book where I've forfeited hours of my time. With wine, I just move on."

"You realize they are watching you, are probably hanging on your every word," she reminded me.

"I just got here. I have a whole country to discover. But I'm genuinely liking what I'm tasting so far." I threw up my arms. "I want to get out to where they're growing these grapes and making these wines!"

The red wines rode on a magic carpet to our tiny table, now overflowing with tasting stemware. Daniela explained what they were, then left us with the descriptions written on the little scraps of paper. The first was a "cool weather Syrah" from a winery in Leyda Valley. I was accustomed to tasting reds closer to room temperature, but this wine had been chilled to around 60 degrees Fahrenheit. The wine was super-ripe with notes of stone fruit and, again, that tortuous river of minerality that I was starting to taste in every one of these wines.

"It's not wine that matters to me, Ariadne, it's where the wine leads me. Wine led me to a novel, and that novel led to a movie, and that movie, ultimately, led me to here. And now to you. And," I said, sensing that I was starting to slur a little, and dumping the remains of the Syrah in the *escupitero* because I did *not* want to get *borracho*, "it's unfortunate that we can't go on a great exploration of this country together. I would pull out all the stops in urging you to quit your job and go on this journey with me."

"You're serious?"

"I am."

"But you have someone coming?"

"I know. That's what's so crazy about all this."

We fell for a moment into the wells of each other's eyes. Ariadne glanced away. Then, she glanced back at me with a worried look. "There's someone out there looking in at you."

I snapped out of the ensconced world of our little romance, turned and saw a terribly anxious Silvio, hands tenting his forehead, gazing in. When he saw me he waved. Then he wedged his bowling ball shape through the narrow entrance and bustled over to the table.

"Silvio, what're you doing here?"

"Are you okay?"

"Yeah, I'm fine. This is Ariadne. I met her on the plane."

"Nice to meet you," he said quickly, then trained his attention back on me. "You're sure you're okay?"

"Why? I'm here drinking Chilean wines. And I'm enjoying them so far."

"Barrio Lastarria can be dangerous," he said. "I wanted to make sure you were okay."

"I'm fine. How did you know I was here?"

He waved off the question as though it were an annoying fly. "We have an interview tomorrow at nine," he announced.

"Silvio! Why do you keep springing this shit on me? Our agreement is that I would come here to discover your great wine regions"—I pointed to a map on the wall of Bocanáriz that depicted the twelve regions that made up Chile's wine industry—"That is what I came here for. Not all these fucking interviews, pardon my Chilean."

For some reason this made him laugh. But he had his own agenda. "Yes. And then tomorrow we get you your car."

"Good. Because without a car, that you promised, the only wine region I'm going to discover is Bocanáriz!"

He pulled up a chair and sat down at our table. He sampled some bread and dipped it into a puddle of olive oil. Perhaps it was impertinent of me not to invite him to sit with us. "You like the wines?"

"Yes," I said, with annoyance in my voice.

"Good."

"What time tomorrow?"

"Nine."

"Change it to ten."

"I can't."

"Please change it. I need to sleep."

Silvio glanced over at the beautiful, almost seraphic, Ariadne, haloed in golden light. Maybe being Latin he understood the preeminence of romance and *amor* over obligation. And maybe that's being culturalist, but I don't care.

"We would like to be alone, Silvio. Thank you for checking up on me. I will look out for the *banditos*!"

Ariadne stifled a laugh with a fist cast to her mouth.

Silvio straightened to his feet. "Good, I will pick you up tomorrow morning." Before he left he craned his neck to the left and right like a wary camel, as if looking for something. "See you tomorrow," he said, then bustled out and strode up José Victorino.

I was shaking my head. I turned to Ariadne and said, "How did he know I was here?"

She shrugged. "This maybe is the most likely place for you to come. I don't know."

"Do you think I'm being watched?"

"You are *definitely* being watched," she said.

I got up to go to the bathroom. I strolled past a private room with a long table and about a dozen men and women seated around it like a miniature version of *The Last Supper*. Bottles and bottles of wine, and plates and plates of food, cluttered the table. Faces were florid, flushed with happiness. It looked like a Goya painting, if he had painted Chileans. Though, in my ear I could make out, aside from Spanish, both English and French.

When I came back from the bathroom, Daniela was entering the private room bearing more food. "Who are these people?" I inquired.

"MOVI," she said.

"MOVI?"

"*Movimiento de Viñateros Independientes*," she said.

My smattering of Spanish made the words intelligible. "I would love to join them."

"They are having their monthly meeting."

"I see. Could you introduce me?"

Daniela went in and spoke to one of the men at the end of the table. He was a handsome guy with a two-day's growth of beard and the sun-weathered face of a farmer, but eyes with the keen understanding of an intellectual. He waved me in.

"This is Nick," Daniela introduced.

"Hi, I'm Miles," I said.

"I know," he said. "We've been hearing about your visit."

I blushed. "I didn't want them to make a big deal about it," I explained.

He shrugged, as if it didn't concern him. Then, he picked up a bottle of wine, set a glass in front of me and said, "Here, taste the real Chile." He poured me a red wine.

"What is this?"

"Old vines Carignan."

As I sipped it, Nick spoke in Spanish to the rest of the assembled. He placed a hand on my shoulder and introduced me to the rest of the group. They toasted their glasses to me.

"This is an extraordinary wine."

"You do not know how extraordinary. Come to Maule if you get a chance," he exhorted.

We exchanged business cards. "I will," I promised.

"Here, try this," he offered, picked up another bottle and poured me a half glass. "We are big believers in the future of Carignan," he said, a little bombastically. I was no stranger to bombast, so I liked his bombasticism.

It was another interesting, gorgeously earthy wine, a wine the likes of which I hadn't tasted before. I didn't know much about the Carignan grape, except that it was common to the south of France.

Nick started to tell me about these vines that he and some others had discovered growing wild. They had been planted years ago under some governmental plan to invest in the emerging wine industry, but politics and the changes in the country had desolated them, left them unattended for years.

Suddenly, I realized that I had abandoned Ariadne and I wanted her to share in all this wine socializing. I excused myself and went back out into the restaurant.

She was gone. The table was empty. I raced out on to José Victorino to look for her, but it was like trying to find an impish child in a veritable swarm of shoppers at a crowded mall.

I went back inside and sat down glumly at the table. Perhaps she had gone to the bathroom? But, no, there on the table was her business card with her email and some foreign phone numbers. Next to the business card were a couple 10,000 peso notes. My heart sank. I felt like someone had slugged me in the solar plexus. I fingered her card and stared at it until Daniela came to the table to check on me.

"She said she had to go."

I shrugged. Asked for *la cuenta, por favor* and then finished the remaining wines in front of me.

I took a cab back to the Aubrey, suffused by a piercing feeling of precarity.

At the Aubrey I went to her room and tapped on the door lightly with my knuckles. There was no answer. I didn't want to importune. She had had her reasons for leaving—Laura coming the next day, the long, saturating kiss on the way over that had stung me to the core of my being with so much possibility and which had probably put her in the awkward position of debating whether she would sleep with me.

I walked slowly, loose-limbed, back to my room, filled a glass with mineral water and drank it down, then lay on the bed and stared up at the slowly revolving fan. I could feel a panic attack rumbling like a volcano threatening to erupt and I took a Xanax to help settle my nerves. It would take fifteen minutes before I would really feel the effects. In those fifteen minutes, which felt like an eternity, I reflected again on the rudderlessness of my life. Answers were not forthcoming, certainly not churned out by the fan's paddles whirling above me. Insight was obfuscated. I found myself ransacking my brain in a vain effort to reach some kind of peace about the decisions I had made of recent that had brought me to Chile.

At some point I realized that I was close to Antarctica, a vast ice floe of the soul.

Silvio

The phone twittered next to my bed and I woke abruptly from a terrifying dream where I was homeless, penniless, and all alone in the world, a world I didn't recognize. It was Silvio.

"Are you up?"

"No." I glanced at the clock. It was nearly 9:00 a.m. Jetlag had sent my body plummeting into a kind of irremediable pain. "Can we do this some other day, Silvio?"

"No," he said firmly. "I promise."

"Give me fifteen minutes." I hung up. *You motherfucker!* In the shower, *This is knavery! I came down here to explore Chile, not to be a shill for the Chilean wine industry*, I raged in my head as the water engulfed me in a kind of tropical rain.

Silvio was fidgeting in the lobby when I finally came down, tired, trying to rub the sleep out of my bleary, bloodshot eyes.

"How are you?" he said.

"Fine," I said curtly.

He started to walk me out of the lobby. "Did you sleep well?"

"No. I'm tired."

"This will only be one interview. I promise."

I didn't say anything.

We drove through the labyrinthine Santiago on a hot, smoggy day toward wherever the interview was to be conducted. Silvio tried to confabulate with me, but I just grunted monosyllabic answers like a petulant teenager. He sensed that I was angry. He sensed right.

Santiago is a city of contrasts. It's paradoxical. Modernism has sprung up in the midst of its 19th Century origins. Monolithic skyscrapers rose high into the heavens. Construction cranes were visible everywhere. The city was practically under siege. The almost Himalayan Andes shimmered to the east, glazed by a fine brown mist that was really smog. Sitting at the basin of that great mountain range was similar to San Bernardino east of L.A., where the prevailing onshore winds blow all the pollution. What an incredible view it must have been in the early 19th Century before automobiles and industrialization choked its air.

Half the population of the vast country of Chile lived in Santiago. It was as if the long slender finger of the country, with its diverse climates and topographies, had scared the population into amassing into this one city for reasons of security, the way tribes gather, the way people desire not to be alone in the world. A human need.

I was feeling that human need. I hadn't seen Laura in a year and she was arriving in the evening. Ariadne had left me at the restaurant and it made me feel shitty, as if I had said or done something wrong, as if I had compromised a beautiful evening with that luxurious, insatiable kiss in the taxi, she already knowing that I had another woman coming to see me.

Silvio drove the city's mostly one-way streets like a man in a hurry to get somewhere. He seemed to love to shift gears. It was unnerving me, but I decided not to say anything.

We drove into the underground parking of a wide, ten-story office complex. After the previous day's earthquake I started to grow a little panicky. I employed half a Xanax to calm my nerves. I wasn't nervous about the interview; I was nervous about a ten-story building pancaking on my head, dying in a mass of twisted rebar and crumbled concrete.

Silvio led me to an elevator, up to the ground floor, where we then navigated through a warren of offices with frosted glass partitions like something out of the headquarters of a newspaper in *His Girl Friday*. We sat together on a couch. Silvio, who could turn on this 1,000 watt smile and suddenly look like a politician accepting the nomination at a national political convention, left to go to talk to someone associated with the interview. On the table next to me I saw the day's newspaper. In the lower right I glimpsed something familiar: me! The article, of course, was in Spanish and I couldn't read it, nor did I want to. I was starting to realize that my arrival in Chile was a pretty big deal, or that it had been a slow news day. Oh, another 7 magnitude earthquake struck. Some minor damage, but no one was killed. Lah-di-dah.

Silvio came back and smiled his brilliantly friendly smile at me. "It'll just be a moment," he said.

I nodded. Then I pointed at my picture on the cover of *El Mercurio*. "These guys supported the military coup," I said, half-jestingly.

"Yes. The coup was good for the country," he said.

"Really?"

He nodded vigorously. For a brief moment I feared I was about to be lowered into a scene from *Rosemary's Baby*. But I shrugged it off. I didn't want to get into politics. I knew it was a complicated country as Ariadne had warned.

"I wanted to see Pablo Neruda's house. It's right next to the hotel where I'm staying."

"He was a bad person," Silvio said. Silvio was an educated man. He had gone to school in New York. He was well read. His forbears were descendants of the aristocracy. So, this assessment of the great Chilean poet came as a shock, and filled me with consternation.

"What do you mean?" I asked.

"He had many affairs."

"So, who cares?" Silvio's countenance hardened. "I take it a communist poet is not well-liked in Chile?" I inquired.

Silvio shook his head in disdain. Then, he turned to me, his face lit up by a thought that would take him away from the odiousness of Pablo Neruda. "Your girlfriend gets in tonight?"

"Yes," I said. "Will I have the car to get her?"

"Yes, of course," he affirmed.

I was still unnerved by his comments about Neruda, but I didn't want to press him on it.

A woman came to get us. We stood and followed her into one of the offices where a man sat at a desk with a tape recorder on the table, a pad and pen in front of him.

The woman asked me if I wanted anything.

"Cup of coffee," I said. "And, for the love of God, no Nescafé, please!"

I was introduced to the journalist, a guy named Eulogio. Silvio left us with his beaming smile trailing him out the door. The woman returned with the coffee, another bitter round of Nescafé.

"So, how do you like Chile so far?" the journalist asked me.

"Well, I just got here," I replied. "I haven't been out of Santiago, and I'm dying to travel to the various wine regions in your country."

"When did you have the idea that your characters would come to Chile?"

"Well, I knew it was an emerging wine region, I knew that my main character would have to take his act somewhere else, so when the opportunity arose, I grabbed it."

"What are you hoping to find?"

"I don't know. I guess I'm expecting to find ..." I trailed off for a second and took another sip of the industrial waste known as Nescafé. I flashed back on Ariadne's face at Bocanáriz and a stab of sadness struck me like a doctor's needle when I realized she had, in essence, ditched me. "I guess I'm hoping to find peace," I said, out of the blue, if only because that was the only honest thing I could think of to say at the moment.

"Peace?"

"Yes. Inner peace. An emptying of all my regrets, an exorcism of all my demons. Fame is not what it's cracked up to be," I started in, no doubt somewhat enigmatically to the journalist. "So many aspiring writers out there and what they don't realize is that it's almost worse if you're fortunate enough to have success." Eulogio was scribbling like mad on his notepad. "Hands of great prestidigitation go into all your pockets at once. And, God help you if you're drunk and don't feel them rummaging around in there. People take incredible advantage of you. Your closest friends lie and then you realize they're not your closest friends. Agents, managers, they all want a piece of you, when once they had trouble even returning a simple email. So, yes, I'm looking for a pure way of life. Maybe I'll even meet a Chilean girl and settle down."

Eulogio's eyes bulged like a bullfrog's from the lily pad of his swivel chair. "You would like to meet a Chilean girl and settle down here in Chile?"

"Well, metaphorically," I back-pedaled, suddenly glimpsing tomorrow's edition of whatever newspaper's offices we were at, printing the headline: "Wine Author Looks to Fall in Love in Chile!"

Eulogio asked me what my inspiration for *Shameless* was and I delivered the rote thumbnail, having given the long version so many times it had grown rote. The Xanax was starting, thank God, to take effect and I could feel my passion for talking about various subjects flat-lining. More questions trundled out and I answered all of them with a kind of numb alacrity. In the middle of the interview a photographer came in and started to shoot photos of me. I let him. What did it matter anymore?

"But, I have to be honest with you, Eulogio," I tried to set the record straight, "I really don't like to publicize a book before I've written it. It makes me nervous."

He nodded understandingly. The interview wound to a close. Silvio returned to claim me. Hands were shaken all around.

Silvio walked me back to the elevator. "So, now, we go get your car."

"Yes," I said.

We burst out into the bright sunlight of Santiago, Silvio driving, as usual, like a maniac. He navigated the patchwork of roadways with practiced, if herky-jerky, ease. He talked desultorily about all the construction in Santiago, he advised on some places to go— mostly the south. "You don't want to go north, it's terrible."

"I had heard the Atacama Desert was something to see. I was thinking of driving up there."

He turned to me in horror. "No, you don't want to drive to the Atacama!" he exclaimed. "There are no gas stations for hundreds of kilometers. It is a brutal world. You must visit the south." Which, of course, made me want to go north all the more.

The Fiat 500

"You've got to be kidding me, Silvio!" I nearly shouted, gesticulating histrionically, as I looked at the white Fiat 500, which looked like a ladybug on the wheels of a tot's tricycle. "How am I going to get everything into this thing? We have a ton of luggage. Laura's going to take one look at this toy car and crucify me." As he held the driver's side door open for me I wedged myself inside, not without effort. I slid the seat all the way to its rear position, then reclined it a few inches. It was more claustrophobic than being seated in coach on a Southwest Airlines flight. I gave an anguished backward glance to the rear compartment. Even with the seats down and the back converted into a trunk it was going to be next to impossible to get all of our things in.

"Can we get another car, Silvio?"

"No. You don't know what I went through to get you this one!"

Enervated, I slumped over the steering wheel and just shook my head. I had envisioned a Range Rover for traversing Chile's rough, at times unnavigable, wine region terrain. Also, beleaguering my mind was Laura and meeting her at the airport. Plus, I needed to sleep.

When I looked up, two people had approached. One, a young man, was wielding a large digital video camera in front of his face. The other, a woman, brandished a high-end digital SLR. They were filming as they approached, darting this way and that like dangerous paparazzi.

"What the fuck is going on?" I asked.

Silvio explained. "We just need to get some footage for the car."

"I'm doing ads for Fiat now?"

"No, not ads." He hung his head to one side like a sick mule, as if: *Can't you cooperate?*

"Then, what?" I exploded.

"For the car," he said.

"For the car, for the car; what do you mean for the car?"

"In exchange for the rental," he explained, as if it made perfect sense to him.

Another Chilean approached, this one a smiling young male production assistant. He handed me a glass of red wine. For a moment I thought he had my best interests at stake. But, no, the photographer wanted me to pose outside the car, holding up the glass of wine and smiling.

"So, now what, Silvio, I'm promoting drunk driving?"

For some reason this made everyone, including Silvio, erupt into laughter.

Shaking my head in mock disgust, I capitulated and let them take their fill of pictures. Hell, was this any worse than spilling anecdotes to the technocrati in the Santa Ynez Valley for a lousy five grand? And I was in Chile; who was going to see these photos of me with a Fiat 500, the last car in the world I would buy for this rough terrain?

Life was starting to turn antipodeanly surreal. I had expected to come to Chile under cloak of darkness, meet a few wine dignitaries, be given the keys to a 4-wheel drive, and be sent on my way into the viticultural hinterlands of this great, vast, unexplored country. But the Vintners Association of Chile clearly had other designs on the purpose of my visit. I started to imagine all manner of fatalistic scenarios, but like all things that existed in my head, they usually festered and perished there.

In my new Fiat 500, shifting for the first time since I was in high school and drove one of those noisy death trap VW Bugs high on hashish, I followed Silvio in his spacious SUV into downtown Santiago. I consider myself a pretty good driver, but the Chileans will definitely make you pick up your game! Honking, which has gone out of fashion in the U.S., is definitely the middle finger *Fuck You!* of choice. I tried not to take it personally.

Back in Las Condes, I was ushered by the little roly-poly, shifty Silvio into an Entel office. Silvio asked for my phone and then took a number. We waited. His Nescafé breath was causing me light-headedness. Or was it the proximity to the Andes? We chitchatted about various things related to my trip. Somewhere in the middle of the itemization of quotidian details Silvio outlined more events that he wanted me to put in my calendar: an awards dinner; a big event out at Santa Rita Winery; more interviews. The list was positively daunting.

I tried to maintain my *sang froid*. "Silvio," I said calmly, "I have to get out and see the wineries and meet the winemakers of Chile, otherwise this trip is going to be a bust."

"I know," he reassured me. "Of course. You will. I promise."

"When?"

"We just have these few little things," he niggled.

His number was called by one of the Entel reps. He took my cellphone to the appropriate station. Time passed as I sat wearily on a hard plastic chair. I felt all alone. With Ariadne gone, and the ludicrous fantasy of a love affair evaporated, I started to turn my attention to the beautiful Laura. In my college days I had backpacked around Europe. I had so much fun that the following year I went with a girlfriend whom I had been dating for over a year. We lasted exactly a week before she dropped me off in a rainstorm on a busy highway intersection somewhere outside Barcelona, flipping me off. Maybe I had matured. Maybe Laura and I wouldn't suffer the same fate. I admonished myself to be thoughtful of her. She's just come in from a long flight. She'll be tired. She'll be looking for comfort. Well, she would find comfort at the Aubrey. Or should I switch to the W Hotel? It was $500 a night, but fuck it?

Silvio was talking animatedly to the Entel rep. Apparently, things weren't going well because Silvio was windmilling his arms like a homeless man in Santa Monica who had just been released from a sanitarium. He was talking so fast I could barely pick up even a smidgen of what he was saying.

At some point, an exasperated Silvio returned to explain to me what the delay was. Something to do with activating the new SIM card that they had to install in my phone. Silvio leaped up from the chair and went back for another round of *Lucha Libre* with the Entel rep. I waited. And waited some more. At some point I grew exasperated and, feeling a panic attack breaking on the horizon, went out into the streets of Santiago for some air.

The Las Condes district looked like it had been built overnight. Everything was new. All the buildings; the cars; the roads. If I was looking for an authentic Chilean experience, I wasn't going to find it here.

I ducked into a convenience store, and except for the foreign language that was being spoken, I could have been in Century City. I don't smoke, never have, but now and then when I'm nervous I like to puff on a cigarette. Plus, Laura smoked a little, so I thought I'd get a head start on her. Laura also liked to smoke pot, and I worried about where she might score some. I wondered what the laws in Chile were on pot smoking. Did they send you to a concentration camp in the Atacama for an 1/8? My brain was racing now.

It took some rough-and-tumble Spanish with the proprietor of the store to get me my cigarettes. I really didn't care what brand. I had to use my debit card because all I had was the wad of American dollars on me. The pack of cigarettes came with horrific, vivid, color images of smoke-destroyed lungs and cancerous mouths. It could have had a salutary effect on me if panic anxiety weren't a lesser affliction than cancer caused by cigarette smoking.

I said to the proprietor, "¿*Cambios?*"

He looked at me strangely, tried to be thoughtful.

"¿*Cambios?* ¿*Dinero?*" I pantomimed some ridiculous motions with my hands that suggested anything from turning American dollars into Chilean pesos to bribery, judging by the proprietor's consternated expression. In total exasperation I hauled out the wad of American dollars and showed it to him. "¿*Por pesos?* ¿*Cambios?*"

At first, when he saw the money, his eyes swelled behind his spectacles and I thought they were going to pop out of his cranium. Eventually, he gleaned my meaning and relief flooded him as if he had just learned his newborn had been born with ten fingers and ten toes.

Turned out there was a money exchange place around the corner and I went there. I showed my passport, slipped $5,000 in hundreds in the slot under the Plexiglas divider where a dour-looking man spent a few minutes performing some calculations on a tablet. Then he carefully counted out these beautiful-looking, cerulean-colored 10,000 peso notes. My anxiety lifted a little.

Back out on the sidewalk I lit a cigarette, puffed it for a minute. As I didn't smoke, I grew a little dizzy. My blood raced as the cigarette's vaso-constrictor properties kicked in, pushing my heart into overdrive. I stupidly started to reflect on all the bad decisions I had made in the years since *Shameless* had come out and made me famous, but certainly far from rich. Otherwise what would I be doing in Chile, at the foot the Andes, a guy who didn't like to fly, let alone board a 14-hour flight across the equator? If I thought about a panic attack long enough, one was sure to descend on me as if a deranged animal had lodged itself inside the prison block house of my head.

Silvio materialized on the street looking flustered. "Where were you?"

"Getting change?"

"Do you smoke?" he asked worriedly.

"I do now!"

He laughed. When Silvio laughed, he was human. When he was leading me to the next event that he hadn't warned me about in advance, his knavery manifested itself in a way that was hard to balance with my own sense of what was right, what had been previously agreed-upon.

He thrust out his arm. "Here's your phone." I took the phone from him. "You have a new number."

I held up my $5,000 USD in Chilean pesos, an impressive wad of 250 iridescent bank notes in one hand, and the phone in the other. "I am officially Chilean, Silvio!"

He laughed until his eyes closed with tears.

We started back toward our cars. "What *is* my new number?"

"It's on your phone," he replied. "Now, we go back to the Vintner's Association to meet with De Martino."

"What?"

Grumpily, querulously, I tailed Silvio back to the VAC's offices. Fortunately, the manual transmission came back to me as if some atavistic mechanical memory. At a stoplight, I powered up my smartphone and it effloresced into light. I dialed the prefixes that Silvio had written down on a piece of paper that would get me to an international dispatcher and dialed Jack's number.

"Hello?" he answered. His voice crackled over the shaky trans-equatorial cell connection.

"Jack? It's me, Miles. I'm in Santiago."

"I almost didn't answer, man. The number that came up looked like something from the Middle East."

"I just got my phone all Chilean-ed out."

"What's it like down there?"

"Only been here a couple days. I'm in Santiago. It's sort of like L.A., I guess."

"When does Laura get in?"

"Tonight. We'll see how that goes. They put me in this miniature little Fiat 500."

Jack laughed so hard I had to hold the phone away from my ear. "I'm trying to imagine you in that," he sputtered, before collapsing into laughter again.

"It's good to hear your voice."

"It's good to hear yours, too."

"The offer's still good, man. Come to Chile."

"Man, that's a butt-ass long flight."

"Chicks are beautiful."

"Are they?"

"So far from what I can see. And there's a lot to discover down here. It'll be like old times."

"What about Laura?"

"You two have met. She likes you. Come on down, man. Just go to LAN Airlines and dial in a plane ticket. I'll pay for it, of course. And all expenses are on me down here. What the fuck else are you doing?"

"*Nada mucho, amigo.*"

"All right, I'm coming up on a roundabout here that looks like something I last saw in Athens in the '80s when I was high on LSD."

Jack belly-laughed again and we rang off. I was feeling much improved. Jack, I could sense, was thinking of getting out of L.A. With the Christmas holidays around the corner I knew he would be feeling a little down, his son now approaching eight years old and probably with Babs, his ex-wife. Travel can be salubrious for the ol' Noel melancholy. True, it can also heighten the loneliness, but road trips are one of the best anodynes for hoisting oneself out of the quicksand of despair. And, it *was* good to hear his voice.

I trailed Silvio into the parking structure, sucking in my breath as I thought about the previous day's earthquake. Quick as a wary mongoose he led me back up into the offices of the VAC. Two people were waiting for me in a room. Martino, a handsome man in his forties, with dark hair, stood and smiled and shook my hand warmly. His associate was an Aussie named Guy. Hearing his familiar English, if modulated through an accent, was reassuring.

What wasn't as reassuring was the slide projector and the bottles of wine and *escupiteros* scattered on the rectangular table.

Silvio excused himself to leave me with Guy and Martino. We confabulated for a bit about my visit to Chile, I told them more or less what I had told the various journalists about what I hoped to find, that Chile was a vast frontier "that I hope to explore if I ever get the fuck out of Santiago."

They laughed. But they also had their agenda. The lights were switched off and a slide projector was turned on, sending grainy and over-exposed images onto a wall. Martino started to speak. I didn't come to Chile to be lectured to. I started to silently rage inside my head, but then something happened: the slides turned interesting. There was a dissertation on the soils that I actually found fascinating. Then, in the middle of the presentation, I was introduced, via an electrifying sequence of images, to an extraordinary place called the Elqui Valley where some of their wines were made. They fermented Cinsault in *tinajes*, or earthenware vessels, the way the Chileans did it in the old days. The Elqui Valley wine region looked like a desert moonscape, but the vines were grown on ridiculously steep slopes that looked so barren that it didn't seem anything could possibly grow. But employing sophisticated irrigation systems drawn from subterranean aquifers of Andean snowmelt they grew Syrah on hillsides that only bighorn sheep could possibly traverse.

Martino spoke with a passion about wine that I hadn't heard in a long time. He didn't talk about pH levels, secondary malolactic versus malic and TA (total acidity), oak—neutral or new, French or American—no, he spoke eloquently about the revivification of old traditions in Chile. I felt like I had stumbled upon an old friend, someone who shared my passion for wine, but who had just, in a matter of an hour, exposed me to a world, and to the regions and various mesoclimates in those regions, with an ardor that made me believe he was for real.

We tasted through some uniquely interesting wines: the Cinsaults in the *tinajes*, which had a predictable earthiness and strange, primitive complexity, almost a mystical quality. There were the cool weather Syrahs of Elqui, which we again tasted at 60 Fahrenheit and *not* at room temperature, which were unlike any Syrahs I had had before.

"These are sublime wines," I exulted. "I thought I was coming here to get the commercial tour, but I'm really impressed."

They beamed. Guy said, "You should come to Elqui. It's a cracking place."

"I will. My inbox on my computer is already filling up with requests to come to this winery, that winery. But, I can't possibly visit them all."

Martino leaned forward, his hands folded prayerfully in front of him. "You must come to Elqui and see our vineyards. They're like nothing you have seen."

"I know," I exclaimed, gesticulating to the wall where the images had now evanesced. "It looks like an amazing place."

We all stood and shook hands. Of course I knew what their aim was in taking me through the lecture on topography and geology and all the rest: if my iconic characters come to visit Chile in a novel, then, hopefully, they'll visit and exult in the wines of De Martino and their sales will skyrocket. But they were so passionate in their spiel, and so professional in their not politicking me too strongly, that I left with a respect for the two of them and their extraordinary wines that perhaps I didn't possess when I walked into the room.

Silvio, a little disgruntled, led me back to the Aubrey, for fear that I would get lost. Disgruntled, too, because the traffic was a snarling, barbarous mess. It was difficult to keep up with him. He drove like a man possessed of so many demons. Then I realized that he had a wife and three kids and no doubt other clients he had to attend to.

"I have to tell you, Silvio," I said, as I met him in the parking area, "I really enjoyed that. I'm sorry I've been a pain in the ass. I realize we got off on the wrong foot."

"It's okay," he said. "We have another interview tomorrow."

"You're kidding me?"

"I'm joking," he said.

"Good. Thanks for everything. I don't know about that car, but..."

Back in my room at the Aubrey I showered. When I came out the red light on the phone was blinking. I called down to the desk. There was a message from Laura. Her plane would arrive around 8:00 p.m. I toweled off, dressed and went to the patio restaurant and had a couple double espressos, as I was missing my usual caffeine fix. The Nescafés weren't doing it for me and I needed to wake up.

As I sipped my coffee and reflected over brunch on my life I thought about Ariadne. It occurred to me that at any time, in any place, a person could enter your life and change it dramatically. The night before I had dreamt that I was in a truck, or on a train, I forget, but that there were no brakes. This had become a recurring dream of late, and its interpretation was pretty facile. It had replaced nightmares of finding myself on the top of skyscrapers with no guardrails and monsoon winds howling and my trying to keep from being hurled into the night. Is this the life of the writer, I thought? Yes, of course it is. These dreams supplanted recurring dreams where I was in an airplane piloted by my father. A former captain in the Air Force, he was forced out when, inebriated, he punched out a colonel who was making a pass at his girlfriend, or so the story goes. I bring this up by way of explaining why I might have become an artist, a risk-taker. But, for some reason, later in life I would dream of him captaining a plane, often in distress, with me huddled in the back, unable to offer co-pilot assistance, him totally in death-defying control of my fate.

I killed time back at Bocanáriz. It was mid-afternoon and I was sampling some wines. I was still discovering the Sauvignon Blancs to be stellar, crisp, mineral-y, a palate excitement unlike any I had tried. One from Casablanca looked like water but tasted of the Andes. An Amayna from the Leyda Valley was redolent of toasted oak.

I was still thinking about my father. I had a lot of time to think because I was still alone. After the surgery it was determined he had had a stroke and they conducted a battery of neurological tests. The neurologist sat my mother and me down in a dispiriting room and delivered the fatalistic news: he would never breathe again on his own; he would probably never come to consciousness; if he did regain consciousness, he would be "cortically blind."

"Why don't we honor his wishes and let him go?" I pleaded with him, exasperated.

The neurologist referred me to the cardiologist, as he was the official attending physician on my "father's case." We met with him. He was, as it turned out, adamantly pro-life, and didn't honor my father's living will.

Days and weeks dragged on as my mother visited my comatose father twice a day, heartsick, studying monitors—she was an Army nurse in her youth—watching the blips of his heartbeat, dreading the moment that it would flat-line, standing back when the nurses came in and turned him over to clean him. Now and then I would visit. A nurse once told me to hold his hand and talk to my brain dead father, that he could hear me. And I thought this was a joke, some woo-woo shit, but as time has gone on I've begun to see the value of the spiritual. Once as I did hold his hand, spoke words to him, he squeezed mine slightly, as if he could sense my presence. I don't remember what I said, but perhaps he did hear me, as he teetered on the precipice between the living and the dead.

Several months after the failed surgery I was able to get the hospital social workers to take the attending physician off the case and assign one who was more "liberal." A meeting was called, and that's when the decision was made to pull his feeding tube and increase the morphine. In frustration, I blurted out, "Can't you just give him a shot?" They exchanged uncomfortable glances with one another, then one of the three on the panel addressed me and said, "We don't do that here, here, Mr. Raymond."

Three weeks later he died, essentially, of malnutrition. Less than two years later my mother suffered a massive stroke that changed the fortunes of my family forever.

Daniela returned with more samples of wine. Knowing that I had to get Laura at the airport, I was spitting most of them, but the flashbacks to my father and mother and the tragic finales to their lives compelled me to soften the edges of the memories with a little libation. I was looking for some laughs. I wanted to be one with the Chileans, drinking and having a good time.

I glanced at my watch. It was thirty minutes before Laura was to touch down. If I had had a way of getting in touch with her I would have text-ed her and told her to take a cab, that I had had a little too much. But Laura had already made it quite clear that if I didn't pick her up from the airport she would be very unhappy.

I waved to Daniela and asked for the bill.

I walked out into the teeming crowds of Chileans and their orphaned dogs cruising up and down José Victorino in colorful Lastarria. The night smells were different than they were in L.A. I couldn't quite pinpoint it.

I located my embarrassingly tiny Fiat 500 in the parking structure where I had left it. Its engine roared to life when I turned the key in the ignition. I powered up my cellphone and tapped the Google Maps app. Surprisingly, Santiago seemed extensively mapped. I typed in Santiago International Airport and then put all my faith in the electronic voice directing me there. I started off.

Santiago is a clusterfuck of one-way streets. If you get going down the wrong one, reversing your course and rectifying your error can be aggravating. I tried to get an overall sense of where I was headed—the airport was in the northwest outskirts of the city—but I've always had a bad sense of direction. I'm easily turned around. But I had the power of the Internet on my side.

What I didn't factor in is that Chile's road signs are not for the faint of heart. In the U.S. we are given ample warning of a turnoff. There are at least two, sometimes three, bright green and fluorescent white signs warning you that your turnoff is approaching. Not so in Santiago—or, as I found out, in the rest of Chile. Often one sign is all you get. Often that one sign is mere feet away from the turnoff itself! Worse, my voice navigator had difficulty pronouncing the names of the streets. No wonder Silvio drove like he did! You *had* to be like a Formula-1 racer!

Soon, I was navigating my way to the airport by the stars, as if by divination. Worse, I was feeling the kaleidoscopic effects of the few glasses of wine—even with all the spitting!—and the city was pulsing at me with a dizzying array of lights.

I wanted to have blind faith in my Google Maps voice, but she was driving me insane. At the last moment I would jerk my wheel to make a turnoff, breathe a sigh of relief when it appeared I was on the right path once again, then grew disconcerted when she directed me in a strident, exhortatory voice to "Make a U-turn at the next intersection. Make a U-turn ..."

"Fuck!" I screamed, banging both hands on the wheel, downshifting into second and grinding the gears of the little toy Fiat. Soon I was directed off the main *ruta* that I thought was the right way to go and found myself in a neighborhood, or a barrio as they're called, with shadowy figures skulking through the night. It wasn't a sense of fear so much as one might have in certain areas of L.A., but one of feeling utterly lost.

I slowed next to a Chilean woman and asked her in broken Spanish the direction to the airport. She smiled and pointed and spoke in a Spanish that was so rapid I couldn't understand her. I showed her my cellphone with the Google map laid out on the screen and she navigated it with scissoring fingers in a way that was way more tech savvy than me and finally said, *"Aqui."*

"¿Aqui?"

"Si!" She seemed genuinely excited that she had helped a stranger find his way in her vast city with its Abstract Expressionist's network of roads.

Emboldened by her directions, I putted off again down a desolate street. Dogs roamed in packs everywhere as though I were in the realm of Persephone, their tongues panting. I just wanted to get to the fucking airport and meet Laura and whisk her off to the Aubrey and a dinner of rack of lamb from the Andean highlands and a hearty red from the fabled Maipo. Instead I was in nowhere Santiago, heading uncertainly, in a car that moved in fits and starts like a sick animal chased by the fear of getting lost.

I let my imagination go, while I drove what I thought was in the direction of the airport, now an hour late, to the inconstancy, or fleetingness, of my relationships. The ground under my feet felt friable. Panic rumbled frequently like an aftershock through the emotional geography of my body and psyche. I felt the desideratum of connection, but didn't know how to effect its change. I kept reaching for it with everyone I met. Being alone had its advantages: the world opened up to one. Being with someone carried with it the promise of permanence, as if impermanence were something to be abnegated.

My Google Maps voice warned me of an upcoming turnoff, but there was no sign. I snapped out of my solipsistic reverie and glimpsed jetliners floating in out of the sky, lined up against the Andes, whose snow-capped *arêtes* were visible in the coruscating moonlight.

And then the sign for the *Aeropuerto Internacional de Santiago* turnoff came and went and I was barreling past the airport down an ill-lit *ruta* toward the darkness of the outskirts of Santiago, cursing my inattention, blaspheming the freeway signage, flipping off my cellphone.

Some miles away I turned around and started back toward the airport. I had gone in a maddening pathway of zigzags and circles and still I was no closer to the airport, I thought, than I had started. And, then, suddenly, there was the turnoff again. I veered sharply, and, as I drove into the airport parking lot, I felt the triumph of a teenager who had deflowered a virgin.

Laura

Laura, the Spanish documentary filmmaker I had met in Paso Robles on that crazy alcoholic-fueled trip with Jack and my mother and her caretaker, stood on the curb in front of the main terminal at *Aeropuerto Internacional de Santiago* with a scowl on her face and a piece of luggage the size of a Brit's portmanteau in some Merchant/Ivory period piece. She had other luggage as well, obviously believing me when I advised her, in the most propitious way possible, that this was going to be a long stay in Chile. It looked like she had come for life! And that suddenly scared me.

"Where were you?" she said before she allowed me to hug her.

"I just got this car, I just got my phone operational, these signs..."

"Where were you?!" she shouted at me. She stamped her foot. "I have been waiting here two hours."

"I'm sorry," I said. "It's been crazy ever since I got here."

We hugged finally, but I could feel the tension in her carriage and it wasn't welcoming. In an awkward silence, I rolled her massive trunk toward the car. When we got to the Fiat 500 and I stopped she bent double at the waist and started to laugh. I laughed with her.

"This is what we're going to drive around Chile in?" she asked, incredulous. Incredulous, indeed!

I shrugged.

"I thought you were a famous writer?" she smirked.

"There's fame and then there's fame," I joked lamely. "Come here." I drew her close to me. "It's good to see you. I missed you."

"I missed you, too, Miles."

"I'm sorry about the car. My rep here said he would trade for another."

"I want a jeep," she said.

"I know. I do, too. A fucking Range Rover. How was your flight?"

"Long. I stopped in New York for a couple days."

"New York? I thought you were coming all the way from Barcelona."

"I was. But my plans changed."

I got a sick feeling in my stomach that her changed plans involved another man, but since we hadn't been together in almost a year I didn't feel like I was entitled to any kind of proprietary relationship, let alone jealous inquiry. But it sure made me feel shitty, as I sensed that that's what it was, when I wrangled her portmanteau and other luggage into the impossibly small rear of the Fiat. How I would get mine in for our travels was going to be a miracle!

Laura proved her worth immediately when she took over my cellphone and navigated us back to the Aubrey with no glitches. If a romantic relationship wasn't in the offing—and that was the big IF between us—then, if nothing else, she could guide me to the wineries that the Chilean vintners' association wanted me to visit.

Back at the Aubrey, Laura showered and I busied myself on the computer. My Inbox scrolled and scrolled with requests from Chilean wineries, imploring me to visit them. Suddenly, I felt terribly overwhelmed. Flattered, but overwhelmed.

We dined under the stars, sharing a bottle of wine. Laura was in her thirties, had dark hair and the beauty of a southern European. Her eyes flashed dark. We talked about the current crop of films and we were surprisingly in sync. There was laughter over our disparagement of a certain film that all the critics had gone nuts over.

"I think critics are desperate," I opined. "The Internet is destroying their profession and so they're turning into lily-livered cowards and practically praising everything in sight. Being a film critic is no longer an honorable occupation."

Laura said, "I don't think the films this year had any soul, or humanity. Some of them tried, but it was as though that's all they were doing was trying, instead of really having soul ..."

"... To have soul," I chopped her off mid-sentence, "... it has to come from inside ... I'm looking for that inside again, Laura. I had it once magically in my grasp, but it's like quicksilver, it can leave you so easily. It's so good to see you."

"It's good to see you, Miles."

"I've been talking out loud to myself ever since I got here. Actually, I've been talking out loud to myself the last year."

She looked at me with tired eyes. The wine was making us both sleepy. "What're we going to do tomorrow?" she asked.

"They want us to go to this big winery in Maipo—one of the regions they're very proud of here—but I want to get out of the city. I just came from a big city ..."

"... I know, I did, too!"

"So, let's explore. Let's jam all our stuff in that little Fiat, or leave some of our luggage at the hotel—they're totally cool—and we'll set out and discover Chile. How does that sound?"

"What are we going to do for money? Because, uh, you know we are having problems in Spain now with the Euro ..."

I waved her off and pulled out the roll of $100 bills from my pocket and showed it to her. Her eyes widened. "Tomorrow, we'll exchange a chunk of this into pesos and I'll give you whatever you need, okay? Don't worry about money."

Back in the room, Laura and I undressed and awkwardly climbed into bed. The 3,000 mile long country of Chile beckoned. We lay in silence, staring at the ceiling fan. We were both thinking the same thing.

"This boyfriend back in Barcelona, is it serious?"

"I don't know," she said.

I nodded. Her hand found mine under the sheets and squeezed it. We touched each other some more. And then some more.

Viña Casa Marin – Lo Abarca

The next morning, we found a place in Bellavista near the hotel that changed money. I transmuted $10,000 USD into a whopping $5,400,000 pesos! The 540 10,000 peso notes made me feel like a millionaire; no, an alchemist. The wad of bills I walked away with, after several high level convocations with officials in the back room, must have been an inch thick. There was no way they would all fit into my wallet. I gave half of it to Laura and said, "Here. Hold on to this for me."

She kissed me on the cheek. "I forgive for you being late last night," she said.

"The signs here are insane, Laura," I replied. "They don't give you any warning."

She powered up her cell phone, tapped her Google Maps app and showed it to me proudly. "You now have an expert navigator."

"And you do not know how much pleasure that gives me when you say it."

My phone rang. I saw the number come up—my first Chilean one—and it was Silvio. I declined to answer it. A minute later it rang again, so I started the car and gunned the engine a little and answered it.

"Silvio, how's it going?"

"Where are you?" he asked in a breathless voice.

"Heading to Valparaiso," I said. "My friend Laura came in late last night and ..."

"No, no, no," he stuttered like a machine gun with his finger stuck on the trigger. "We must go to Maipo today."

"No, Silvio, I must get out of town. I must see Chile." I turned on the radio and rotated the dial until I found static.

"No, no, no," he said desperately. "These are very important people."

I turned the static up louder. "I'm losing you, Silvio, what did you say?" He said something I could clearly hear, but pretended not to. "Look, I'll call you when we get a better cell connection. Thanks for the car; it's driving like a dream!" I tapped End Call. Within seconds the notification light was blinking. Fuck it.

"Who was that?" Laura asked.

"My rep. The guy who put this together." I threw the car into first and lurched into traffic. "He wants us to go to this winery that I don't want to go to. There's been a bit of a—shall we say—communication problem regarding what my obligations are. They want me for all these interviews and promotional things, events and the like, and I didn't want to come down here as the customer. I wanted to come incognito."

She grabbed my right arm, the one shifting the Fiat 500 into second, and held onto it with both of hers. "I will protect you," she said. "I know the Spanish mentality. I will throw a fit. I will go into hysterics. They will understand."

"Good. Because I'm Czech and we hide our emotions. Then, one day, we simply flip out. And no one knows where it's coming from."

"But in your writing you are so emotional, so personal," she analyzed.

"Yes, Laura, that is true, but I feel safe in my writing, when I'm writing. The hard part is when I show it to people. Then, they just get uncomfortable. It's like they want me to be personal, in person, but when I get personal they don't like it."

"But this is real art, no?" she asked.

"Yes, exactly. This is real art. I'm trying to focus a laser on my soul to disinter—unearth—the truth." I turned to her, genuinely glad that I had asked her to come. It was a risk. I had only been exchanging emails and phone calls with her the last year, and though the emails had been torrid, you never know until you are with someone if the reality will destroy the fantasy and leave you marooned on its island. All I knew was that I was glad I had someone with me for this Chile adventure. Someone who spoke Spanish. So what if I didn't know this woman, except in a long distance way? I needed someone to, well, keep me fucking sane.

Laura happily assumed her role as my navigator. Being bilingual—her English was impeccable, way better than when we had met a year earlier—she was more than proficient in interpreting the signs. She guided us onto *Ruta* 68, a newly-paved east-to-west freeway that was one sign of Chile's new prosperity. You could see

Chile's emerging Americanization superficially in its major freeways. They were smooth, pot-hole free. Sure, there were peso-gouging toll booths every 20 miles practically to foot the bill, but who cares when you have a beautiful Spanish girl in the seat next to you?

Being below the equator, Chile's November was really their May and it was a warm day. The sky was a very deep shade of royal blue. Retreating behind us were the imperial Andes, snow still frosting their tops. As we drove out of Santiago the topography was arid, almost desert-like. Dwarfed trees sprouted haphazardly in sparsely-spaced arrangements. The hills gently undulated. It wasn't scorchingly hot because the prevailing onshore wind originated from a bitingly cold ocean.

We were headed in the direction of Valparaiso, but would turn off before there, if Laura navigated us correctly, our destination Viña Casa Marin, a winery that I had been advised by the good people at Bocanáriz to visit, because it was exemplary of some of the wines known to Chile.

"It feels good to be out of Santiago," I remarked as Laura fiddled with her cellphone.

"Yes," she said absently.

"What're doing on that phone?"

"Text-ing," she said.

"How're we doing on the roads?"

"When we get to Casablanca we go south," she said.

"Casablanca's a valley," I said, I didn't think testily, but she took it that way.

"It's also a village," she retorted.

I had fixed it in my mind as *Valle Casablanca*, one of the finest wine-growing regions in Chile, and wanted to be sure that she wasn't confusing it. "Are you sure?" I asked.

"Yes," Laura said, flashing me her cellphone where squiggly map lines zigzagged this way and that.

"Well, let me know where the turnoff is," I said.

"It's coming up."

We drove on in relative silence. I tried the radio, but I couldn't find any stations that I wanted to hear. A glance at my phone told me that Silvio had left a raft of messages. I think he and the vintners association were afraid I'd gone rogue. I had. I glanced over at Laura. I didn't want to pester her about her self-adopted navigation role. "Who's Rafael?" I asked, noticing a name on her text messaging with a picture of a handsome young man.

"A friend in Barcelona," she said.

"You're texting him a lot," I said.

"I know, I'm sorry," she said, then swiped the screen and brought up the maps. "Oh, shit!" she said, "we missed the turnoff!"

"Oh, no," I said. "I told them that we would be there at 2:00."

"We have to turn around," she said.

"I didn't see a sign," I said.

"Turn around," she exhorted.

"I'm looking for a turn-off, okay?"

I got off at the next exit, but as it turns out there wasn't a turnaround to get right back on the freeway as there would have been in the States. Suddenly, we were driving down a two-lane country road in the middle of nowhere. Laura, now intently focused on her Google Maps, was trying, it appeared, to guide us to our destination.

"Well, I know we're headed south," she said.

"Great. Soon we'll be in fucking Patagonia," I said, growing exasperated.

"You don't have to be like that, Miles. You said yourself the signs here sucked."

"Yes, I didn't see a turnoff for Casablanca anywhere," I replied in a mollifying tone.

On the positive, the countryside had turned lusher. Vineyards bloomed into view, beautifully manicured rows of vines. Being their June we could see grape clusters hanging pendulously from the vines. I started to laugh maniacally. "Fuck, I don't care if we're lost. We're in Chile. We don't have a care in the world. Who gives a fuck if we don't get there until tomorrow!"

"I will get us there," Laura said. "Okay, there's a turnoff coming up for Lo Abarca, so take that."

A moment later we were at a fork in the road. The one that went where Google Maps had instructed us was dirt.

I stopped the car and left it idling. "You want me to take this turnoff?"

"Yes, that's what Google Maps says," Laura said defiantly.

"Okay," I said. "You're the navigator."

We both hopped back into the car and fishtailed down the dirt road. We didn't see any other cars. I was starting to get worried, but I didn't want to press Laura for confirmation that we were headed in the right direction. A funnel of dirt spiraled like a horizontal twister from behind the Fiat, which wasn't built for these kinds of roads.

Laura became more focused than ever on her Google Maps. "Okay, we need to turn here," she instructed.

I halted the car at even narrower dirt road. "Are you sure?" I said, as nicely as I could, fearing a night in the 500, angry at a Spanish girl who probably knew how to demonstrate her infuriation at our calamity worse than me.

"Yes!" she said, demonstrably.

"Okay," I said, surrendering to her exhortation. "But, it's clear that we're lost. You will admit that, won't you?"

She raised her cellphone and held it up in front of my face. "We are here"—she tapped the screen with her index finger—"and here is where we are going. We are very close," she said defiantly.

"Okay," I said. "I mean, it doesn't look good, you will admit that."

"I will get us there, Miles, okay?"

"Okay." I slipped my vial of Xanax out of my pocket and fingered a 1 mg. pill, powderized it and let it dissolve under my tongue. In fifteen minutes I wouldn't care if we were headed off a cliff and hurtling into the icy Pacific.

Soon the dirt road turned into a rutted asphalt road, and I found myself dodging pot-holes like a dirt bike champion.

"We're getting close," Laura said.

"Despite the total absence of people, I have no doubt that we are," I said, trying to disguise my sarcasm.

As we bumped along the asphalt road in disrepair we toured through villages that looked abandoned. Here and there the poor and disenfranchised of Chile, hardworking farmers, were walking along the sides of the road, almost always trailed by packs of mangy dogs. It was a hardscrabble country that we were in, far from the economic miracle of Santiago with its Andean high skyscrapers, but I felt like I was finally burrowing into the heart of Chile.

And then we were in the tiny town of Lo Abarca. I pulled off the asphalt road, parked on the dirt, and we both got out. The first thing you could smell was the sea. A mist had developed over its icy waters, but above the mist was a sky so Mediterranean blue that it took your breath away. There was a stillness, a quiet, that I hadn't experienced in years. In L.A. you are constantly assailed by noise. Unless you're one of the lucky few and live high in the hills of the Pacific Palisades, or wherever the rich muckety-mucks of the entertainment world live, you are in a city of constant noise and light.

I dialed the number for Felipe, the vineyard manager of Viña Casa Marin. "Felipe. We are here. We made it."

"Good," he said. "I will be with you in a minute."

I turned to Laura. She had lit a cigarette and was puffing it nervously.

I leaned against the car next to her. "Give me one," I demanded. She handed me her pack and I tapped out a cigarette. She flicked at a plastic lighter, but it took a couple times because the wind off the ocean kept blowing it out. Finally, I got it lit.

We glanced all around us. On steeply-sloping hills, vineyards climbed and rollercoaster-ed everywhere. "It's beautiful here, isn't it?"

"Yes," she said. She shivered and I hooked an arm around her.

"Are you glad you came?"

"Yes," she said, none too convincingly.

A few minutes later a 4-wheel drive, with wide, off-road treaded tires braked to a halt next to us. Felipe climbed out of his rugged, mud-streaked jeep and greeted us warmly. He was late twenties with short-cropped dark hair, the countenance of a movie star and the physique of someone who did CrossFit on a regular basis.

"You made it," he said, smiling. "Hi, I'm Felipe."

I took his extended hand in mine. "I'm Miles and this is..."—I started to say my *girlfriend*, but stopped myself—"... my friend Laura." We shook hands all around.

"I will take you up to the house, is that okay?" he asked.

"We'd probably like to get something to eat."

"Conchita will be coming up from Lo Abarca to cook you dinner. You have menus, you can choose what to order."

"Okay," I said. "And we'll need some wine."

"You have all the wine you need," he said, laughing, "at the house." He swept his arms across the rolling vineyards. "We make wine," he said. "Tomorrow you will hear our story."

We hopped back into our cars and followed Felipe up a winding series of switchbacks through beautifully manicured vineyards that glowed iridescent green in the fading light of day. We climbed higher and higher, maybe 1,000 feet, maybe higher, until the ocean rose into view. It was mere miles away and I wondered how grapes could agriculturally prosper this close to an ocean so cold.

At the top of the highest knoll, Felipe came to a stop in front of a simple two-bedroom structure that commanded a sweeping, 360-degree, panoramic view. Vineyards stretched everywhere like ribbons of green and brown candy. The wind off the ocean was chilly as we followed Felipe inside what they called their Villa Marin. He showed us around the cottage, acquainted us with the Internet, presented the menus that he would give to Conchita who would come to cook for us, then showed us the wine. A lot of wine. I had a feeling that Laura would soon need a glass after a long day of dead-end roads, appalling signage, and a world we were both unfamiliar, and a little unsettled, with.

Felipe made us feel at home, though. He handed me a cellphone and said, "If you have any problems, you call this number"—he showed me the first one on the Contacts list—"and someone will come help you, okay?"

"Okay."

"I loved your movie," he said.

"Thank you."

"We are so happy you have come to Chile. You will find some great wines here."

"I already have," I said. "Bocanáriz in Lastarria."

"Ah, Bocanáriz. I know them well," he said. He pointed at the menus. "I recommend her soup. It's really delicious."

Laura and I scanned our menus, checked off what we wanted, then handed them to Felipe. He smiled, then took off, leaving us on the top of the hill that ruled sentinel over the vineyards of Viña Casa Marin.

I could sense that Laura was still a little out of sorts from having just flown in the previous day, so I suggested she take a shower while I brought in all the luggage.

When she emerged from the shower with wet hair and a towel knotted around her breasts, I had a cold glass of Casa Marin's Sauvignon Blanc waiting for her. The wine was as pure an expression of Chile as I had tasted. Sometimes people in the wine world say that if you taste a Burgundy in Bordeaux it won't taste the same as if you had it in Burgundy and vice versa. I was beginning to wonder if the same wasn't true of Chilean wines.

"Feeling better?" I asked.

"Yes," Laura said, smiling, pulling on a robe and knotting it at her waist.

We took our wineglasses and drifted out onto the porch. We found two hammocks and, like seals on slippery rocks, maneuvered ourselves into them. The sun was traveling fast now toward the west, as if pulled down by the mist that flooded in from the ocean and obliterated the water from view. Above us, even though it was still light, stars had started to coruscate in the highest reaches of the Chilean empyrean. For the first time in weeks I felt at peace. I looked over at Laura and I could see that she was staring pensively at the horizon.

"Look, Laura," I broke the silence, "I know that we've had nearly a year of a long distance friendship, or whatever you want to call it, and that this was an experiment. But, no matter what happens, I'm glad you came, because I needed someone here in Chile with me. I feared being all alone. All my life I've feared being all alone."

She listed her head to one side and met me with her eyes. "I'm glad I came," she said. "And this wine is incredible."

"Isn't it?"

We turned our attention to the vineyards unfurling everywhere around us. Some were dappled with sunlight and others were slipping into the tenebrous light of shadow. Where the fading sun still struck a vineyard, the green of the summer vines was iridescent with color. A light breeze from the ocean audibly rustled the leaves. In the far distance you could occasionally hear one of the lost *perros* of Chile. The upper reaches of the sky continued to blue, coloring to indigo. The silence, the serenity, was almost overwhelming. Soon, the bottle of Sauvignon Blanc was almost gone, and our frayed edges had been remediated.

A mini-truck bounced over the humped dirt path that wound up to our cottage and stopped next to the porch. A stout woman in her forties with thick black hair streaked with gray stepped out. Silently she went around the back of her truck and produced two large baskets covered with red-and-white gingham cloths. She approached and introduced herself as Conchita. She spoke almost no English, so Laura translated.

"She's here to cook our dinner," Laura informed me.

"Great," I said, feeling nicely euphoric from the wine.

Laura told a smiling Conchita that it was okay to go inside.

"Should I open another bottle?" I asked Laura.

"Sure," she said. "What else are we going to do?"

I followed Conchita inside. Laura's tone of voice was tinged with hostility, I thought, but maybe she was just tired and feeling edgily petulant. I found one of Casa Marin's Syrahs, uncorked it, brought out two fresh wineglasses to the porch, and poured Laura a glass. She was puffing her third cigarette. I handed her the wine and then wriggled myself back into the hammock, wondering what I could do to improve Laura's mood.

The Syrah was astonishing. Bright cherry and redolent of the earth. "What do you think of this wine?" I summoned Laura's appraisal.

"Mm. I like it," she said, forcing a smile. She turned to her cellphone, then rested it face down on a table. "I can't get a connection," she complained.

"They have Internet," I offered.

She snorted a response.

"Besides, whom do you need to call? Doesn't it feel liberating to be totally unplugged?"

"No," she said contemptuously.

A gust of wind swept up the vineyard and I shielded the dust that blew across my face. I started to drink more of the Syrah. I had gone a year without wine, but I knew coming to Chile I would have to get back into it, though I had promised myself that I would be abstemious. But there was something about Laura's mood that was troubling me. I felt bad that I had charmed her into coming to Chile with me, and now, from her body language, it seemed like she felt all alone, or was having second thoughts. For me, it was freeing to be away from my writing, in another country, closer to Antarctica than the equator.

Conchita came to the door and declared that dinner was ready. Laura and I shared a wonderful meal of a traditional chicken soup, salad, and bread. Dessert was a quivering rectangle of chocolate flan. Laura seemed in a better mood after having gone around to the rear of the cottage to find a better Internet connection. Either that, or the wine was ameliorating her doubts for having come so far for an uncertainty with a man she barely knew.

Conchita cleaned up after us, then said goodbye and left us to ourselves. I uncorked a third bottle, yet another Syrah from the Casablanca Valley. Day had transited to night and the sky, with no ambient light visible anywhere in our universe, was densely speckled with stars. I had no background in astronomy, but I could clearly make out the Big Dipper. A night sky like the one we were marveling at showcased whole galaxies, a veritable river of stars that streamed deep into the black hole of infinity.

"The sky is amazing, isn't it?" I remarked to Laura, hooking an arm around her and drawing her close.

"It is," she said before leaning the weight of her body against mine, reassuring me of something that I was feeling.

"If you ever wonder whether there are forces more powerful than us, whether everything can be explained or not, all you have to do is look up into a sky like this and you realize just how insignificant you are, how eternally stupid we as humans are, how we'll never be able to explain *that*." I pointed to the heavens.

"No, we cannot know everything," she said.

I ventured a kiss. Her response was willing, but not passionate. A year ago in a winery tasting room in the Santa Ynez Valley she had hungered for me with an almost animal-wild ferocity. Now, it was more hesitant, as if she were having doubts about us, this inchoate relationship that we had both fantasized would bloom in the unknown world of Chile.

"I think I'm going to go to bed," she said. "I'm tired."

"Okay. I'm going to stay out here for a bit and see if I can find myself in the stars."

She smiled. We kissed again and then she disappeared inside.

I sagged into one of the lounge chairs and filled my wineglass with Syrah. The wine tempered my unease. The sound of the vine leaves, now invisible, rustling in the night seemed to trip through my soul like a thousand smooth stones skipping over water, erasing everything and turning me *tabula rasa*, as much as that might be possible. For some reason I shuffled through the women in my life like cards in a deck. I laughed when I banally thought of the dumb, cliché analogy that some were aces and some were queens and many others were just numbers. What did it matter, when you were lying in the ER, how many women you had had? What mattered is what you had done, that you had at last known a deep and abiding love. Since I had no children, all I had left was my writing. And now it was resting immortalized in an archive at my *alma mater*. Was that enough?

I glanced toward the bedroom. Through the window I could make out the silhouette of Laura sitting up in bed playing with her phone. She was text-ing frantically, maniacally, addicted to the device that seemed to be her lifeline to a world she hadn't wanted to leave.

I returned my thoughts to the night sky. It seemed to hoist me upward. A bird screeched and it startled me. Something moved through the vineyard, then stopped. I could make out a pair of luminous green eyes casting their gaze at me. Then they evanesced as quickly as they had materialized. I reached for my wineglass. Was I hallucinating? I panicked a little, then inhaled deeply and exhaled slowly. What was there to be worried about? The universe was going to take me into its vast cosmology, whether I liked it or not. I wasn't going to be earthbound forever, that I knew for certain. And what was this time on earth, but suffering and pain and, yes, here and there, intermittent lacunae of joy? But it had mostly been suffering. Why did people so crave happiness? A multibillion industry based on antidepressants and yoga retreats had sprung around this craze. Our life slogging out on this earth was never about happiness, I concluded, as I sipped the rest of my wine and straightened uncertainly to my feet. Our life on this earth was only about one thing: glimpsing consciousness before we were reeled back into the great maw of unconsciousness.

Viña Casa Marin

Sunlight spilled through the venetian blinds, waking me with a start. I had a mild headache, but otherwise I was feeling rested. Something stirred in my groin, but I could already hear Laura up and about in the main room. I crossed the hallway to the bathroom, shaved hastily, showered and dressed. When I came out into the bright living room Laura was busy on her laptop.

"I'm getting a good signal," she said cheerfully.

"Good," I said, walking over to her, grabbing her shoulders with both hands and giving them a squeeze. I heard movement in the kitchen and whispered, "Who's that?"

"Conchita," Laura said.

"Oh, right."

A moment later, a demurely smiling Conchita appeared from the kitchen with plates of food. Fresh squeezed juice, cold cuts, scrambled eggs, and bread with butter and little hillocks of jam. Laura and I sat down across from each other and dug in. I needed the food to offset all the wine from the previous night.

"How did you sleep?" I asked Laura.

"Very well," she answered.

"Are you having doubts that you came to Chile?" I asked her.

"No," she answered. "Why?"

"Well, I sensed you were a little distracted last night."

"I was, yes."

"Is it something you want to talk about?"

"No, I'm fine," she said.

We ate our breakfast in silence, now and then commenting on the wonderful food, looking up at each other and smiling. At one point I extended a hand and touched hers and she returned my touch with a little squeeze.

"The stars were amazing last night," I said.

"Were they?"

"I got totally lost in them. There's something about the skies here."

"So, what's going on for today?"

"Well, Felipe—the guy who brought us up here—is going to give me a tour of the vineyard. And then we're going to drink wines with the winemaker, Maria Luz, I think is her name."

Laura grew a thoughtful look. "I'd like to go see Pablo Neruda's house in Isla Negra."

"All right," I said agreeably. "By yourself?"

"I'll be fine. I've traveled the world." She leaned her head forward and smiled into my face. "I got us here, didn't I?"

"That's true." I drank some more coffee. "Okay, then, we'll meet back up at their winery in Lo Abarca and drink some wines."

"Okay," she said. The arrangement made her happy. Perhaps we had already spent too much time together and needed a little time apart.

I called Felipe on the cell he had given me and told him I was ready for the tour. Laura gathered some things together and held out her hand for the keys to the Fiat, and I surrendered them.

"Do you know how to get out of here?" I said.

"Sure, just go down the hills. There are signs, remember?"

I enveloped her in my arms and we kissed. "I wish I could go with you to Neruda's. I really wanted to see where he wrote so much of his great poetry."

"I will take a lot of pictures," Laura said, holding up the digital SLR that she had brought along for the trip.

I waved goodbye as she drove off. Back inside I made small talk in my smattering of Spanish with Conchita, who was still cleaning up. She offered me the menus for that night and I filled in both Laura's and mine. Then, Conchita left, leaving me to wait for Felipe.

I sat out on the porch. The fog that had flooded in overnight had retreated toward the ocean, beat back by the burning sun of Chile's summer. An ocean breeze had already started to come up and a few local raptors were soaring like paragliders on their updrafts. Everywhere I gazed I could see vineyards. I had never seen a wine

region quite like Casablanca Valley, though technically we were in
Lo Abarca, a sub-appellation.

Felipe, a laconic guy, arrived in a veritable cloud of dust in his
mud-streaked 4-wheel drive. He shook my hand and asked me how
breakfast was and I told him it was wonderful, thanking him
profusely for his hospitality.

"Where is your Laura?"

"She wanted to go to Isla Negra to see Neruda's house there," I
said. "I think she has a crush on him."

"Ah, Neruda," he said. "You will know the politics of a Chilean
when you bring up Neruda," he said cryptically.

"What do you mean?" I inquired as he directed me to his 4-
wheel drive.

"There are those who just want to forget and move forward," he
said. His countenance grew introspective as he turned over the
engine. Then he turned to me with the broadest smile, his white
teeth flashing in contrast to his onyx-black hair. "I just want to
make some good wine."

"All right."

"What did you drink last night?" he asked.

I told him about the Sauvignon Blanc and the Syrah, described
them as rapturous, unlike Syrahs I had had from the Rhone, from
Australia, or even Napa. Very different in style.

"You will see why," he said.

Felipe navigated the narrow dirt roads through the vineyards that
he knew like his boyhood home. The son of the winemaker and the
founder of Viña Casa Marin, he knew every vineyard row and what
was planted, as he had grown up on this farm. Now and then we

would stop and he would take me right up to the vines and point out certain salient features. The clusters were, in some cases, very small and, he explained, in a somewhat tragic tone, "Sometimes we don't get these berries to come to ripeness. Not enough sun."

"I'm amazed," I added, "that you're able to grow grapes so close to this very cold ocean."

"It is hard," he said. "And then there is the wind, too. You can get 'shatter,'" where the clusters are, how do you say, agitated?"

"Yes."

He stopped his 4-wheel drive and we climbed out. He pointed to the vineyard before us and said, "These first few rows block the wind for the rest of the vineyard. They sacrifice themselves for the other grapes."

I was taken aback. "They literally give themselves up year after year for the sake of the vineyard?"

"Yes," he affirmed. "And even then sometimes we don't get them to the sugar levels we're looking for."

"Who would be so insane to plant vineyards so close to the ocean?"

"You will meet my mother," he said, with a wry smile on his face.

I tented my forehead with my hand to shield the hot sun, which was now arcing toward its zenith in the sky. "I don't think I've ever seen, with my own eyes, a vineyard in the foreground and an ocean in the background. Nowhere. I'm sure it exists, but I haven't seen it."

He smiled. Even though he was only in his late twenties, Felipe's handsome face was fissured at the corner of his eyes with tiny wrinkles. It was evident that he had spent a lot of time in the sun, working these vines. When he told me that there were only a handful of vineyard workers on the nearly 100 hectares, with the exception of harvest when more were brought in, I said,

"You must work hard here?"

"Yes," he said. "Sometimes I wish I had another life. These grapes can cause me so much grief, but I love my vineyards like children."

"Do you have children?"

"No," he said wistfully. "Some day. And they will farm this property because it'll be in their blood."

We drove on, stopping frequently. The soil was a red clay, and mineral rich. I had never seen soils like this. He and his mother believed, like most winemakers, that wine was made in the vineyard and not in the winery. "Wines made only in the winery are not good wines," he said. "They are mass market wines." He swept his gaze over his vineyards. "You must have good grapes."

We continued to drive through the vineyards. Felipe explained why Syrah was planted in one section, Sauvignon Blanc in another, Chardonnay in a third. Altitude, soil, amount of sunlight, it all factored in to where they had chosen to plant a certain grape variety. To the untrained eye it might look like rolling green vineyards haphazardly planted over steep hills and down in little glens, but there was a science, and an intuition born of experience, that determined for them where the grapes were to be planted.

"But this cold ocean," I kept coming back to. "It must make it difficult to get these grapes to come to ripeness in some years."

"Yes," Felipe said, "some years we get so little, not even enough to make few barrels. But this is the risk that we take. When we have good years they can be very good, especially for the Syrah and Sauvignon Blanc."

"But Syrah is typically a warm weather grape?"

"It is," he agreed. "But we Chileans, we are a young wine industry, we are still experimenting. We have a long way to go."

"Your Sauvignon Blancs are world class," I said.

"Thank you."

"It's so beautiful here," I said. I realized when I said that I was glad that Laura had split off from me and gone off to see one of Neruda's three homes. Sometimes men, even heterosexual men, prefer the company of other men. We keep our emotions in check, we often speak more laconically, and there isn't the frisson of tension that there is when a man is in the presence of a woman.

"I don't understand women," I suddenly blurted out, *à propos* of nothing.

Felipe laughed. "You will never understand women." He gently cupped a small cluster of grapes in the palm of his hand. "And we will never understand these grapes," he said.

We stood for a moment in silence. The wind buffeted us on the slope. It was chilly, even though it was the middle of summer and the sun overhead was hot. "This is the perfect marriage of cold and hot, isn't it?" I remarked, gesturing to the ocean, then pointing up at the sun.

"You know something about winemaking," he said.

"No, not really, Felipe. People *think* I do because of who I am, but I really know very little about wine. But what I've seen so far in Chile really impresses me. The Sauvignon Blanc I had last night was every bit as delicious as any Sancerre I've ever had in my entire life. But, you are battling the French. They think they are the gods of wine. And, yes, they make some pretty sublime shit. But think of Chile, think of its incredibly, radically diverse topography. You've got this freezing ocean to produce the acids, a mere hundred miles away you have those imperial Andes and their mineral-rich snowmelt. You have these amazing volcanic and alluvial soils, and if you just—my God!—if you just don't fuck with it too much, think where you'll be in fifty years, a hundred? The French have been making wine for half a millennium, probably longer. It's just trial and error, trial and error."

"I'm not sure I understood all of what you just said, but it sounds like you are passionate about the future of Chile's wines."

"Yes! I get excited when I stand in a vineyard like this and you tell me that vines suffer for other vines. It's analogous to the process of art, Felipe—similar to writing," I amended. "You suffer and suffer through all those bad experimental novels and poetry to find the one that hits a nerve. Winemaking is so much like writing, like the process of art. There are things you can't control. There are almost supernatural forces sometimes that influence the final product. All we can do is do the work and hope for the best. And then try again."

"You should visit the Atacama," he said.

"Is there wine there?"

He laughed out loud, showcasing those gleaming white teeth again. "No. It is the driest desert on the earth. There are amazing telescopes up there. When you talked about the supernatural, I think you will find it there."

"In the Atacama Desert?"

"Yes. It's in the north of Chile. Where 'The Disappeared' went."

"The Disappeared?"

Felipe's face suddenly clouded over. His speech grew hobbled by an inexplicable emotion. He stared fixedly at the ocean and the fog that was now flooding back in. It was as if he were staring at the heart of Chile and, in the face of its vast and complicated presence, was nonplussed. He seemed to be hurtling back in time to a place that perhaps was one of incomprehension. Without looking at me, he said, "Do you want to taste some wine?"

"Yes," I said.

He turned to face me with a smile that seemed ravaged by tragedy or worry about his grapes or something I didn't comprehend. "And meet my extraordinary mother."

"I'm looking forward to it," I said.

We bumped along a dirt road down the steeply sloping hills, Felipe holding his 4-wheel drive in a low gear.

"Such an extraordinary property you have here," I said.

"Yes," he said.

We arrived in Villa Casa Marin in Lo Abarca. The Fiat 500 wasn't there and I feared for a moment that Laura got lost on her way to Neruda's Isla Negra house, but then put that worry out of my mind.

Felipe led me into the small winery. On a second floor, with picture windows, he introduced me to his mother, Maria Luiz Marin. She was an attractive woman in her fifties, I guessed, with a wiry frame and bird quick eyes. I'm so used to meeting winemakers who are overweight blowhard drunks, usually intoxicated by mid-afternoon and roaring on and on about something or other, that it was kind of a mild shock. Maria Luiz was very composed, perhaps even a bit nervous.

"Your vineyards are beautiful," I said. "I heard you planted them yourself?"

"Yes. Not all," she said. Her English, as it turned out, was a little spotty, though better than my Spanish, so Felipe translated for us.

We congregated around a wooden table. Framing us on all sides were stainless steel fermentation tanks, barrels (though not many), presses, de-stemmers, conveyor belts for sorting, the usual array of winemaking equipment.

While Maria and I talked, Felipe brought bottles to the table for us to taste. We started with one of their entry level Sauvignon Blancs. We sampled. It was a simple, beautiful wine, unmanipulated, as were most all of her wines.

"What is your story, Maria? When did you start this vineyard?"

"Oh," she said, then looked off, as if searching for a starting point to begin.

In her decent, but broken, English, and in my *muy mal Espanol*, I learned that Maria grew up in and around this area of San Antonio Valley close to the sea. Her father drank wine, but was not a winemaker, nor a connoisseur. For some reason — love of her father? — this was important to the understanding of her narrative. She went to the university to study agriculture. Bored out of her mind, she was on the precipice of quitting, not sure what she wanted to do with her life, when she decided to enroll in a viticulture class. "I had an *epifania*," she said, a wry smile creasing her face.

"Yes, I understand epiphany. I've had one or two in my life, especially with certain women."

They both laughed. Felipe poured us their Cipressa Sauvignon Blanc, their high-end one, from a small vineyard. Again, like many Chilean Sauvignon Blancs, it was translucent as water but had such a minerally depth of flavor.

"This is an extraordinary wine," I said. "My God, I can taste the ocean air in it!"

Felipe said that some winemakers will leave the juice with the skins for a while to extract just those flavors.

"And the minerals. It's like this wine is a pure delivery system of the *terroir*. Chilean *terroir*."

Felipe translated for his mother and she blushed a smile. "Yes," she agreed. "Very well put."

"I'm a writer. They pay me to come up with that stuff. Well, sometimes they pay!"

They both laughed at my self-deprecation.

"So, you had an *epifania*?"

Maria continued with her story, Felipe pouring more wine and continuing his running translation.

Maria's *epifania* was that she would devote her life to the growing of the finest grapes she could produce. A headstrong woman, and with some money saved, she chose an 80-acre property a mere 2-3 miles from the ocean, an almost insane decision for a viticulturist! Particularly the frigid Pacific in this Chilean valley. A grape grower is going to battle frost, too many days where the temperatures never get hotter than 70 degrees — in other words, a viticulturist's nightmare. But Maria was stubborn. She fervently believed that grapes could be cultivated here in this inhospitable region. Not only ripen against insuperable odds, but produce wines of stellar quality.

But, unfortunately, this steeply-sloping property was a veritable forest of eucalyptus trees and the Chilean government had it agriculturally zoned as #5 — meaning, forest, don't touch. Maria was undeterred. The old lady she bought the property from was concerned when Maria informed her that she was going to rip out the eucalyptus trees and initially refused to sell her this rugged parcel of rolling, windswept land. I asked her if this was because she had some affection for her eucalyptus forest and Maria shook her head vigorously from side to side. No, the old lady was afraid that Maria, whom she knew as a child, was going to go broke growing grapes in this cold climate!!! Maria eventually convinced her to sell. Her troubles were just beginning. Maria attempted to persuade the government to change the zoning from a #5 to a #3—agricultural. They refused. She pestered them. They were intransigent. They didn't see that grapes meant jobs, meant a potentially exportable product. Like many things in Chile, things don't happen fast. Not only don't they happen fast, many things they do flat out don't make sense. Frustrated, Maria had the trees uprooted in total defiance of the government.

I stared at her in disbelief, agape. "You had the eucalyptus forest razed without the government's permission and planted grapes? In our country you would be thrown in jail! Didn't they know what was happening?"

"Of course," she exclaimed, then launched into another rapid-fire explanation in Spanish which her son translated. The government was slow in attending to her zoning changes, and they were apparently also slow in getting around to stopping her. Then, when they tried to stop her, the news media caught on, and she became a local celebrity, a sort of grape *revolutionista* if you will.

Maria smiled drolly at the memory, then glanced up at her son. It was good PR for her nascent winery, was more or less what she confided, somewhat chagrined at the admission.

As the sun bent toward the ocean, the sunlight poured through the wide windows of the second-floor room. The wineglasses piling up in front of us now—we were on to her remarkable cool weather Syrahs—were coruscating in the golden light. As if she had never told her story before, Maria explained in detail about the difficulty of growing grapes so close to the ocean. She talked about how the weather changed, literally, from hour to hour, and how that affected the grapes, how within her 80 acres she could identify many tiny little micro-climates. These austere, beautifully crafted wines that showed, like so many wines of neighboring Casablanca Valley, the pure quintessence of the *terroir*. If they can wild ferment, Felipe translated, they will, because they believe that commercial yeasts deleteriously affect the flavors. If they can cold soak their grapes— i.e., juice in whole clusters with skin and seeds to pull out as much of the earth and saline air from the ocean as possible—they will. They used little or no oak. Secondary malolactic on their whites was blasphemous to them. Like many Chilean winemakers, it's sort of a fashion —or tradition— to have a "consultant." Almost every winery maintains one on staff. Maria had one, too, but she let him go when he didn't get when she told him: "I just want the wines to reflect that"—and she swept a delicate arm around her, gesticulating to the vineyards where she and Felipe grew Syrah, Sauvignon Blanc, Pinot Noir, Riesling, Sauvignon Gris and a little Gewürztraminer. As Maria talked about her passion for wine, winemaking, and, particularly, viticulture, I was blown away. I had never met anyone in the wine world who had so defied nature—and the authorities!—to produce a product, against all odds, with such integrity and dedication. I almost got teary-eyed because she reminded me so much of what I'd gone through to find some success as a writer. This woman had lived a hard life. This woman was salt of the earth, the real deal. You could see it reflected in her proud, sun-weathered face, the intense black thumbtack eyes of a woman who refused to listen to the remonstrations of those who believed she couldn't succeed. And there were many.

Just then, Laura appeared, led up to the second floor by one of the vineyard workers.

"Laura, come sit down. This is Maria Luiz. She is the winemaker here."

They politely shook hands.

"How was your day?" I asked.

"Neruda's place was *magnifico*," she said, flushed with excitement.

"Have some wine," I said. "Try these Sauvignon Blancs. They're staggeringly, knee-vibratingly delicious."

Laura smiled at me and sampled the wine. "Mmm," she said. "These are *muy delicioso*." She reached a hand behind my head and massaged the nape of my neck. I wasn't sure why she was being affectionate all of a sudden, but with the wine and Maria's personal journey story, I was feeling her finally coming around to Chile the way I had started to.

"It's just such an incredible story, Maria," I said. The wine was making me, as it was wont to do, a little grandiloquent. "I feel such a connection with your suffering for some reason. Your story brings tears to my eyes." I slurred, feeling a little inebriated. "Don't cry for me, Chile, not Argentina!" I said, raising my glass in a toast. They laughed.

Felipe uncorked a long slender-necked bottle, produced four fresh glasses, and said, "Do you want to try some of the Riesling?"

"Yes, please," I said. "I would."

Felipe poured us generous amounts. In the glass it was almost amber in hue. On the nose, as I swirled it appraisingly in my wineglass, it had that classic German Riesling petroleum aromatic. In the mouth it was explosive: intoxicatingly plump fruit, bright acidity, and it traveled for eons in the back of my mouth.

"I never would have thought you could do Riesling this extraordinary this close to the ocean."

"Only one vineyard," Maria held up her hand. "Felipe didn't want me to plant it." Felipe shrugged. "He wants me to plant more Sauvignon and your Pinot Noir."

"Pinot Noir could do well here," I said, giving some support to Felipe.

"Yes, and we make it, but I want to try Pinot Gris, Gewürztraminer ..." Maria trailed off. You could see the viticultural explorer in her. She had no patience for wineries that produced a replicable flavor profile year to year. She was on the leading edge, and wanted to continue to be on that leading edge. Felipe, perhaps fearing the economic realities of getting Chilean wines to the market—and it was a challenge coming from a country so far from the major wine drinking countries of the world—leaned toward the more conservative.

"I want you to try something special," Felipe said.

"We've been sampling nothing but special wines!" I exclaimed, my voice now booming in the room. "Fuck! These are incredible."

Felipe found four more clean wineglasses and placed them in front of us. Outside the windows I noticed that a few ominous-looking clouds had started to scud in. Felipe opened the bottle and poured us all generous pours. In the glass the wine was the color of black cherries, densely opaque.

"This is a Syrah that I've been cellaring in the Andes at a friend's," he said.

"Wait a second. This is a wine you've been what?"

"Cellaring in the Andes. I believe the conditions up there make this a special wine. It was in barrel for almost two years."

"Cellaring in the Andes is, what? Like champagne in limestone caves in Champagne?" I asked, incredulous.

He looked at me as if he were surprised. "Of course. It matters where the wine is resting, don't you think?"

"Let me see," I said, pretending circumspection.

There was a moment of silence as we all tasted the wine. Like other Syrahs I had had since coming to Chile this was sampled closer to 60 degrees than true room temperature. For me, at least, it made the wine show more opulently and not so hotly alcoholic. Too warm and a lot of wines stretch out like obese people on clothing optional beaches.

We all sipped, oohed and aahed the wine. Felipe was clearly nervous about what we would think. Time in the barrel had definitely softened it. Again, there was that mineral component that I found so distinctive of Chilean wines. Unlike old world French Syrahs, which can taste of barrel and floors of barns, there was something elevating about this Syrah.

"I never would have guessed this was a Syrah," I said to Felipe. "It tastes like an amalgamation of a bunch of great grapes. I might have guessed Grenache."

"*Granacha*! We must plant some *Granacha*," Maria said in a rising tone that brought everyone to laughter.

"Do you like this wine, Laura?"

"Yes, very much," Laura said to everyone. "It's like a great Rioja."

"Rioja. Ribera del Duero," I said. "I don't know what cellaring it high up in the Andes does to it, but there's something ineffable in this wine that I can't quite put my finger on."

Felipe smiled warmly. Maria was looking a little tired. The clouds had now started to close off the sky and the winery darkened, casting us all in silhouette.

"Looks like rain," I said.

Felipe looked consternated. "No, it doesn't rain in December."

"Don't you want the rain?"

"No," Felipe said. "We do not need the rain now." He hurriedly started to cork the bottles.

"I guess we'd better be getting back up to the cottage," I said.

Yunta de Bueyes

We followed Felipe back up the sometimes vertical rises of dirt switchbacks that led to Villa Marin, our little cottage on top of the hill. Laura, for some reason, had apparently had an unexpected enantiodromia at Neruda's and was touching me and kissing me almost wildly. Given the first two days of querulousness I didn't know if it was issuing from the wonderful wines, if Neruda had evoked something in her with his love poems, or what.

"You had a good time at Neruda's?" I asked her.

"Yes. An incredible house. Of course it is all touristy now. But you could imagine what it would have been like back in the '50s. He's got all these nautical and marine-themed artifacts and knickknacks. And the way the waves crash against the rocks, you can see the inspiration of this great poet." She kissed the side of my face and whispered in my ear, "The way that wine country inspired you to write your great work."

"Neruda I will never be. A Nobel I will never win. We are in a Fiat 500 heading up to a little two-bedroom with a view of a vineyard. I think that'll be about as lavish as it gets for me."

Laura laughed and kissed me again. A fulguration of lightning tore a jagged line across the blackening sky. The mushrooming clouds looked positively portentous. A handful of raindrops fell from the changing skies and spotted the dirt-smeared front windshield in a leopard pattern.

"It's going to rain," Laura said excitedly. "I love the rain!"

We continued behind Felipe on the tortuous switchbacks leading to the top of the highest knoll where Villa Marin was. When Laura and I climbed out of the Fiat we were slaphappy. Not in anger, but more in jesting protest, I kicked the Fiat 500 and exclaimed, "This fucking little piece-of-shit car. We need a Range Rover!"

As Laura retrieved the half-empty bottles of Casa Marin's finest, I approached an anxious-looking Felipe.

"Hopefully, it will not rain too much," he said.

"Mold and mildew, huh?"

"This soil is very clayey." He kicked at the ground and produced a diminutive cloud of red dust. "The rain makes it very slick. Hard to drive."

A few more raindrops spattered the ground, each raising a puff of dust, as if liquid bullets strafing random targets.

"Thank you for the wonderful day," I said.

"My pleasure," said Felipe, smiling through his concern. He kept gazing off anxiously at the horizon where the storm was gathering.

A moment later Conchita came up. This time she was in a different vehicle, a four-wheel drive. She climbed out and conferred with Felipe. Then, Felipe turned to me and said, "She will cook you dinner now. But she wants to get back because she's afraid of the rain."

"Okay," I said.

Felipe shook my hand, glanced one more time at the skies, sucked in his breath, then strode back to his car.

Sunlight still dappled the porch with its sweeping views when Laura emerged, showered and freshened up, with the bottles of wine and some wineglasses she had found. She poured some of the Syrah that had been cellared in the Andes.

"What is your next book, Miles?"

"I don't know."

"Am I in it?"

I turned to her and smiled. "I will try to go easy on you."

She jabbed me in the shoulder with her fist. We sipped the wine. It was softening our moods. A few more raindrops fell, but the storm was still hovering out over the ocean, though gathering force.

"You know that Neruda's remains were disinterred?" I said to Laura.

"No, I didn't know that."

"They think the CIA assassinated him with the help of Pinochet. That he didn't die a mere two weeks after the coup from prostate cancer."

"What does that mean?"

"It means that certain powers wanted a Nobel Prize-winning poet dead." I turned to her. "That's a huge burden for an entire country to bear. If it's true. But apparently a former CIA operative admitted that he knew another operative who impersonated a doctor and gave Neruda the lethal injection of poison that they think killed him."

"Wow," she said. "Then Neruda was assassinated?"

"Apparently. The United States practically owned Chile when Salvador Allende was democratically elected on a socialist platform in '73. You had powerful interests here and powerful interests in our country who wanted to make sure that socialism didn't succeed in this country. It wasn't about the infamous Domino Theory and the spread of Communism. It was, as always, about money." I turned to Laura. "We know that the CIA, in collaboration with their puppet Pinochet, assassinated Allende. We know many people went missing, were persecuted and tortured, that over a million people fled the country for fear that they would be murdered. So, it makes sense that they would kill Neruda. He was Chile's greatest, and most eloquent, megaphone to the world. Unfortunately, he was a devout Communist."

"How do you know so much?" Laura asked, pulling on a sweater she had brought out.

"I don't," I said, "but whenever someone is doing something wrong to another, whether it be man to man, or country to country, or whatever, the bottom line is rarely ideology. It's money."

"Yes, we have a lot of problems in Spain now because of money. Everyone is fighting all the time." She hooked her arm inside mine. "I'm glad to be here with you." We kissed.

The door opened and Conchita stood there and said, "*Bien.*" She forced a smile, then tilted her head toward the sky. Her son, who had driven her up, was standing by their mud-spattered four-wheel drive, puffing nervously on a cigarette.

Conchita hurried us through the meal, but Laura and I didn't mind. She cleaned up while we ate, then said goodbye in a hurry as if she had other mouths to feed. A light rain had started to fall as the clouds pushed in from the ocean with the force of Mother Nature's lungs exhaling one of her tumults. Soon the porch was being peppered with heavy raindrops and the sound was cacophonous! Laura, drunk on wine, went out into the rain and started dancing, as if she were an American Indian whose crops hadn't yielded a kernel of corn in five years. I joined her in the rain and we both danced under the threatening skies until we were bedraggled and soaked in our wine-induced delirium.

The dark sky fulgurated with jagged shards of lightning, followed closely by booming crashes of thunder that seemed to invisibly explode, as if the universe might implode and come collapsing down on us at any minute and transform itself back into total nothingness.

We made love in the bedroom for the first time since that night in Paso Robles a year ago and Laura was on fire. Her dark hair and fierce catlike black eyes bore into mine as she cavorted on top of me, in hopes, I thought, of exhausting all her doubts and anxieties about having come to Chile.

She lit a cigarette in the dark and smoked it absently. "I don't want a relationship, Miles," she announced matter-of-factly. "I like you, but we are different. I feel like you are searching for something different." She turned to me. "I feel like you will always be searching and I need for my heart to be in one place. Does that make sense?"

"Yes," I said, resigned.

There was a pregnant pause. The rain, now unleashed in all its fury from the cathartic heavens, drowned out the silence and I wanted to go to it. But, instead, "Is that all you have to say?" she asked.

I shrugged. I wasn't happy that yet another relationship wasn't going to work out, but I had fatalistically come to the realization that this was my lot in my life. There *was* truly nothing else to say, and I was being honest when I didn't feel like analyzing it. A year of emails and a long-distance telephonic relationship had produced a fantasy that was now clearly all out of proportion to reality. Unfortunately, for me, I was lying naked in bed with the woman who had just informed me that she wasn't interested in pursuing a relationship, we were high on a hill in the middle of nowhere, in the country of Chile, and the rain was ensconcing us in all its spectacular fury. Happiness should have been within arm's reach, but it couldn't have been farther away.

I turned to Laura and smiled, "Let's just have fun, okay?"

"Okay," she said. She snuggled up next to me. "I love the rain, don't you?"

"Yeah," I said.

"Did I depress you?" she asked.

"I don't know what depression is," I said absently. "Maybe the rain is all there is. Maybe this moment with you is all there is."

"Yes," she said, extinguishing her cigarette with an audible sizzle in a glass of water. She looked down at me. Her black hair streamed over the sides of her face and tickled my chest. "I try not to dwell on the past. I try not to have regrets. I try to live in the moment." She lowered her head to mine and kissed me on the mouth. "And the moment right now is us. In Chile. In the rain."

"Yes," I said, suffused by a chasmic loneliness suddenly.

We fell asleep amid the now torrential rain. I woke in the middle of the night from disquieting dreams—homelessness, destitution, the usual. Laura was lying on her back, snoring lightly. I tiptoed quietly out into the living room. I wanted to smoke a cigarette, but it was raining so hard that I couldn't go out onto the patio to have one. On the coffee table I noticed Laura's cellphone. Stupidly, I picked it up. It lit up, as if by a motion sensor that had suddenly activated. I tapped the text icon. There was a very long string of texts in Spanish from someone named Sergio. I couldn't read it, but the word *amor* appeared more than once. Snooping, I tapped the icon for her picture gallery. A nude photo of Laura came up, the same woman now sleeping peacefully in my bed. It was a cellphone video and I tapped Play. Laura—my Laura!—was staring straight into the camera, smiling coquettishly. Then, she reached down into her crotch and began masturbating. It might have been a turn-on, I suppose, except for the audio, which was not just the rustling of sheets, but the voice of a man in Spanish, apparently urging her on. Laura started to masturbate with more salacious vehemence and the voice on the audio grew more animated—as if he were masturbating, too!—so much so that I had to tone down the volume. When he, bare-assed naked, set the cell down so that it was now a static shot and joined her in the frame, I frantically hit Pause on the cell's player.

I set the cell on the table, face down, then crossed the living room to the bathroom, knelt before the toilet and threw up. I didn't vomit because I had had too much to drink; I vomited because of the loneliness that now invaded me seeing Laura, a woman I thought I had a chance with, about to fuck another man. Of course she didn't want to explore a relationship! She already had one ongoing in Barcelona. God knows what excuse she had employed to tell him why she was traveling to Chile. I tried to throw up again, but there was nothing left. It was as if my stomach were a sinkhole and I had fallen into it.

I sat up on the couch all night trying desperately to expunge the *moving* image of Laura fucking another man. And no doubt recently. Disgusted as I was, I started to pullulate sexual fantasies with her. My imagination was a twisted tangle of despair and desire and, at the bottom, there was nothing but a dark mine shaft that sank deep into the earth's core of depression.

I must have fallen asleep because when I awoke there was a great surge of pleasure issuing from my groin. Laura was on her knees before me, my cock in her mouth. I raked a hand over my face. She looked up at me with her doleful black eyes as if, *Is this okay?* A glance to the coffee table and I noticed that her phone had been moved. No doubt she had realized that I had been invading her privacy, had watched the cellphone video and now was making amends by fellating me.

Regardless of the convolutions of emotions that now roiled between us on this isolated hilltop in the antipodean country of Chile, I had no intention of stopping her. Through the windows raw dawnlight filtered in. The rain was still falling in a steady downpour. Laura twisted and turned over my cock as if performing a dance with only the movements and gyrations of her head. Desire geysered up in me and I started to lose control of my senses. Hours ago, with that video, she had desolated my soul, and now she was bringing it back to life, watering it with her salacious sexuality.

The ground started to tremble. I heard myself say, "Oh, my God." I had never had the sensation of the ground actually moving under my feet while having sex, but it was happening! I noticed that the couch was moving, its legs banging up and down on the hardwood floor. The blinds started rattling as if a desperate mariner was clinging to them like a foundered mast. The lamps started rattling. Wineglasses slid off the table as if pushed by a disembodied hand and crashed to the floor ...

Laura looked up. "It's a fucking earthquake!" she shrieked, her face now disorganized in terror.

I came out of my moment of near-ecstasy to find the entire cottage dramatically shaking. "Get to the door frame, get to the door frame!"

Laura flung open the door and braced herself against the frame. Silhouetted against the pink dawn, she looked like a woman crucified on the cross of both terror and prurience—I'll never forget that image as long as I live! As wineglasses and wine bottles continued to crash to the floor I buried my head in my arms and curled into a fetal position until the earthquake had passed.

When we were both pretty certain the *seismo*—as the Chileans call it—had spent itself, we hurriedly dressed to assess the damage and our shattered nerves. We hugged each other tightly, as if we were headed to the altar, which we clearly were not.

"It's okay," I said. "They have these all the time down here."

She looked at me with fear in her eyes, as I once remember a cat looking at me after it had been struck by a speeding car. "We have to get out of here, Miles."

"All right. Okay. Let's just relax. I'll call Felipe."

"No! We have to leave now."

"Okay. Don't go Spanish on me!"

"That's not funny," she retorted.

"I'm sorry, Laura. Okay, let's go."

Laura raced into the bedroom and started to pack. I called Felipe on the phone he had given me. There was great unease in his voice.

"Are you all right?" he implored.

"We're fine. But Laura wants to go."

"Don't try to drive out of there," he insisted. "You'll never make it on those roads."

"It's all downhill."

"Wait for us to come get you."

"All right," I said.

Laura came into the room with her bags packed. She walked right past me out into the inbound morning. I trailed after her. Beyond the cement patio there was wet dirt. As soon as Laura's foot touched it her leg kicked out from under her like one of the Rockettes and she fell hard on her ass. I rushed over to help her. Fortunately, her fall was cushioned by the mud.

"Let's get the fuck out of here!" she screamed at me.

"Calm down, Laura. Felipe's coming up to get us."

"Fuck that!" she cursed. "I want to get out of here." Her black eyes had transfigured into a veritable conflagration.

"We can't drive out of here on these roads in that car. Those tires can't handle it," I said, my nostrils flaring in anger.

There was another flash of lightning in the threatening morning sky. Rain started to empty from the skies again, only exacerbating Laura's increasingly dismayed state of mind.

"I'm driving out of here right now!" she blared, bent over at the waist.

Laura raged her luggage out to the Fiat. I shook my head to myself, then crossed the patio in an effort to help her. The rain-soaked earth was now a billabong of slippery clay. You had to walk a step at a time, as if mincing over a booby-trapped dirt road. Walk at a normal pace and you were destined to topple over. It was on this slick surface that an hysterical Laura attempted to wrestle her luggage into the Fiat.

"It was just an earthquake," I said. "We get them in California all the time. It was no big deal. I'm guessing it barely registered a six on the Richter Scale."

She looked at me like an escapee from a lunatic asylum. "You think I'm crazy? This whole country is sitting on a fault line." She wrangled her largest bag in, then zigzagged to the porch, her feet sliding out from under her as she slithered over the wet clay-ey surface, grabbed her carry-on bag and asked, "Are you coming?"

I looked out over the vineyards. The narrow dirt roads were puddled with water and the rain was still pouring down. It had been raining all night. This dense packed clay could not absorb all the water, so it just pooled on the surface where it created a silicone-slick foundation. "No," I said, disgusted. "I'll wait until Felipe comes up to get me."

"I'll see you at the bottom," she said. "Where are the car keys?"

I reluctantly handed her the keys. "Don't go, Laura, it's too dangerous."

"I've got to get out of here." She staggered to the car, slipping and regaining her balance several times. The engine turned over and she ground the gears into first. Mud spit out from the back of the spinning tires like Gatling guns firing red clay bullets. The car barely moved. When it finally erupted into movement it fishtailed violently left and right. The more frantically she worked the clutch the more the wheels spun in an effort to find traction where there was none. Then, suddenly, the car shot forward, but the first time she attempted to turn it spun out of control. The little car had whipped around 180 degrees and looked like an angry wasp in a jar trying to get out. She gunned the engine, tried reverse, with another loud crashing of gears, but the car just spun helplessly in place.

Finally, exasperated, she surrendered to the impossible conditions. She slowly opened the door and climbed out. "Fuck!" she screamed, waving her arms at her unseen persecutor. Then, losing her balance, she crumpled to the mud in a heap. She started crying.

I rushed to her as gingerly as I could over the treacherous ground to help her. Hoisting her up with my hands hooked under her armpits, I got her to her feet. I dragged her through the mud back into the cottage where the cellphone that Felipe had given me was ringing. "Take a shower, Laura, let me figure this out."

Resigned, she hauled her muddied and bedraggled self into the bathroom to get cleaned up.

I answered the phone. It was Felipe. In a rising tone, he said, "I can't get the four-wheel drive up to the villa."

"Oh, shit." I was thinking more about Laura than I was myself. Her rage had dismayed me. "What're we going to do?" I asked, feeling helpless. "Maybe the Vintners Association could fly a helicopter in," I suggested, trying to strike a mirthful elision in the concatenation of my growing despair.

"That may be a possibility," he said in all seriousness. "We may have another idea, too."

"Because, here's the deal, Felipe. I'm up here with a woman I barely know. She's kind of freaking out on me. Looking at these roads, we wouldn't be able to drive this car out of here for at least 3 days. And that's assuming the rain stopped, right?"

"Yes," he allowed. "We will figure something out." From the tone of his voice you could tell he felt badly, and you could also sense that he was worried.

"I mean, if you can't get your four-wheel drive up here ... how are we going to get food?"

"I know," he said in a voice as reassuringly as he could manufacture. "Just hang tight. We will figure something out."

"How bad was the earthquake?" I ventured.

"Not too bad. Seven, maybe."

I set the cell down just as Laura returned from the bathroom. She slumped onto the sofa in a fit of pique, but emotionally spent, and thus shut down. Much of her anger had abated and she now seemed resigned to letting it play out, realizing that her fate was now out of her control. "What's happening?"

"They couldn't get the four-wheel drive up," I said. "They're figuring it out."

She shook her head, then her body shivered. I hooked an arm around her and she let me pull her toward me.

"It's going to be all right. There's nothing we can do. I promise you they're not going to let us die up here."

"That's encouraging."

"And the earthquake was just an aftershock," I lied.

"Fuck, if that's an aftershock, I'd hate to be in the one that caused it!" She looked up at me with frightened eyes. "Earthquakes freak me out. They had a huge tsunami here in 2010. Thousands of people drowned."

"Relax," I said. "The good news is we're at a thousand feet elevation. No tsunami can get to us. Of course, the bad news is, with all this rain, no four-wheel drive can, apparently, either."

Laura trembled in my arms. I hugged her tighter.

"Would you like me to make some breakfast?"

"Okay," she said.

I found some eggs in the refrigerator. On a table in the kitchen there was a basket piled with onions and peppers and I whipped up an omelet. I uncorked a bottle of Casa Marin's finest Sauvignon Blanc, their Cipressa, and poured us each a fortifying glass. I figured we both needed the liquid courage. To hell with the opprobrium of morning drinking!

The wine animated both of us and momentarily ameliorated the sticky situation. I had forgotten all about the sex video and my vomitus reaction to it. I think we both realized that this was a relationship that had no future, but I was hoping to buy some time. I didn't want to be all alone in Chile, a prisoner of my celebrity. Without a mirror to my soul, I feared for my sanity.

Villa Marin's phone rang and I picked it up. It was Felipe. "Okay," he started. "We are coming with the *yunta de bueyes*."

"What?"

"You will see. It is our only chance, short of calling the Chilean Coast Guard. We need to get your car off the mountain," he said. "And we will. Then, we will bring you down."

I hung up and turned to Laura. "They are coming to rescue us with the ... *¿yunta de bueyes?*"

"What?"

"You speak Spanish."

"Oxen?"

"I don't know. He said they were coming and they were going to get the car and bring us down off the mountain. We're scheduled to be in Matanzas, this supposedly gorgeous beach resort, later this afternoon. If we don't check in to our cabin, they threatened to give it to someone else."

Laura picked up her wineglass, threw her head back and drained it. Then she refilled it, not with a compulsive drinker's defiance, but in fearful resignation to her now sealed fate. "This is fucked up, Miles." She tossed her head back again and nearly drained that one.

"I don't think I've ever had oral sex in an earthquake."

"And you may never again," she taunted.

"Oh, yeah." I grabbed one of her wrists and pulled her toward me. We kissed and I could tell the wine had liberated her. We moved tangle-footedly into the bedroom and made love like newlyweds. Sometimes apocalyptic moments inspire the lascivious in us humans, as if, in our last gasps of breath, survival forsaken us, our only desire is to propagate the species.

The rain stopped and a rainbow had formed over the vineyard-carpeted hills to the south. We marveled at it on the patio. An hour or so later we heard the clanking of what sounded like steel cowbells. We both straightened on wobbly legs. Down one of the steep paths that led up to the hilltop villa I could see four men, one of them Felipe, driving a pair of oxen who were marching sluggishly, but obstinately, up the slick muddy hill. Across their necks was hung, like a pillory, a weathered wooden yoke.

"¿The *yunta de bueyes*?"

"The yoke of oxen," Laura translated. "I thought you were joking me in Spanish."

"Apparently not."

The four men and the pair of oxen trudged slowly, but progressively, up the steep hill until they came to a thudding halt at the patio where Laura and I stood, framed by the rainbow and wearing the florid countenances of tragic lovers who had imbibed a little early, which, of course, made us less tragic.

Felipe spread open an arm, "The *yunta de bueyes.*"

Laura and I both burst out laughing. Laura doubled over, then toppled to her knees she was laughing so hard. *"Yunta de bueyes,"* she kept saying through her hysterical, eye-watering laughter.

Felipe clearly found the humor in it, too. We also both knew that there was no way we were going to get that Fiat 500 down those oil-slick switchbacks without some good old-fashioned locomotion.

"Fuck, man, this is whack!"

Felipe instructed his men, two of whom had coils of thick rope slung over their shoulders—and who, incidentally, *weren't* laughing (!)—to lash the *yunta de bueyes* to the Fiat 500.

I did the only sane thing I could: I got out my Canon camera and started snapping photos.

The *yunta de bueyes* were herded in front of the 500. They had the look of serious oxen! The heavy ropes were tied to each end of the massive wooden yoke, then to the front bumper of the 500. The trick was going to be to keep the Fiat from gaining speed on the descent and bumping into the oxen—who probably wouldn't have felt it they were so massive.

Felipe climbed into the driver's seat of the 500. His men unloaded Laura's luggage because they wanted the car as light as it could be. Felipe promised a concerned Laura they would come back for it—and us! One of the vineyard workers, shod in heavy boots, stood next to the oxen. The other two men positioned themselves behind the 500 to push it. Felipe put the car in neutral and was going to steer and work the brakes.

A command was issued, and then the worker next to the oxen struck their backside lightly with a switch fashioned from the branch of a tree. Nostrils flaring, they started forward, their massive shoulders flexing like boa constrictors in burlap bags. Laura, in her mad attempt at a getaway, had dug the wheels pretty deep into the mud, but the mud and the toy Fiat was no match for the powerful oxen. They pulled that little car out as if they were Chile's version of AAA.

With Felipe behind the wheel and working the brake, the oxen pulling with all their formidable strength, and the two vineyard workers pushing from behind, my promotional car slid off down the hill. Now and then it shimmied from side to side on the slick, clay surface, but the oxen were resolute, fearless in getting to their destination.

The *yunta de bueyes* briefly brought Laura and me together. She was going to be saved by the oldest towing company known to mankind and have a story to tell for the rest of her life that would draw laughter in whatever language she told it in. All I had to say was *yunta de bueyes* and we both collapsed in collective laughter.

Soon the 500 had disappeared over one of the knolls. A half hour later Felipe and his three vineyard workers, along with the faithful, indefatigable *yunta de bueyes* slogged back up the hill. Felipe asked for our luggage and we brought it out to the living room. The rain had started up again. The vineyard workers meticulously shrouded our bags—two of which were almost coffin-sized—in plastic sheeting.

Felipe handed Laura and me rain coats and said, "Put these on. Your shoes are no good. We're going to take you down on the *bueyes*."

"What?"

"Come on," he said. Laura, concomitantly laughing and looking a little unsettled, let Felipe help her on to one of the oxen. He showed her how to hold the yoke with both hands. Then, it was my turn. I climbed astride the ox next to Laura's and grabbed my side of the yoke. Almost simultaneously, we looked at each other and our faces disorganized into the kind of laughter that saves marriages.

We started off with a broken lurch. I had never ridden an ox before. Jokes poured out of me fast and furiously, a cathartic liberation of my tortured soul like I had never experienced before.

Matanzas

We made it back to Viña Casa Marin. Maria Luiz and Conchita greeted us as if we were returning from a war where casualties had outnumbered survivors. Our butts were saddle sore from the oxen, but we were both glad to be rescued from the hilltop. Hilarity flowed profusely. Conchita had prepared a proper return-from-the-war repast and we ate ravenously and drank copiously their stellar wines, as pure an expression of Chile's *terroir* as I could only imagine. And still so much to discover!

After we had said our goodbyes, Laura and I crammed ourselves into the now despised and much-derided Fiat 500, obviously the worst vehicle imaginable, once you got off Chile's interstates, for these pot-holed roads and impassable vineyard trails. What was Silvio thinking? Emails to him to get a new car were met with non-replies, or assurances that he would try.

With Laura navigating we motored our way south from Lo Abarca to Matanzas, a tiny, drowsy fishing village that was renowned for being a mecca for windsurfers and kite-boarders. My connection at the Aubrey had recommended a place there called Olas Matanzas where they rented cabins shelved onto a hillside that overlooked the ocean.

The storm clouds that had brought the anomalous summer rain had started to clear, leaving ragged edges at the periphery of the sky, and a vast hole of blue above us where the sun shone down hotly. We stripped to our T-shirts and put our sunglasses back on. I don't know if it was my imagination or not, but it seemed like Laura had doubled her 3-4 cigarette a day habit. A part of me wanted to bring up the sex video and the Sergio texts, but I didn't think it was any of my business. Perhaps she had left her phone out in an unlocked way because she had wanted me to find out. I met a woman once who was so miserable in her marriage that she fucked her husband's best friend in a blatant demonstration of the fact that she wanted out of the relationship. Perhaps I had been too ardent in email over the past year and a fantasy had bloomed and swelled all out of proportion to reality where there was, in reality, nothing but desert.

I thought about what I had been hearing about the Atacama Desert and the famous astronomers who made pilgrimages there with their colossal telescopes to search the heavens for the origins of life. Would they ever find it? Or, was it not really about finding it, but the search itself? I was talking to myself again, even though there was someone sitting in the seat next to me.

"How're we doing?" I asked Laura, referring to her navigating us to Matanzas.

"We're fine. On the right road. I think."

"You think?"

"These are the worst signs I have ever seen," she said.

"Yes," I agreed. "The Commissioner of Roads should sue the university he attended for back tuition."

That brought a chuckle to Laura. "We're looking for the G-80-I, whatever that is," she said. "And any signs to Navidad."

"Okay," I said, "I'll keep my eyes peeled."

In Chile, road signs were scarce, as if whoever created them and erected them was on a strict budget. Worse, they were often placed just before a turnoff as if they had hired knuckleheads with no sense of how long a motorist traveling at a certain speed might need to anticipate a turnoff. Seeing a turnoff sign at the last minute, and the only one leading up to it, I often found myself veering sharply to make the turn, not sure if it was the right one, or speeding past it and hurling imprecations at the road I needed to be on now fleeing past me as if it were some magical highway to heaven that we were forever destined, like star-crossed lovers, to miss.

We stumbled our way into the quiet town of Navidad. Packs of Chile's lost *perros* roamed everywhere, their heads sunk low, their lives reduced to nothing more than foraging for scraps of food and puddles of water. We stopped at a small *tienda* and bought some fruit drinks. The sun was dipping in the west now and I wanted to get to Matanzas before it grew dark and we found ourselves fumbling around lost in another new place, only to end up arguing again. I knew then and there that Laura and I weren't meant for each other, but I wanted to keep her around as long as I could, as long as I dared, to stave off the loneliness that I knew would descend on me. The thought of her traveling with me for the next three months was almost unthinkable at this juncture. Judging by her body language, by her expressions, by her frequent text-ing, I thought it was obvious she was missing someone on the other side of the world. And I knew only too intimately how much that could hurt.

I dodged the pot holes in a narrow, sinuous asphalt road that led to the ocean. We climbed through twists and turns until we emerged, like those Chilean miners hoisted finally out of that mine shaft, at the edge of a cliff that looked out over the ocean. Matanzas. The view was jaw-dropping, heart-stopping, lung-emptying! My friends at the Aubrey hadn't steered me wrong. They said I would find peace there. Even Laura had stopped her obsessive text-ing to take in the breathtaking scenery.

We clambered out of the car at the first overlook we came to and gazed down at the blinding ocean. Large, powerful waves, groomed by an offshore wind, wrapped around a point and broke with a hollow ferocity. Windsurfers and surfers sped across their textured faces, gliding adroitly, and building up tremendous speeds. The waves crashed against black rocks that contrasted sharply with the deep blue waters. White, black, and blue, my favorite colors; the colors of my soul.

We got back in the car and coasted down the damaged road into the tiny town of Matanzas. Past the town we found the sign for Olas Matanzas and I braked in front of the reception cabin. Inside, our reservation was handled with the typical Chilean lack of celerity, but we were tired and didn't mind.

A young man in a golf cart then led us to our cabin. It was a modest two-story, wood-framed structure set in a gently sloping hillside where other similar cabins were situated, all of them afforded spectacular views of the staggeringly beautiful, strong ocean.

We dragged our luggage into our cabin, bone-weary. The young man gave us a mini-tour of our accommodations, then left. As I went upstairs to unpack, Laura went into the bathroom to take a shower. From upstairs I heard a scream. I raced down the narrow spiral staircase.

"There's no hot water," Laura complained.

"Fuck," I said. "Maybe it takes a few minutes for the water heater to kick in."

"I'll just take a cold shower and pretend you're not famous," she joked.

"I'm glad you still have your sense of humor."

"It's wearing thin."

I left her alone to take a cold shower—she needed one! —and I went back upstairs, powered up my laptop to get on the Internet. After a brief Google search of Matanzas restaurants I noticed there was basically only one game in town: Surazo. Laura could use a nice dinner and we both could use some wine.

Surazo was set on the beach at the southern edge of the town of Matanzas. We walked into it from the sand as if we were shipwrecked mariners seeking refuge from a gale that had capsized our boat. Night had yet to fall and the sky was bleeding and billowing orange and mauve. The wind had shifted to onshore and the ocean was now shark-toothed with jagged whitecaps. Windsurfers skimmed the rough water at high speed across the ragged waves, performing aerial maneuvers in the frigid waters.

We were seated at a table in the simple wood-and-glass framed building. The menu looked promising. There were some great Chilean wines and we ordered a bottle of the Amayna Sauvignon Blanc, one of the many wineries I was hoping to visit.

I reached a hand across the table and held Laura's in mine. "Look, Laura. I know this was a mistake. I know you have someone back in Barcelona. But I just need for you to stick this out for a bit. I don't want to be all alone here by myself."

She smiled wearily, then took another sip of her wine. "I should have said something. We just met a month ago."

"Looks like it's gotten pretty hot and heavy in a month," I said, then tapped my index finger on her phone.

"You saw?" She rushed a hand to her mouth. "Oh, my God."

"I didn't mean to spy. It was just lying there on the table. I'm sorry."

"I'm so embarrassed," she blushed.

"Don't worry about it."

"I'm sorry, Miles."

"Don't worry about it, Laura," I reiterated. "It doesn't matter. I wasn't going to move to Spain anyway, and you sure as hell weren't going to move to L.A., who can blame you? Who would want to live in that abominable and venal city?"

"I really like you, Miles," she said, relaxed now that I didn't care she had a boyfriend she was keen on, had two glasses of wine under her belt, and was off that muddy hilltop and the muscular backs of those *yunta de bueyes*.

"For a moment, we can have *un gran romance*," I said, using the Spanish she had once used to refer to our weekend affair a year ago in Paso Robles that had resulted in our being here together in Chile.

"Yes," she said, smiling.

I upended the Sauvignon Blanc, summoned the dilatory waiter and ordered a Casas del Bosque Syrah. The Amayna Sauv Blanc had hit the spot of a still-light-outside get-going wine, but the Syrah, with its velvety trimming, whetted our palates for the wood-roasted lamb and the encroachment of night. We ate and drank to repletion, then walked a zigzag trail back to our cabin. The upstairs bedroom showcased a commanding view of the ocean. A full moon, with no ambient light to speak of, touched the ocean like stardust and magically made it materialize out of the dark like an image appearing on photographic paper in a developer's bath. As our eyes, like owls, adjusted to the dark, and their irises opened wider and wider, the ocean coruscated like mica struck by a fierce sun. All one could hear was the crashing of waves. And where the waves broke they erupted into brilliant phosphorescence before spending themselves on the black sand shore. We had sex—because it wasn't lovemaking anymore—against this painterly backdrop and enjoyed it for its physical ephemerality and nothing more.

We laid awake and shared a cigarette. I couldn't believe how bright it was outside, how preternaturally silver the ocean glistened. And the moon looked gigantic in the sky, as if, being in Chile, the earth had shifted and we had grown closer to the cosmos. Perhaps we had! An eerie peace descended over both of us.

I broke the wave-crashing silence when I whispered, "I just don't want you to leave me and I end up like Malkovich in *The Sheltering Sky*."

For some reason this made her laugh. Laura knew her Paul Bowles, knew her Bertolucci, evidently. Knew the existential crisis of the artist. "What's going on tomorrow?" she asked.

"I have some wineries to visit. You don't have to come, if you don't want to."

She didn't say anything. The moon, through the window, sagged low in the sky where it haunted the night with its luminous girth. A moment later I could hear Laura snoring lightly. There's nothing lonelier than being in bed with someone who doesn't want to be in bed with you. It was confusing. With confusion came doubts. With doubts came barriers. I was talking in my head again. How many relationships exist with these barriers *always* erected? And more getting erected every day?

I slipped silently out of bed, pulled on my clothes and walked down a serpentine sandy path to the beach. The ocean reeked of rotting seaweed. I came across the ghastly sight of a sea lion who had met a grisly fate. A section of his body had been bitten out, as if by a shark or a killer whale, of which there were many in these frigid waters. I instantly thought of Hemingway's *The Old Man and the Sea*, and then I thought about my own travails in the viper pit of the film business where even if you bring in a catch, by the time it gets to shore, it's often been devoured by unscrupulous agents and venal producers and you, the writer, are left washed up on the beach with little or nothing to show for your years of suffering and hard work.

I walked on, the shoreline lit brightly by the powerful moonlight. A lone dog the size of a golden retriever padded past me. He stopped and looked at me as if perhaps I might have something for him to eat. I opened my arms and said, *"No comida, perro."* He seemed to understand, threw me a sorrowing face, then wandered on, perhaps to the trash bins outside one of the restaurants.

The thunderous surf drowned out my thoughts. I hadn't been in Chile long, but for the first time in my life, with a more than modest success under my belt, I felt like I had arrived, I felt like I didn't have to go in that room and turn on the computer and write. For years this is how I lived my life. Except when I was making films, I wrote. I wrote six days a week, always taking Sunday off to recharge my imagination, push the work down into the unconscious and let *it* work on it. Writing came easily to me. The hard part was taking it to the world: friends, lovers, wives, agents, producers, the whole gauntlet of disparate sensibilities who can either damn you with faint praise, praise you all out of proportion to your worth, or kill the project you poured a year of your life into, or more, with trenchant criticism that would later turn out to be wrong. The writer's life is a Sisyphean one. Even if he gets the boulder to the top of his personal goal hill, and even if he has a success, he starts again with a new boulder, at the bottom of the hill, with the blank page.

Here in Chile I had gone completely *tabula rasa*. I had decided I wasn't going to write, or even think about writing, if I could help it. I was going to let myself go to the world that I found down here, south of the equator, as far away from California as I had ever come. Perhaps I had a fantasy that I would find love with Laura, but that clearly was not in the narrative anymore, and I lambasted myself on that moonlit beach for fashioning such a ludicrous one.

I glanced at my watch and I was shocked to see that it wasn't even midnight. In a gesture of defiance of time, I removed the cheap watch and hurled it into the ocean. I suddenly didn't want to know what year it was, what day it was, what time it was. I didn't want to know when the deadline for finishing a certain project was, self-imposed or imposed by some abusive head of development. I wanted to empty my soul of all my regrets. All they were doing was eating me alive, dragging noisily behind me like the tin cans on a *Just Got Married* car speeding off into the tragedy of divorce. Just as I wanted to expunge the past and, with it, all the monsters who had made my life a living hell, I wanted nothing to do with the future. I wanted the future to be in the here and now, and though that wasn't going to be entirely possible, I wanted so badly not to preordain anything. I no longer wanted to believe in the promise of anything because the promise of things happening, especially for a writer, is a living hell of future regrets.

I turned and faced the tumultuous sea. The waves pounded the outside reef with a relentless energy generated from strong winds and storms far out in the black amplitude of the ocean. Above me stars, planets, meteors, comets, whole galaxies, looked arrested in motion, but I knew that they were moving, were constantly in a state of flux. When I was twenty years old, I reflected, I believed I could read a huge swath of the world's literature, see most every film that had ever been made, that one day I would reasonably know what made me and others tick. Thirty years later I realized I knew next to nothing. Instead of vouchsafing me answers, life had given me nothing but befuddlement. I understood, at best, the horrible nature of man, the cruelty of the animal that anthropologists would tell is by far the cruelest mammal on the planet: man, himself. But I didn't understand the Byzantine ways of love. I only knew, as another wave crashed and spit foam into the air, causing me to pause in my internal dialogue, that its mysterious properties were the only anodyne to that cruelty.

The Mapuche

Laura was still sleeping when I woke in the morning. I made some horrible instant coffee, which barely gave me a buzz, wolfed down a banana, wanting to get out of there before she awoke. I left a note saying that I had some wineries to visit and that I wouldn't be back until later in the afternoon.

On my Google Maps app I inputted my destination near Pichilemu. I was headed for a vineyard property that grew Sauvignon Blanc close to the ocean. Pichilemu is a famous big wave surfing break and I was hoping to have lunch there and perhaps watch the surfers ride the giant waves that wrapped around Punta Lobos. The day apart, I hoped, would be salubrious for Laura and me.

Following my Google Maps app, I drove due east out of Matanzas on a bad road that the Fiat 500 just wasn't designed for. I drove through colonnades of towering pine trees, slowed through seemingly deserted villages where the stray dogs outnumbered the residents. About an hour into my journey, Google Maps wanted me to veer off onto a dirt road. In Chile, sometimes dirt roads are preferable to the paved ones, but they're not, as I learned, to be looked askance at. So, I took the turnoff that I was instructed to take.

Soon I was climbing on the dirt road through some rugged terrain. Google Maps kept showing me I was on the right course for the vineyard property, so I barreled forward, thinking of that pathetic fool in Germany who drove into the Rhine and drowned in his BMW when his computer-voiced guide exhorted him to turn left when she meant for him to turn right.

I pushed on, up hills rutted by the recent rains, the only car on the road, the only human in existence. Several times I debated turning back, but the blue icon on my phone representing my vehicle showed that I was making tremendous progress.

Suddenly, the road I was on turned nasty. What was once a relatively smooth graded road now was carpeted with sharp rocks that kicked up inside the wheel wells and produced an awful racket. What provided traction for the right vehicles was clearly destroying the undercarriage of the 500. Soon, I heard a thumping noise. The steering wheel kept veering to the left. The car slowed, seemed to hitch forward like a spavined jackass, then just started hobbling.

I braked to a halt and climbed out. The sun was high in the sky and beating down on me with a searing ferocity. A quick inspection proved what I had feared: the left rear tire was flat. Not just flat, totally shredded as if a wheat combine had trampled over it.

"Fuck!" I hadn't changed a tire in a long time. In the U.S. most people don't change tires anymore as modern communications and inexpensive AAA solves most of your automotive mishaps. Not so in Chile. Not when you're on a dirt road in the middle of nowhere, between the lyrically-named villages of Matanzas and Pichilemu, don't speak the language, are tired, prone to panic anxiety, and a little hung over. My phone was useless. Other than Silvio 200 miles away in Santiago and Laura in Matanzas, whom I would never call in a million years under the circumstances, who was I going to call?

I found the manual in the glove compartment. In the rear of the car I rooted out what looked like the kid's toy version of a tire changing kit. The jack appeared tiny, flimsy, fit for a bicycle maybe. I kicked at the car because there was nothing else to do to vent my frustration. Then, I clambered down on the dirt and maneuvered the jack into position. It was a ludicrously slow process, but I eventually managed to hoist the left rear of the car off the ground. With the cheap lug wrench I popped off the hub cap to give me access to the lug nuts. I put the lug wrench on one of them, but it wouldn't budge—and I had five to get off! I positioned the lug wrench horizontally and slammed down on it with my foot. My tennis shoe slid off, the lug wrench banged hard against my ankle bone, and I fell to the ground like a wounded infantryman.

"FUCK!"

I started to panic. Fifteen miles, I had calculated, in this hot sun with no water was going to be brutal, if not downright insane, if I decided to hike out for help. *Stay with the car*, a man stranded in the middle of the desolate Baja Peninsula had been warned. The next day they found his body at the edge of the ocean, in a burrow of sand he had dug for himself, his flesh picked apart by vultures, nothing left but his skeleton and the sockets where his eyes once glimpsed an untrammeled world.

I squatted down next to the annihilated tire and, for some reason, the image of the half-devoured sea lion dead on the beach under the moonlight throbbed as an eschatological omen in my head. I was tired, dehydrated, cursed myself for not bringing along anything other than a Styrofoam cup of Nescafé that was now long gone, when I heard the strangest sound. I turned and saw a man on a white horse approaching me. For a moment I thought I was hallucinating. (Chile is a country that can induce hallucinations! One moment you're stuck on a hilltop and oxen are pulling you out, the next you're at some fabulous winery being fêted by the aristocracy.)

The man and his horse stopped next to me. The horse blubbered air through his nose. The man was deeply tanned, almost to the point of looking African American. But he bore the distinctive features of the indigenous Mapuche Indians. He wore a red bandana and his countenance was stoic, mirthless, almost as if he were a relic in a museum.

"*Hola*," I said.

He nodded briefly without uttering anything, looked past me at the tire and the woeful Fiat 500. I grabbed the lug wrench with both hands and pantomimed my inability to budge the lug nuts. He seemed to understand. His impassive presence was scaring me. He looked like a fierce warrior whose countenance bore hundreds of years of his peoples' suffering.

Slowly, he climbed off the horse. He smelled autochthonous, if earth and indigenousness can be defined as an odor. He kept his gaze trained on the tire. I stepped aside. He placed the worn leather boot of his right foot on the lug wrench, pushed down hard once with the force of his strength and the bolt gave up the ghost. He performed the same thing on the other four bolts effortlessly, then he handed me back the lug wrench.

"*Gracias.*"

"*De nada,*" was all he said. I started to reach for my wallet, but he waved me off, appearing offended. He climbed back onto his powerful white horse, made a clicking sound with his tongue and clopped away, as if he were in no hurry to get anywhere. I watched him trot off. I wanted to get his picture, but I had heard that Indians didn't like to have their pictures taken because you were robbing them of their soul. In reality, the Mapuche, in a strange ineffable way, had given me back my soul.

Bolts unstuck, I went to work and got the laughably miniscule doughnut spare on. I got back in the car, turned around and retraced my route, driving extremely slowly over the sharp rocks. Another flat and I would be royally fucked.

I limped into Navidad and pulled into what looked like a service station. Used tires decorated the outside of the structure. I showed them my shredded tire and they seemed to find great hilarity in its irreparable condition. A bad mix of Spanish and English resulted in my being directed to another shop where they thought maybe I could be helped.

I continued down to a shop with a weathered sign hanging askew on which was hand-painted *Reparador* and *pneumaticos*. A smiling man came out who spoke a little better English than the previous *reparadors*. He, too, broke into the same look of utter dismay when he saw my ravaged tire. He held up a finger, then turned and disappeared inside his shop. One of the lost *perros* of Chile ambled by. He stopped close to me, begging for a treat. I had nothing to give him. And he had nothing to give me. I bent down and petted him and he was so grateful for the affection that he nuzzled up next to me, filthy as he was.

The *reparador* returned, barking into a cellphone. He turned to me and said, "I have this tire, but it comes from San Antonio."

"How long?"

"*Una hora.*"

I looked at the doughnut on the left rear of the Fiat, knew that I still had some dirt roads to traverse to get back to Olas Matanzas and decided to wait. "*Bien,*" I said.

Mr. *Reparador* sprung into action when I pulled some 10,000 peso notes from my pocket. He plucked three of them ($60) out of my hand, which I considered a bargain.

I couldn't believe I didn't have Laura's number. How stupid of me. I guess I didn't think we'd be apart. I tried emailing her, but the data connection was so slow I couldn't get my Gmail account to come up. In frustration I drank a beer at an outdoor café. Then another. After my third beer I went back to the *reparador*'s shop. The *pneumatic usado* (used tired) still hadn't arrived from San Antonio, but Pepé promised me it was en route. I glanced at my watch. It was almost 6:00 p.m., and the sun was bending off toward the west. Laura would start to wonder about me if I didn't make it back for dinner. I debated driving with the doughnut—and no more spare for a back-up! —to Matanzas to salvage what I could with a no doubt distraught Laura, when a mini-truck roared into view.

Pepé roared with delight, "*Aqui está.*"

As the sky turned to deep blue and the lonesome dogs lolloped by, Pepé went to work on fixing the tire. An hour or so later, he was done. I kept hearing the phrase *muy suerte* on the *pneumatico* because I guess the Fiat had these ridiculously small tires that weren't common in Chile. I tried to tip Pepé another 10,000 Chilean pesos, but, like the Mapuche, he waved me off. Then he hugged me. I couldn't remember the last time a repairman in L.A. hugged me. Hell, if one had I might have been concerned! But there was something natural about it. Pepé knew that I had had a long day, that I was out on a dirt road in the middle of nowhere. He got that I was scared and lost and missing my *amiga novia Laura*.

Laura; Women

I found my way in the crepuscular light back to Matanzas, smashing into pot-holes left and right with my *usado pneumatico*. It was dark when I parked in front of our cabin and climbed out of the car. Waves pounded the shore with an inexorable intensity.

I called out Laura's name as soon as I entered, but there was no answer. I climbed the spiral staircase to the bedroom, but it was empty. Something looked different. Then it hit me: half the luggage was gone! I snapped on a light and found a piece of paper staring me in the face on the comforter of the bed.

> *Miles,*
> *I took the bus to Santiago. I was able to change my plane ticket for a flight tonight back to Spain.*
> *I know that you are searching for something here in Chile, but it's not with me. Yes, I have someone in Barcelona whom I started seeing and I do miss him, but that's not the reason I left. I left because I'm homesick, and I don't think I could live the life that you live.*
> *I'm sorry, Laura*

Outside the picture window the moonlight had begun to illuminate the crashing waves. I needed people suddenly, and I needed a lot of them.

I showered and pulled on some fresh clothes and walked at a brisk clip toward Surazo. They showed me to a table where I sat all alone. I ordered a bottle of Metatic Syrah and started in on it with a mind to obliterate Laura's leaving. If I had had her number I would have called her. My lifeline to Chile was suddenly cut off.

Next to me was a table crowded with roistering young men and their girlfriends. The men, good-looking, athletic, young, spoke English, so I straightened to my feet and introduced myself. Turns out they were windsurfers who were in Chile for their winter. Next they would be on to Hawaii, circumnavigating the globe in a circuit that sounded romantic.

The wine flowed. Soon, their table was a full-blown party. Tipsy from the wine, I had them in stitches with my story of the flat tire and the Mapuche Indian who had "saved" me. They were empathetic when I told them that my "girlfriend" had upped and left. A couple of them seemed to have recalled her from the previous night. They remembered, in particular, her exotic beauty, her mane of black hair and ...

"Okay, stop!" I roared. "Enough. She's gone!" I waved my arm in the direction of the waiter. "*Camarero, otra botella de vino!*"

More bottles were delivered to the table and more pesos fountained out of my wallet in ejaculatory ecstasy. My generosity knew no bounds when I was lonely and bereft and needed company. Hell, my Spanish was *mucho mejoro*!

"Okay, you guys, I need your help," I said, after I had paid for everyone's dinner and wine. "I want you to follow me just out of town." They looked at me, baffled. "Trust me, this has to be done. Okay? Wait for me."

I hustled back to my cabin, clambered noisily and drunkenly into the Fiat 500 and drove back down to the restaurant. The two couples got into their mini-trucks and followed me the short distance out of town. Just north of Matanzas the road climbed to the stunning overlook that Laura and I had stopped at when we had first come into town.

I parked the Fiat 500, but left the engine running. The two mini-trucks waited, with their lights burning into the night, as I put the car into Drive and leaped back as it started to move forward toward the precipice. Driverless, it crossed the thirty or so paces of dirt before it launched itself off the cliff. As if drawn by a powerful magnet of curiosity, everyone rushed to the edge to see the white Fiat tumble end over end on the dirt, until it finally crashed to a halt on the rocky shore. Unlike in the movies, it didn't erupt into flames.

I cupped my hands around my mouth: "FIX IT AGAIN TONY!"

A celebratory cheer went up. They had been on the receiving end of my risible, and miserable, relationship with the Fiat 500, and they, too, viewed the decision to junk it as my liberation from "vehicular oppression."

They drove me back to Olas Matanzas. We exchanged high-fives and thank you's and then I went back inside, all alone. I opened another bottle of wine, poured a glass, and climbed the stairs to my bed. At some point it occurred to me that the woman who was going to make this journey with me was now on a flight back to Europe and I was once again, in the middle of nowhere, this time without a car.

I slept fitfully. Disquieting dreams plagued me, hounded me like Dobermans. I was homeless, staggering alone in deserts. Bankruptcy lurked at every corner. Nothing made sense. I was sleeping on couches and itinerantly peregrinating from abode to abode, an unshowered roustabout. My dead parents, in one dream, came back and admonished me again for having chosen the life of the writer. I went in and out of sleep like a mariner dipping and rising through turbulent seas. The previous night I had been so at peace with the moon out my window. Now my life was a whirlpool of panic. If only Laura had just stuck it out another week. But I didn't blame her for leaving. What did I have to offer? I didn't want kids; I didn't want marriage; hell, I didn't even know if I wanted to live with someone!

Sure, I wanted companionship because when you go *tabula rasa* like I had in a strange and foreign land like Chile your foundations have crumbled. Words spew out of you to no one and the mirror that another person, especially someone who understands you, holds up to you, to keep you in check and sane, is shattered. The loony bin beckons. I trembled in my loneliness. The wine, good as it was, didn't help anymore. I was having an existential crisis and didn't fully realize it. Repressed feelings were surging up into my already troubled psyche with unexpected force and I didn't know how to contain them. The moon, instead of looking preternaturally beautiful, as it had the previous night, now appeared lugubrious, saturnine, the cold disfigured eye of an ogre! For some dumb reason, as I ranged through thoughts from suicidal fantasies to moments of artistic glory, I went through the women I had been intimate with in my life. None of them had really understood me, except my ex-wife and ... Maya. But Maya was with a new man now, so that door was closed off the way a storm cloud closes off the sun. But, with Maya, I came to the realization that love wasn't confusing. And because it wasn't confusing there were no doubts, there were no hesitations, there were no barriers. This is how I had felt when we had made love in Santa Ynez. I realized that this is what I was looking for, but the timing had never been right. Fame had transformed me into a borderline despicable person, until fame leveled me with its other side: what have you done for me lately?

The night before I had been inhaling and exhaling slowly. Laura had been snoring lightly next to me, and though I knew we weren't going to build a relationship, there was a comfort in knowing that she was there, that we had come to an understanding about what she meant to me here in Chile: her knowing the language; her being someone I could talk to. Perhaps, after thousands of words of emails, I did harbor the fantasy that something more was there, even if I knew the true test of a relationship is annealed in the cauldron of being together twenty-four hours a day, seven days a week, making mutual decisions, and then, after a long day—missed turnoffs, bad restaurants, showers that don't work—finding the romance that was once there on a weekend in California's wine country when nothing except hot sex and the fantasy of romance was at stake. Nothing, except pure carnality, flesh tearing at flesh, words of heightened adoration blurted from inebriated brains through slurring lips and slobbered into the pretty ears of women who only wanted to be adored. That's not love. It's not even the promise of love. It was only sowing the seed for hurt.

Part III

Jack to the Rescue

Salmon-hued light jarred me awake. My head hurt. My mouth was Saharan. And then it hit me: the Fiat 500 was belly-up on the rocks on a beach in Matanzas, giant waves swatting it like a cat pawing a dead mouse.

I pulled myself together and walked the short distance to the Olas Matanzas office and informed them that my car had been stolen. They were deeply concerned, very apologetic. I admitted that I might have left the keys in the car—stupid me, *muy borracho*! They immediately phoned the authorities.

An hour later two *Carabineros de Chile* were standing solemnly at my cabin. A serious-looking young man and his partner, a young woman. They asked to come in. I told them who I was, whom the car belonged to, and wondered about a ride back to Santiago. They filled out a report and departed. Apparently, car theft in Chile was as enterprising as it was in the U.S.!

I phoned Silvio and told him what happened.

"Your car was stolen?" he asked, incredulous.

"Yes. I'm going to need to get back to Santiago somehow."

"Take the bus," he suggested.

All my frustration suddenly boiled over into rage. "I'm not going to take a fucking bus back to Santiago. And I need another car. And not some fucking toy. I've got wineries to visit. I've got a novel to research! Your project's about to go down the drain and be pulverized in the disposal like a puckered lemon if you don't get me something four-wheel drive and big enough to carry my luggage!"

"I will see," he said.

"Otherwise, I'm heading to *Aeropuerto Internacional de Santiago* and am out of here." I ended the call. With my thumb and forefinger I massaged my temple. Laura's Ylang-Ylang perfume lingered on the pillow, and it haunted. Lack of sleep had thoughts Ping-Ponging around in my brain with little purpose. A bus back to Santiago? Fuck, it might have been my only option.

I called Jack. It would have been early back in L.A.

He answered groggily. "Miles?"

"It's me."

"Where are you, dude?"

"I'm in the gorgeous fishing village of Matanzas. The wine is awesome and the chicks are fucking hot, if a little on the Catholic side, which means they like to be spanked."

He chuckled groggily. "What happened with Laura?"

I told him what happened with Laura.

"Fuck, man, that's raw."

"Yeah, I'm still trying to expunge that porn video from my amygdala."

"You're what?"

"Area of the brain for cognition and filthy thoughts."

"I was worried about you."

"Yeah, and she took ten grand from me before she left."

"Miles. You crack me up. You just don't know how to handle women."

"I'm a romantic, what can I say? Romantics get roistered in the ass. Look, I had an idea. Why don't you get on a plane and come down here and finish this trip with me? I'll go online right now and get you a business class ticket to Santiago. It's all on me. Fuck it. I need someone who understands me. I can't take this country alone. It's too big and weird, but the wine is amazing, dude, and I've made some connections. We'll be going to some extraordinary places. What do you say?"

"Chile?"

"What've you got going on?"

"Not a whole lot. Up for this A.D. gig on a pretty big film, but I already interviewed for it, and if it happens it wouldn't be for another month."

"Then, come on down. It'll do you good. It'll do us both good."

"Chile, huh? I've never been south of the equator."

The *Carabineros de Chile* returned to my cabin. They beckoned me to their patrol car that looked more like a Humvee outfitted to fight Al Qaeda in Afghanistan. We drove a short distance out of Matanzas to the top of the cliff and the scene of the crime. We all climbed out and gaped over the edge. There were a few more *carabineros* down on the beach where the Fiat 500 now looked like a crumpled sheet of writing paper.

"Is that your car?"

"I believe it is," I said absently, with no emotion.

On the cliff, with the waves crashing in the deep blue sea and the sky a cobalt blue, they conducted a little interrogation. I don't think they thought for a minute I had any motivation to ditch the car the way I had, but they went through the motions of an investigation. I didn't tell them that when I was a teenager I once saw the flashing lights of a cop car in my rearview mirror while smoking marijuana and drinking beer. Instead of stopping I hit the accelerator, swerved left, swerved right, pulled into a driveway, then hoofed it home, waited until morning, then called the cops and told them my car was stolen. Cops bought it hook, line and sinker.

I took a bus back to Santiago from Matanzas. It was not a fun trip. For five long hours, I bounced on a seat that was designed for a convict heading to Folsom. But when a cab deposited me at the Aubrey and I got checked back in, showered, and hit the bar, I was in heaven. Chile has this extraordinary way of making your life miserable one moment, then hoisting you to a ledge of wonderment and appreciation of all that is salutary in life.

And then, like a dream, there was Ariadne, sitting all alone at a table with a menu hiding her face. I approached her. She smiled. "Look who's back."

"May I sit down?"

She opened her arms to me.

I sat down across from her. We swapped stories about our days in Chile since we had checked out of the Aubrey. She told me she had flown over the Andes to Buenos Aires to see a man who danced the tango. Apparently, he also performed the mambo with her credit cards.

"It was a disaster," she said, waving her hand theatrically, and refilling her wineglass.

"Why do we get into these romantic entanglements?" I asked.

"I guess we're always searching for love," she said.

"Yes, the great C. G. Jung once said that he had plumbed the depths of the psyche, he thought he understood so much about man, his neuroses, etcetera, but the one thing he never understood was love."

"Yes," she said.

"I think God or whomever—and I'm an anti-deist, by the way— did a number on us. He made sex so wonderful that we started, as we came more and more into our ego-consciousness, to conflate, and confuse it with love. There should be no confusion, it should just feel right. And yet we let ourselves get on planes and fly through Andean passes to someone we think is going to change our life, return with stories of identity theft and a broken heart. Or, look at me: I'm ten thousand lighter in the wallet and wondering what the hell I was thinking asking someone I only knew over a weekend to come travel the country of Chile with me for three months. How was that ever going to work?"

"I guess for you, you can mine some good material for your next book."

"Yes. But I don't want to have to suffer for my material anymore."

Ariadne laughed. "It's good to see you. I wasn't looking forward to eating alone."

"Neither was I."

"What's on your agenda?"

"My friend Jack flies in tomorrow. We're heading to the Maule Valley with this guy from MOVI to see the real Chile, supposedly. You're welcome to come with us."

"I'd love to, but I have meetings all week in Santiago."

"You'd like my friend, Jack, he's a fun guy."

"I'm sure I would."

A silence fell. We exchanged flirtatious glances. I couldn't tell if she was attracted to me. Not needing more rejection I was loath to make a move. But then the wine took over. "You're a beautiful woman, Ariadne."

"Thank you," she said.

We talked and drank and ate until the restaurant shuttered and the candles winked out. Then we took a walk through the raucous weekend night streets of Bellavista. We might have kissed at one point, but it wasn't to be. Back at the Aubrey we hugged and then went back to our separate rooms.

Jack

God, it was good to see Jack. He came out of the Customs line and he embraced me with a bear hug in the main lobby of the airport.

"It's good to see you, Miles," he said in his booming voice, a little more booming than normal due to some over-imbibition on the long flight down. He sat me down. "Man, what have you been eating down here? You've put on weight!"

"Have I?"

"You've got to go light on the tacos."

"They don't eat tacos down here, fucking culturalist!"

Jack laughed. I helped him out with his luggage to the new Fiat that Silvio had procured, a car I had never heard of called a Qubo. It was like Fiat's version of the now defunct Honda Element, with way more room than the 500 and tires that could handle rough terrain. With Jack, with Maule, with MOVI, I had a feeling that we were heading into rough terrain!

I sensed that Jack needed a beverage so I uncorked a bottle of Casa Marin's cool weather Syrah. Jack smacked his lips at it as I maneuvered us out to *Ruta* 5 and aimed the Qubo south.

"I'm so glad you came," I said, feeling a sense of relief.

"What happened to Laura?"

"Fuck, man, the chick had a video on her phone of her masturbating in front of some guy. Do you believe that?"

"I'd believe anything these days," he said. "Damn, this wine is good."

"Yeah, and we're headed to where it's going to get really good."

"So, she just up and left."

"Yeah, it wasn't the porn video—which I think she left out for me to discover—it's just one of those things, you know? When we were up in Paso we were lit up like Christmas trees, and then all the emails that followed, none of it was fucking real. But you put two people in a car, in a foreign country, now that's the true test of whether a relationship will work." I turned to him. "Give me a sip, will you?"

He handed me the glass and I took a sip. Then, I held up the glass to him.

"Just like old times," I saluted him.

"Just like old times. Road trip. Chile. Man. I'm excited." He clapped his hands together. "Where're the chicks?"

"We'll have to find out."

"It's good to see you, Miles. I don't get to see you much these days."

"You're looking good."

"I cut back on the grape a little. The kid, you know."

"How *is* the little guy?"

"He's doing well. In Little League now."

"How's Babs?"

"She's doing very well. Things have normalized."

"You're not thinking about getting back together, are you?"

"Well. I did some pretty bad things, as you well know. But, there have been discussions."

"No shit?"

"Yeah."

"Hard to rekindle the romance when you get that whiff of new pussy," I remarked.

"Yeah, but you don't have a kid in the picture," he responded.

"But, you're in Chile now. We're outside the 100-mile rule. Way outside!"

Jack eyed me with that wolfish gleam in his eye. "That's right, brother. That's right."

"What'd you tell everyone?"

"That Miles was in a hospital in Santiago with acute panic anxiety and that he needed someone to help get him out of the country alive."

I laughed. "Did you know that Pablo Neruda, back in the '50s when communism was banned in this country, escaped across the Andes on a burro?"

"No. Didn't know that. Don't know my Neruda."

"I've run into these strange pockets of crypto-Pinochet loyalists down here. Weird country. I haven't seen a lot of it, or not enough of it yet. Insanely beautiful in a lot of places."

"What's the novel you're going to write?"

"Hell, I don't know. I suppose I could write a satire about how disorganized they all are down here, but then that would make me sound culturalist. There's a ton of wealth down here and, like in the U.S., only a few are in possession of it. So, I guess my character could fall in love with the leader of the student communist party and lead a revolution against the aristocracy."

Jack laughed. "You might not get back into the country."

"And I don't know why they keep pushing this Carménère grape variety. It's not a winning marketing strategy for their wine. They need to get the world excited about their Sauvignon Blancs the way New Zealand did. So, I guess my character could stage a protest with winegrowers holding up signs, 'No More Fucking Carménère!'"

Jack laughed and poured himself some more wine. He passed me the cup and I sipped it. Mountains reared into view, the Andes to the east, and lower, rolling, forested hills to the right.

"So, I don't know what I'm going to write," I said. "I'm still looking for the book." I turned to him with an arch smile. "Maybe I needed you to come down and give me some material."

"Hey, dude, your book didn't do *me* any favors, if you know what I mean."

"You were flattered."

"Well, some others weren't quite so appreciative of your fine fictive skills."

"Just trying to make a living."

"It's cool, man, it's cool." He sipped some more wine and stared out the window. "Where're we headed?"

"A winery. Lapostolle. Grand Marnier fortune. We've got rooms there overlooking the vineyard."

"You're living the life, Miles. Still living the life."

"I'm not happy," I said. "I feel a little like a prisoner of my own insidious design. I mean, it was fun for a while, then you realize that all this fame and celebrity is a kind of cliché curse. People use you for things. People want to glom on to you. Agents try to arm-wrestle you into deals that you don't want to get into. Your writing suffers. The bar is high and no matter what you do next you're automatically going to be criticized. And the women are devious. You're taken in by them, but you can't decide if they're using you or not, if they want something from you or not. Oh, sure, eventually you find out, one way or the other, but I guess what I'm looking for is a kind of truth in a partner that has eluded me my whole life."

"Chile is spiritualizing you, dude."

"It kind of is. I don't want to believe I've lost my sense of humor, but I feel like I've grown more introspective. Or is this just the function of age? As we pass our acme and start the declivity we turn to the more contemplative. I mean, you'd think we'd want to find *more* humor in our encroaching mortality, but instead we grow more grimly realistic about everything." I turned to Jack. "Chile's too serious for me in some ways. The country's barely over two decades out of a military dictatorship. It's like they're still in shock. And what's sad is that they have these beautiful wine regions and these lovely wines and these humble people, but the ownership of this country is in the hands of a few, which isn't a good thing as we know from our own country."

"Not only has Chile spiritualized you, it's politicized you."

"I know. I came down here to discover their wines—and I have! They're transcendent, many of them! But the country makes you wonder where they're headed. You want the best for them, you know what I'm saying?"

The time had flown driving with Jack. It felt wonderful to have my old buddy with me. Not because Chile's a scary country—it isn't; it's incredibly safe—but because it's a foreign country, because it's south of the equator, and, as a result, I was feeling disenfranchised, cut off from America, my home, the apartment I had given up, the world I had left behind. I didn't mind being a roustabout. In a way that's how I had always lived my life. Never toiled at a real job, always managing, somehow, to get by on my writing. But life was never secure. And in the proverbial peaks and valleys there were more valleys than peaks. And even the peaks seemed more like barren hillocks in a range of imposing mountains.

Three hours south of Santiago we turned off the interstate in the town of San Fernando. We stopped at a gas station. Jack thought it was hilarious when he discovered that the gas station rented showers.

"Government order. You must shower once a day. Otherwise they can arrest you for smelling like a three day-old *lomito*."

Jack laughed. "What's a *lomito*?"

"This nasty-ass sandwich that's sort of a tradition."

We climbed back into the car. While I fiddled with my Google Maps app Jack plugged his iPhone into the car's auxiliary sound system and let loose with, for some strange reason, a bit of Marvin Gaye. Which hit the spot.

"We need something all-American," he said. "To get you out of your funk."

The road west out of the small town of San Fernando was a decent two-lane straight-away that shot through small villages and many roadside stands selling fruit and other comestibles. Within 40 miles we had come to the tiny town of Santa Filomena de Cunaco. Vineyards were planted everywhere, as far as the eye could see. The sky above was a brilliant opaque hue of blue.

We angled off on a dirt turnoff for Lapostolle Winery and meandered on a bumpy road through verdant vineyards drooping with grape clusters. To the east the Andes loomed magisterially.

"Have you ever seen mountains that high, Jack?"

"Never."

"Majestic, aren't they?"

"I can't imagine Neruda humping it over them."

"Probably apocryphal."

"Probably. Whatever *apocryphal* means."

Pretty soon, in the distance we could make out the winery, the main building and the four *casitas* on the hill. We climbed a steep grade, then braked to a halt and got out. Jack stretched his arms out to the view.

"Beautiful."

"This is so Chilean," I said. "Just when you think you're headed into a slum you end up in the middle of a beautiful property like this."

We were greeted in the main reception area by a young woman who was waiting for our arrival and who spoke fluent English. We plopped down on sumptuous sofas in the great room of the lobby with its pitched raftered ceiling and panoramic view of their vineyards. We were in a five-star resort and we both needed a five-star resort just then. Life had not been easy for either of us.

A man in his thirties took us up a winding hill to our individual *casitas*. They were lavishly appointed, beyond sumptuous. Gargantuan beds, bathrooms that could wash and bathe an entire family simultaneously, with all the luxury that a bathroom that size would have, motorized blinds, views so heartstoppingly staggering you wished you never had to leave.

I took a long and luxurious shower, the showerhead wider than a Frisbee. Underneath it, I felt like I was in a tropical rainstorm.

Refreshed, in a change of clothes, I text-ed Jack. He text-ed back. I coasted down the pathway to his suite, which was equally spectacular. He was grinning from ear to ear. "Now, all we need are a couple Chilean girls," he said. I smiled. "Bring 'em up here and it's all over," he said. "Hell, I don't even have to lie to them!"

I laughed. "Come on, let's get something to eat."

We sauntered together down the dirt path back to the main building and took seats at one of the tables on the patio. We were maybe 500 feet above the floor of the vineyards that were now lushed out in foliage. To the east the snow-capped Andes rose high into the sapphire-blue sky.

As we admired the view, a woman approached us with menus. We confabulated about the serenity of the place, then responded in the affirmative when she asked us if we wanted any wine.

Colchagua Valley is inland and the grape varieties tended to the more Bordeaux-like, with Cabernet Sauvignon and its accompanying cousins like Cabernet Franc, Merlot, Petit Verdoux, Syrah, Carignan, and the ubiquitous Carménère. Their whites were predominantly Chardonnay. They presented us with three of their lower rung wines to sip. The sun beat down with a merciless ferocity, but we were canopied under a large umbrella and only felt the cooling breeze that snaked in through the valleys off the cold Pacific.

"There's a guy down in Patagonia who farms two hectares of Pinot Noir," I said to Jack.

"We got to get there."

"It's on the itinerary, brother. Just stick with me."

"And get this: there's a guy down here somewhere who is wanted by Interpol for inventing fragment bombs and can't leave Chile, and *he* has a winery. Then, there's MOVI, this small organization of trailblazing winemakers just south of us in Maule Valley who source grapes from 80 year-old vines. There's tons to discover here," I said.

"Looking forward to it," Jack said, sipping his wine and looking about as relaxed as I'd ever seen him.

An elderly couple came and sat at the table next to us. We made small talk about what it was like to travel in Chile. They were from Sweden. They had visited all the great wine regions of the world. To them Chile was the next frontier. I couldn't have agreed more. Even though the wine press hadn't caught up with Chile's promise, we all agreed that the geographical and topographical diversity, the mineral rich Andean snowmelt, the volcanic and alluvial and granite soils, and the close proximity to the cold Pacific continued to promise that Chile should do very well with Burgundian grape varieties. The surprise bonus was the Sauvignon Blanc and their beautifully nuanced cool-weather Syrahs. We nattered on about how they could better market their wines, get a wine trail with real tasting rooms. When they found out I had written *Shameless* they blushed at the recognition of the movie that had made me famous. I didn't feel famous. I didn't tell them that I felt lost and alone in the world. When they asked me why I had decided to come to Chile instead of another country—New Zealand or Australia for example—I waxed emotional:

"I think I wanted to change my life. I don't like being in the entertainment business anymore. It's changed. It's not about art anymore, movies are a business more than ever dominated by corporations and bottom lines. Maybe if I found a Chilean woman I could find my way to a simpler life." The wine was loosening my tongue. My candor silenced everyone. "People think I'm a rich man," I blubbered on. "That's so far from the truth. I'm not only not a rich man, but I'm impoverished by having spent so much time in a business that's filled with venal and downright cruel people. I'm looking for authenticity."

Our food arrived and was placed on our white-clothed table. The sun moved past its zenith and began the second half of its diurnal parabolic arc over the rolling hills to the west. Raptors rode the ocean breezes that blew through the vineyards, marking the blue sky with their soaring black forms.

As lunch concluded we were joined by one of Lapostolle's winemakers, Andrea. She was a Chilean in her thirties, married to an American, and whom Alexandra Lapostolle, the eponymous owner, had granted permission to do a project where she worked with different wines from different regions, though often with the same grapes. Chile was still so young. Everyone was experimenting. Andrea got us excited. But, first she wanted to show us around the property.

In her four-wheel drive she drove us around the biodynamically-farmed vineyards. She told us that they didn't use any chemicals to combat disease and fungi, they composted, recycled, planted by astrological cycles ... I was transfixed by her passion, her passion for her country, her country's potential to become, in the next fifty years, one of the great wine producers, with its dozen unique regions, in the world.

Afterward, she led us on a brief tour of Lapostolle's extraordinary winery. It was essentially a colossal cylinder that had been bored five stories into the granite rock ground. As the wines aged, the barrels were lowered deeper and deeper until finally they came to the bottom floor. The money in Chile for these wineries—Santa Rita, Perez Cruz, Concha y Toro—seemed vast, as if the possibilities were immense.

"Fucking poetic," I whispered to Jack, as we stood in the cavernous depths of the deepest part of the winery, the air cool and smelling of must.

After the tour we met up in a second-floor boardroom that overlooked the winery's immaculate property. Andrea wanted us to taste her Syrah project. She had used the same grape variety, but had sourced it from uniquely different regions, as far north as the forbiddingly harsh desert-like Elqui Valley to her own Colchagua, as well as seaside Leyda and Casablanca, and neighboring Maule and Cachapoal. They were all so distinctly and wondrously different.

"I love how you're experimenting with wines down here, Andrea. It's only going to get better and better. Chile has everything to make spectacular wines. It just needs time. They need to let the innovators rise like cream to the top." I held up my wineglass and, in a moment of tipsy magniloquence, said, "And there should be more women winemakers who make wines with finesse and femininity."

She smiled broadly. "Coming from you, that's like being blessed by Bacchus."

Jack laughed at that one, as I blushed from embarrassment.

A little while later we were joined by her husband, Matt, a free-lance photographer. He was as American as American could be. He talked about how he had found his way to Chile, met his wife, and fell in love with first her, and then the country. We skirted the issue of Chilean wealth inequality politics because it was a touchy subject, especially when it edged into their fascinating world of wine.

I said, "I only know what I taste in the glass. And I've had superb wines from Casa Marin and Amayna and Casas del Bosque, Metatic and de Martino and even some from the big guns, Santa Carolina and Santa Rita. The range is amazing. But the difference I'm seeing is that in our country the big wineries don't choke off the small ones. It's a more level playing field. It's more of a meritocracy. If you make good wines, even in tiny batches, you can succeed."

The attractive couple looked at each other and smiled.

Matt turned to us asked us what we were doing for New Year's Eve.

Jack, his face florid, said, "Why? Do you know a good party to go to?"

Matt smiled. "We will take you to the Count's."

"The Count's?" I asked.

"It will be a uniquely Chilean experience you will never forget," Matt promised.

We sipped and spit, sipped and swallowed, and drank until the sun was broken in half by the mountains it was magnetically drawn to. We hugged all around, then Jack and I returned to our *casitas* for a siesta. I couldn't sleep. All I could think about was Maya, for some reason.

Maya

I logged on to my computer, checked my email. My inbox was inundated with requests to come to dozens of Chilean winery properties, way more than I had time to visit. I was so overwhelmed I didn't know what to do, so I opened a blank Compose New Email and typed in Maya's email address. I hadn't written her since I arrived in Chile.

> *Dear Maya,*
>
> *I've been in Chile for nearly a month now. It's an interesting country. There's almost a Wild West feel to the place, as if, in this nearly 3,000 mile long country*

with only 15 million people, half of them in one city (Santiago), the possibilities are endless.

There are 12 distinct wine regions here and although I've only visited a few, I've tasted wines from all of them. I heard about a guy down in Patagonia growing Pinot Noir. I spent a few days at a viña property so close to the ocean it would make you cry, vinifying Sauvignon Blancs and what they call cool-weather Syrahs that possess depths of flavors that are positively to die for. You would love it down here.

Laura, the woman who met me here and who was going to travel with me, has left. There was nothing awkward about her leaving, other than the fact that she just, well, was gone one morning. Sure, I felt hurt. But I knew it wasn't right and I knew it wasn't ever going to work from the moment she arrived. What scared me was being in a foreign country, far away from home, all by myself. You know how I get up in my head and start to imagine all manner of crazy things, how panicky I become. So, I asked Jack to come down, and he did. But, he can't stay very long—kid and everything—so I thought I'd reach out and see if you wanted to come to Chile for a few weeks, or even a week, it doesn't matter. I would show you this country and you would, in turn, keep me from sucking the marrow of my own brain and going mad where I have a thousand friends, and no friend, all at once, if you know what I mean.

How are you? I still remember our night together,
its intensity, the sapphire-blue flame in your eyes …
     Love, Miles

I must have fallen asleep because when I woke it was dark outside and my laptop had slipped off my thighs onto the bed. I had been dreaming, but the dreams were indistinct. Once again, as per usual, my dreams were of being rudderless at sea, homelessness, destitution, deprivation, and I woke feeling glad that I had a roof over my head and a friend just down a short dirt path.

I showered, then went to find Jack. He wasn't in his room. I meandered down the path and found him in Lapostolle's infinity pool swimming laps, of all things. Was he trying to get back into fighting shape in hopes of winning his ex-wife back?

We had a great repast on the patio with two other couples who were estivating on the property. Wine and terrific food flowed. I loved it at Lapostolle, but there was something gnawing at me. It was the dominion of the privileged. I wanted to see the real Chile.

MOVI

Nick Sublette met us at a roadside restaurant in Maule Valley in the tiny town of San Ignacio. He was a barrel-chested Canadian who had emigrated to these parts to make wine. He met a beautiful Chilean, fell in love, married, and started to produce wines. To him, Chile was all about old-vine Carignan and the great Maule Valley. I had promised at Bocanáriz that I would make it down to Maule and that if I did, asked him if he would show me around.

We followed him out in his truck across a summer-desolated landscape to a vineyard farm-cum-horse ranch owned by an Italian woman and her absentee husband. The rolling hills and sparse shrubbery, the hot sun and incessant flies, made me think of an Africa savannah.

We mounted spirited horses and cantered through vineyards with Nick. He told us about the loose confederation of winemakers known as MOVI (*Movimiento de Viñateros Independientes*) and how they weren't against the Vintners' Association, but rather were another aspect of the Chilean wine culture. Critics had discovered them and they were making a mark, but getting their wines into the distribution pipeline was proving to be a daunting challenge.

We rode through vineyards that almost didn't resemble vineyards. I'm used to seeing modern agronomy—trellising, neat rows, vines planted a specific distance apart. These vines seemed to be growing wild. And, indeed, Nick had come to them as if an explorer to a forest, found Chileans who were tending and harvesting them the old way. He wanted to harness that tradition. He saw value in preserving that tradition. He was both new school and old school.

We stopped at a shack of a house where an old couple, their faces worn as saddles, weathered by years in the burning sun, were pouring homemade Carignan out of jugs. It wasn't the kind of wine that would get 90+ scores, but there was something so earthy about it. Something so close to the land it made me believe that wine didn't have to be about this refined palate. Sure, an experienced palate could distinguish between great Burgundies from famous vineyards, perhaps, but wasn't it just as important to taste simple, real fermented grape juice from vines that grew as the gods meant them to be grown?

Back at the ranch we were treated to a sumptuous lunch of traditional dishes and some Carignan and Cinsault rosés that were delicious. Laughter abounded. I was losing myself in the real Chile, far away from the hustle and bustle of Santiago. My spirits were not only buoyed by the wine, and by the horseback ride which seemed to take me back in time, but also by its opposite: modern technology. There was an email reply from Maya.

> *Dear Miles,*
>
> *I was thinking about you, wondering if you were doing okay. I'm glad you're having a great time.*
>
> *After two years, Cliff and I decided to call it quits. In respect for his privacy I'd rather not go into the details.*
>
> *I would love to come to Chile. If you still want me to. If the offer's still good.*
>
> *Maya*

On the tiny keyboard, my heart swelling a little, I hurriedly wrote her back:

> *Dear Maya,*
> *Please.*

After lunch we followed a crazy-driving Nick on a tortuous path of pot-holed grated dirt roads deep into Maule Valley.

"Maya's coming?" Jack asked, a bit incredulous.

"She says she is."

Jack smiled, then raised his sunglasses back up to cover his eyes. We were both still wearing our wide-brimmed sombreros and looked like inebriated gauchos in our Qubo as we continued to follow Nick deeper and deeper into the hinterlands of Chile.

We finally arrived in the tiny town of Curaco. It looked abandoned. Nick explained that many of the buildings had been destroyed in the 2010 earthquake that devastated southern Chile.

We were met by José, a Buddha-faced, relatively young man, who was a winemaker.

"José's one of the winemakers keeping alive the traditions here in Chile," Nick informed us.

We trooped together down a deserted street in the postage stamp-sized town and entered a building whose façade was under re-construction. Inside, the floor was made of dirt and the adobe walls spiderwebbed with fissures. Nick explained that the earthquake destroyed more than half the town, many residents fled, but this particular adobe building, which was a former winery, had somehow miraculously survived.

José and Nick led us into a dark, dank room. On one side there were dust-covered bottles dangerously stacked on top of one another in no particular order. In another corner of the room there was a large egg-shaped, clay-and-mud *tinajas*, about chest high. Wordlessly, José produced a crowbar and chipped away at the hardened clay until he had pried open the bunghole. He set the crowbar aside and then proceeded to wriggle the bung out of the top. Nick, loving this performance, was grinning from ear to ear.

"This is the real Chile, isn't it?" I asked rhetorically.

"This is the authentic Chile," Nick replied, just as rhetorically. "This is why I came here."

After he had pulled out the bung, José ran plastic tubing down into the *tinaja* and, using the pressure of his mouth, produced a stream of red liquid from the colossal vessel. He let it go into a glass beaker, then poured waiting wineglasses that Nick provided.

We sampled all around. Astonishment greeted our palates. In this dank, earthquake-destroyed building, where sunlight poured in mote-swirling shafts of light, I could have been tasting the finest Burgundy or Barolo known to man. I searched for words to find the superlatives. More wine flowed. Nick translated from José questions that I was asking him about how long he kept the wine in the *tinaja*.

"It is all instinct and feel, he says," Nick translated. "He does not go by any set plan. He does not put wine in bottle because he has to move inventory. He does what he feels."

"I'm liking what he feels," Jack said, his face growing florid. And mine, too!

José and his beautiful wife and five children treated us to an extravagant peasant lunch in their modest house. We talked about the earthquake and the repairs to the village and when the residents would, if ever, return. We discussed the future of Chile, its wine business, and all agreed that one day it would be producing some of the finest wines in the world.

"France has been making wine for hundreds of years," Nick said. "We've only just started, really. There's so much more to experiment with. Chile, like wine, needs time."

My mind went back to Bocanáriz where I had met Nick and where I had gotten my introduction to Chilean wines. And to think I had journeyed this far, to the tiny earthquake-ravaged town of Curaco, to find this glorious Cinsault in an earthenware *tinaja*, in an utterly dilapidated building, was a truly magical moment for me.

"Nowhere in California would you find this," I said. "Nowhere on the Pacific Coast either. I don't know about Europe, but this is truly special."

Everyone smiled.

One of José's young daughters held up a magazine named *Tell*. She flourished it in my face and gestured at the picture on the cover. In Spanish she said, "Is that him?" pointing at me.

Everyone laughed. There I was, leaning against the Fiat 500 with a glass of wine in my hand.

The Count's New Year's Eve Party

Andrea and her husband Matt met Jack and me at the entrance to the winery around 9:00 p.m. to caravan to the Count's.

Matt had said, "You cannot miss The Count's New Year's Eve bash. It's something to experience."

"Experience is what I'm looking for," I had told him. I had spent too much time in Santiago and I needed to get as deep into Chile as I could.

We followed a fast-driving Matt and his wife in a westerly direction toward Pichilemu. As we drove along the perilously narrow two-lane road there were outdoor stands set up with grills blazing and meats cooking and Chilean men and women drinking beer and wine and their children running around helter-skelter.

"What do you know about The Count?" Jack asked, as I maneuvered to stay apace with Matt and Andrea.

"Nothing," I said, "except that his place was destroyed in the 2010 earthquake and he rebuilt it at great expense, and that apparently he has some truly interesting friends. And it's *the* party if you're in the know out in these parts."

"Chicks?" Jack asked.

"I would imagine so." I turned to him. "Hey, wait a second, you and Babs are trying to get back together."

"Hundred mile rule, baby. Five thousand mile rule. And we're trying. And something I didn't tell you." Jack looked off. "She was living with a guy for two years who wanted to marry her. So, it's not like she's a saint or anything."

"Were you jealous?"

"Dude! What do you think? My kid's over there. A new guy is pile-driving her. Okay, I made my bed and had to lie in it, but, you know, jealousy's a weird thing, man. It's worse if you have an image in your head of him, too."

"Yeah, I know," I said, remembering Laura's video on her cellphone.

We had turned off on an unilluminated road. Dirt was funneling out the back of Matt's four-wheel drive like a horizontal dust cyclone. I had to ease up on the gas a little and back off because it was enveloping us to the point where I couldn't see the road anymore.

"With Laura, I mean, I'm not trying to be judgmental here or anything, but what possesses someone to have porn videos of herself on her phone? It's just so not a turn-on for me. Where do you stand on the issue?"

"I've done it all, Miles. I've experimented with practically everything—with women!—and I'm with you on this one. Once you get into that kind of shit, I don't know ..."

"When is it love and when is it just sex? And—more important—can the two ever be one in a perfect confluence where both are better than they've ever been with anyone else you've ever been with? I mean, I've had love, with Victoria, but the passion fizzled, went south. And I've had euphoric, orgasmic, sex—with Laura, for example—but the feeling, the connection, just wasn't there. And then I've had just friendships with women that were amazing, and sometimes almost preferable."

"Something's changed with you since you came to Chile," Jack remarked.

"I don't know. I'm living out of a suitcase. I don't like being alone. Before the novel I was alone for ninety percent of the time for nearly a decade. Maybe traveling around down here has amplified that feeling, I don't know. I mean I just don't know what's so great about all this kinky sex, not that I have any problem with it. I go back to my original question that inspired this disquisition on sex and love: what the fuck does it all mean? Who cares? We've gotten so far up into ego-consciousness we've lost all sense of what being human is worth. In other words, what will meaningfully resonate when they hang the morphine?"

"You're on a roll, brother."

"Well, finally, I have someone I can talk to who knows me like you know me."

"I think Chile's been good for you. Deep."

"I wasn't sure when I first got down here. They were twisting and pulling me this way and that, wanted me to attend this function, this awards dinner, go to this winery and that winery, videotape me, I mean, it was fucking bizarre."

"They just love you, brother!"

"I guess. I mean, maybe that's the way it's done down here, even though I was very clear to them that I wanted to come incognito and not have all this attention. Fuck, man, I've got a novel to write, and I don't want to promote it before I've even *written* it, if you know what I mean."

"It's ass backward," Jack said, shakily pouring a little more wine into a wineglass, handing it to me, now that we were on dirt roads and out of reach of the many drunk driving checkpoints that the Chilean *carabineros* are fond of impromptu setting up to entrap unsuspecting sots. So fond, there's a phone app that updates and tells you where they are so you can avoid them!

"But Chile has been good to me. And there's more I want to see. It's been good for me to get out of L.A., that fucking nasty film business, those crapulous souls digging in for one more spec script that they hope will bring them fame and fortune. And I was part of that fantasy, desperate climb to the top. But what it does to people ... I don't know, Jackson, I just let it all go when I gave up all my possessions and came to Chile. I haven't written a word. All I've been doing is traveling and meeting new people and watching people living their lives and not thinking about Hollywood and dreaming about doing deals and one day being back at the Academy Awards. I love film, but there's something so perfidious about that place, and what it does to your sense of reason and humanity, and how when you meet those with power what narcissistic jerks most of them are, and you wonder: what am I on this earth for? Who cares about me? No one cares about me up in that fucking hellhole. They only care about you if there's a deal on the horizon, and they'll sell you down the polluted river in a heartbeat just to do the deal, even if it's not something you want to do."

Matt was still blazing the trail, barreling ahead of us, dirt hurricaning out the back of his vehicle. It was so dark outside the stars exploded in the sky.

"I don't know if I can go back to that place. I feel unshackled here. My brain is aflame with new ideas, new possibilities, a life without trying to climb that chickenshit rung to the top in Hollywood. And, yet, it terrifies me. I need somebody here with me. I thought maybe Laura would be the one, but it was silly to think that a year of emails and telephonic communication was ever going to solidify a relationship. Fuck, man, after today, that guy with the *tinajas*, I could see myself living in a little village, just writing my books. I mean, with the Internet we can be anywhere, right?"

"You'd move to Chile?" Jack asked with disbelief.

"Look, it's been a whole eversion process for me. I feel like my whole being, my soul, my heart, just extruded out, left that world behind. I gave up my books ..."

"You gave away all your books?" Jack chopped me off.

"Yes. Donated them all. Even my precious collection of first edition Jungs. I want to be free, unfettered. I don't want to be tied to anything, nothing material. I want to lose myself in life. But I want someone to be with me, precisely because we need that someone to hold a mirror up to ourselves. If only to chronicle our journey. If we do it alone, we die alone, and having written about it is not the same as sharing the journey with someone else."

"You're going all sentimental on me," Jack remarked.

"No, not maudlin, not me. My cynical self is still very much in tact, I can assure you. But, you know, I don't have anyone, Jack. You've still got parents, siblings; fuck, a kid! And maybe an ex-wife back in your life. I don't have anybody, Jackson. Parents are dead, no kids, wife remarried and *with* a kid, and I'm estranged from my only brother. I feel all alone in the world. I dream troubling dreams about *being* alone, for Christ's sake. I'm wandering in deserts—especially fucking deserts!—and I'm searching for oases, I'm searching for someone. Or I'm marooned on the roofs of skyscrapers and there's no guardrail and the winds are monsoon-strong and I'm about to be blown into oblivion. I think about our two great trips together, and how we shared something together on them both, but your life is with your son, maybe Babs, you've got work in L.A., you're not a writer, you're not banging your head against the system like some lunatic in a padded cell like me. That's how I feel in that fucking place." I took a swig of wine and handed the glass back to Jack. "And the traffic fucking sucks!"

Jack roared with laughter. Then he leaned back. "You've got big hair."

"What?" I looked in the rearview mirror. My full head of salt-and-pepper hair had blossomed out like a windblown tumbleweed.

"Your hair. Are you using some new conditioner or something?"

I started laughing. "No, this is Andean hair." Jack laughed. "Everyone down here who has hair has it. Especially the men. The water is so fucking mineral rich that your hair explodes on your head." I raked my hand through my wavy hair. "It feels thicker. Feel it."

Jack ran his fingers through my hair. "Fuck, man, that's wild. You've become Chilean!"

"I know. Against my will. I've got Andean hair!"

We both fell into laughter.

Matt and Andrea turned down yet another dirt road. We started seeing lights again, illuminating a long adobe wall that bounded the pot-holed dirt road. Then we came upon open bonfires in 8'-wide diameter adobe pits, their crackling flames licking the sky, and shooting sparks off everywhere. There was something Bacchanalian about it, as if we had arrived in Chile's version of Hell and were about to consort with the denizens of this wonderful and strange and deeply complicated country.

We braked to a halt in a forest of cars, most of them of the four-wheel drive variety. We were road weary. We had come at least 50 or 60 miles from Lapostolle and we were in another world. Dogs yowled and prowled the property, Cerberus and the hounds of Hades everywhere!

Matt climbed out of his car and came over to us, "Okay, we're here. We've got a bit of a walk to the Count's."

"Lead us to your dignitary," I exclaimed, realizing I'd imbibed enough to hear my voice rising in volume.

"Wow, this is wild," Jack said. "What's the deal with all the dogs?"

"Don't worry about them. It's a thing down here. They wouldn't think of euthanizing them. And, yet, ironically, you hardly see any homeless people down here. Families take them in. They're an amazingly compassionate people. They suffered a lot in the Pinochet years. A lot of them are in denial about just exactly what they did suffer."

As we walked through the gates, the hounds of Hades were positively ubiquitous. They barked incessantly, but not menacingly. I was used to it, but Jack was still a little circumspect. When he saw all the guests walking casually into the Count's compound and ignoring the dogs, he started to relax.

I stopped at one point, tugged at Jack's sleeve and made him halt, too, and beckoned him to look up at the sky. The empyrean was an amplitude of twinkling stars. "Fucking believe that sky, Jackson. You ever see anything like that?"

"Never," he said.

"I heard in the Atacama Desert, where there is zero humidity, that it's ten times as amazing."

As we approached the Count's house there were bonfires everywhere lighting the way. Dogs had been supplanted by people, and what a crowd it was! I had been accustomed to some of the conservative stuffed shirts in Santiago and the rustic farmer winemakers, but this was a whole other animal of Chile I hadn't seen since touching down. The Count clearly nurtured a wide circle of friends. He was an Italian expatriate—some say he had to leave Italy under scandal—and his lover was high up in the Chilean government, a fact that many people knew, and which would have gotten the official thrown out of his high-ranking position, but which everyone pretty much overlooked. As a result, the crowd that Jack and I came upon was right out of *La Dolce Vita* and *8 ½*, with even a soupçon of *Satyricon* thrown in for good measure. Certainly, the bonfires created the effect and the impression that this was not a wine function in Las Condes. This was the heart and soul of Chile, as envisioned by an ex-pat Italian. This was the place, the party to be at.

The Count's *residencia*, or *hacienda*, or whatever everyone was terming it, was architecturally unlike anything I've ever seen in person. Imagine a colossal, single-story rectangle with the center cut out and open to the stars. The house, itself, was a series of interconnecting rooms that you had to transit through to get from one to the next. At any point you could step out and be in the center courtyard and be showered by the infinity of stars and planets in the most brilliant cosmology anywhere. If you kept walking, eventually, after a labyrinthine journey through everything from bedrooms to museums with Chilean antiquities, you'd end up back at the room you'd entered.

As Andrea drifted off to say hi to some people, Matt took Jack and me to meet the Count, stationed in the courtyard center where most everyone was congregating. Bonfires lit the courtyard as if something deliciously evil was going to happen! The Count was a man in his fifties with nut-brown skin and thinning dark hair. He shook my hand profusely as if I were a long-lost friend who had

253

journeyed from miles away to see him. I later learned that many at his party had done just that.

"It's so good of you to come, Miles. I'm a big fan of your book and your movie."

"Oh, come on, Count, you're just saying that."

"No. I've read your book more than once, and seen the movie many times."

"In the publishing industry they call me a hack."

"Oh, no," he said, dismissing the criticism. "You are Mark Twain and Jack Kerouac in one!"

"Well, I'll take the compliment. And I admire your literary tastes."

"You should see his library," Matt said.

"I'd love to."

"Get some food, get some wine, get some champagne!" the Count said gaily. "It's New Year's Eve."

Massive grills were barbecuing cuts of meat from all parts of the cow, Matt explained. Jack came back from one of the many wine stations and handed me a glass of bubbly.

"Here's to you, brother!"

I clinked glasses with him. "No, here's to you. Thanks for coming. I would never have seen this without you."

"Don't go all mushy on me now." Jack swept his large head around on his tall frame as if he were a lighthouse and his face emitting a long traveling beam of light. "This is fucking incredible. Some fucking hot chicks here, too."

I glanced around. Several hundred people had now gathered in the football field-sized courtyard. They were all ages; they were dressed, many of them, like circus performers, or Mardi Gras attendees. "Yes, there are," I finally said. "Yes, indeed-y, there are."

Other guests converged on the Count. He always wore a ready smile for them. Matt, who was a close friend of the Count's, was eager to show us around the *estancia*, as he referred to it. We started in one of the main rooms. Matt explained that the 2010 earthquake had more or less razed the property, and that the Count feared rebuilding but, in the end, was so in love with Chile that his heart told him to go ahead with the massive reconstruction project. "So, not only is this a New Year's Eve celebration," Matt said, "it's kind of an open house party for the Count and his house."

I followed Matt into a kitchen. Chilean women of all ages scurried about preparing fresh appetizers. In the crush of people rivering anaconda-like in opposable directions through the vast house I threw a backward glance to Jack. He was chatting up a pretty Chilean woman. Jack raised his glass of champagne to me and threw me that impish wink of his. I guess he reasoned that in the new year all his transgressions would be forgiven. Jack never believed in regrets or dwelling on the past. He lived consummately in the moment. I, on the other hand, was swamped with regrets, castigated myself for mistakes I had made, which made it difficult for me to live in the present without the termites of remorse gnawing away at my already beleaguered soul.

I trailed a loquacious Matt, who rambled on about the Count's history, through a bedroom and into a high-ceiling-ed art gallery. It was a hodge-podge of paintings and Chilean artifacts, including earthenware pottery and sculptures. We paused and looked around at the art, then Matt elbowed me on, "Let's go into the library," he suggested. "You're a writer. You'll appreciate it."

I followed him into the Count's library. It was a capacious room, bounded on all sides, floor-to-ceiling, with books, books and more books. I took in the whole of the massive room from its center, as if wanting to engulf myself in the books as an aggregate. I grew wistful thinking of my own modest book collection and how I had donated its volumes away, how I now owned nothing but the clothes on my back. And here was the Count, firmly ensconced in a home, a dwelling he could wake every morning to and discover objects that would give him a sense of comfort, a sense of peace, these objects validating his existence, making him feel like he belonged in the world. I didn't feel like I existed. The ground beneath me felt friable, like it did at Casa Marin, like it did when I landed in Chile and thought I had left the known world and journeyed to a place to research a novel, but instead had unwittingly found myself plumb-bobbing the depths of my very soul. I wanted out of my head. And here in the Count's library, at his spectacular *estancia*, I found it, my *epifania*: the objects of one's life that imparted meaning to that life. These great tomes were part of his life. He had spent hours with each of them and they all had no doubt etched an immutable imprint on his soul. Mine had, too, but now they were just paper in someone else's library, or, God forbid, part of a landfill. In passing them on I had not passed on my soul, I had only passed on objects of no personal connection to those individuals because it was I, me, who had invested those objects with soul. And the same here for the Count.

"No wonder he rebuilt, Matt," I muttered. "He needed this connection to the narrative of his life." Matt tossed me a strange backward glance. Though I got the impression he wasn't much interested in metaphysics, I didn't care, I was talking about myself, I knew it, and I just had to keep talking for fear that I would go mad in the vast silence of my head. "He needed this library. He needed to dust his books off and start over. Without them he would feel like he was nothing but stardust, carbon, whatever we're made of. He needed not just the physical manifestation of his life, he needed this rebuilding of his *estancia* for the very reconstruction of his soul!"

"Miles, I need to get you some more champagne."

"No, this is beautiful, Matt. This wealthy man who builds this place out in the middle of nowhere, seismically unstable Chile, an earthquake utterly demolishes it—he probably knew it was an inevitability!—he's, as you told me, in emotional ruin, but he regroups, he rebuilds. And though I'm sure there were many who couldn't and had to suffer other—worse!—fates, his rebuilding almost brings tears to my eyes because that's all that life is, Matt: a tearing down and a rebuilding, a tearing down and a rebuilding, of our soul. Until we get it right."

"But we never really get it right, do we?" Matt said.

"No, we never get it right, but it's in the fantasy that we're going to get it right, it's in the trying that we're going to get it right, that we're going to come closer to the truth of who we are." I turned to him. "And then there better be someone there with a net to catch us. Like your Andrea."

"Yes," he said. "She's beautiful."

"You don't want to lose her. I've lost too many, Matt. I've fucked it up too many times." Emotion, fueled by champagne, was starting to hobble my speech.

A tuxedo-ed waiter broke into my philosophical musing, bearing a tray in one hand with a small village of glittering and golden champagne flutes. I took one and Matt accepted another.

"Here's to you, Miles," Matt toasted. We clinked glasses. Threw them back.

"Chilean bubbly?"

"Absolutely," Matt said. "I don't know the winery, but we do it all down here."

"That you do," I said, feeling a tide of emotion flooding my being and making me wax sentimental. I produced my cellphone. "Is there a connection out here?"

"It's the Count, man. Come on. He's got Internet!" Matt roared with laughter.

"Yeah, that's ridiculous, I know," I said. "When I was getting ready to come I was so naïve about South America that I asked Silvio if you had credit cards down here. He thought that was pretty funny."

Matt laughed. He recognized someone and waved. He broke away from me and left me alone in the library. I sagged into the couch, engulfed by all the books, reclined at an angle and stared up at them in the saffron-yellow light. Tremendous literary collections—Voltaire, Tolstoy, Austen, Dostoevsky, Chekhov, Woolf—and many art books—Van Gogh and Cezanne, et alii.— and many, many books in Spanish some of whose great authors I recognized—Marquez and Fuentes and Cervantes and the great

Chilean writer Roberto Bolaño. Almost all of the books were hardcover, and I surmised that most were first editions—the Count would have first editions! I reflected on my own relationship with books, how I was so proud to finish one and place it on my modest shelf in my student apartment in San Diego, thinking, believing, hoping, that it was another rung on my personal achievement ladder to hoist me out of that backwater navy and war armaments town. Books drove me to the future, arrested my soul, opened doors to other worlds, and in those worlds I discovered new doors, and those doors swung open to even greater dominions of revelation and new truths. And I wouldn't have known it. There were great films, too—Fellini, Renoir, Buñuel, Wilder—who ferried me to new regions that I hadn't seen before. But it all started with books. The transformative power of art. And now all my books were gone, donated away. Sure, I could replace them, but replacing them would never be the same.

Sorrow suffused me. I could hear the New Year's Eve chatter and the sound of a band striking up filtering in through the other rooms and ricocheting off the tiled floors. I felt so removed from them suddenly. I wanted my books back. I wanted someone in my life to replace everything I had given up in my *puer aeternus epifania* moment of madness. Now? Now, I wanted to sink my feet into the earth, this Chilean earth and feel the taproots of my soul slither deep like serpents into the mineral rich soil and find me a toehold, anything, anything but this feeling of being dispossessed of everything except my perfervid mind and my panic-stricken psyche.

The Count's books towered over me from all sides, immense walls of words and spent intellects. Where he had run out of room he had stacked them horizontally in the spaces on top of the rows of books and on top of the bookcases themselves. They spilled everywhere. It reminded me of a literature professor's office, except that the room was adobe, cast in yellow, artisanal throws, hand-crafted by Chileans, spread on antique sofas imported from Venice and Rome. What a room to live in, I thought!

I reached around to my back pocket for my cell phone, switched in on, got a connection, went to Gmail and wrote Maya:

> *Maya,*
> *You wouldn't believe where I am right now. Come to Chile. We'll go to the Atacama Desert. Please.*
> *Miles*

I could feel a smile creasing my face. Whether Maya would come or not I had no way of knowing. I only know that I had asked, and that was a major first step for me! Suddenly, there was a notification on my phone.

> *Miles,*
> *I'd love to. When?*

> *Maya,*
> *Asap. Get a flight to Santiago, connect to Calama. Let me know and I'll meet you at Aeropuerto Internacional de Santiago. LAN Airlines. I'll send you my flight info.*
> *Love, Miles*

15 minutes later, as I listened to the party, still warmly enveloped by the Count's impressive book collection and hung deep in thought, came the following:

> *Miles,*
> *I can't wait to see you.*

With the email was an attachment. It was a copy of her plane ticket. I set down my phone. The smile widened on my face.

I was so relaxed I didn't want to move. The books, Maya's email, the fact that she was coming to Chile to take the hand-off from Jack, was just all too good to be true. I started to straighten to my feet ...

Suddenly, there was a jolt, as if the Count's building had been struck by a missile. Then, everything started shaking, but this time more violently than at Villa Marin. The shaking was so violent I was knocked to the floor. The walls started to grow ellipsoid-like as if I were having a psychotropic drug flashback. I tried to clamber to my feet, but the force of what was shuddering the house was preventing me from regaining my footing. My bearings were gone. For a moment I wondered if I were having a stroke, and this is what it felt like to be my mother when I found her collapsed on the floor with a dazed look on her face, virtually cataleptic. Was I having a stroke? A heart attack? Or was it a *grand mal* panic attack, the kind of which once sent me in a siren-blaring EMT vehicle to the ER where doctors and nurses found me caterwauling for the baby Jesus and the Virgin Mary? What the fuck was going on? As if from a bathysphere I heard screaming, crashing of objects shattering. I tried to regain my balance, get to my feet because now the ceiling was splitting apart and the wall sconces and molding were buckling!

Then, all at once, the bookcases listed forward, imploded into the center. Books cascaded everywhere, their canvas back covers flapping like the broken wings of a dying flock of birds that had suddenly decided to take wing *en masse*! There were books everywhere, like lemmings hurtling themselves off cliffs. I flung my arms in front of my face, reared back, and made the sign of the cross—as if God would help me! A devout anti-deist!—to protect myself from the plummeting books. They struck me hard, those books, they lashed at me as if I were being stoned by them for all my transgressions, everything I had done wrong in my life! They toppled from on high, slammed into my vulnerable body, literary bricks from an old house under demolition. They crashed down onto me, my whole life those books, as if wanting to weigh me down, smother me in them, the books that I had recklessly given away coming back at me from the dead and hurling themselves at me like old lovers whom I had spurned or cheated on, or worse!

Down for the Count

No one knew how massive the earthquake was, or where its epicenter was located. Jack and Matt and several others found me buried under a pyramid of books. When the earthquake struck everyone managed to get out into the courtyard or outside the perimeter of the Count's *estancia*, except me. Matt had remembered leaving me in the library and that's where they rushed to find me.

Because the room was fortified with huge oak beams it had remained remarkably intact. Even the roof had not completely collapsed. But it was difficult to dig me out. Matt and Jack threw books off of the pile to get to me. (Later, Jack would laugh that when they finally uncovered me in the pile I was holding a glass of champagne aloft! One of those bizarre images you can witness in the aftermath of a natural disaster.)

After they had pulled me to my feet, determined that I wasn't dead and there were no broken bones poking up out of my flesh, they dragged me across the rubble into the courtyard. My biggest fear was panic and claustrophobia from being entombed and mummified under all those books, but once I was gulping air again I regained my sense of equilibrium.

People were milling about everywhere. The electricity was down and the *estancia* was eerily dark, like a catacomb, but the bonfires were still burning and you could see the silhouettes of the guests, as if shadowy figures from *La Dolce Vita*, not knowing where to go or what to do. Nonplussed. Discombobulated. People asking one another if everyone was okay.

"You all right, Miles?" Jack asked.

"Yeah. A little shaken. Buried alive in books!"

"Fuck, man, that was powerful."

We looked around at the Count's *estancia*. Unlike in 2010 it hadn't come totally crumbling to the ground, according to Matt, who was scurrying inside and out of the building and hugging Andrea, his wife, relieved that she was okay. There was a certain calm in the people that Jack and I didn't exactly share because they were accustomed to these earthquakes.

"I'm guessing a 7.5, and centered pretty close!" an amped-up Matt assessed.

Suddenly, we heard a man bawling. Mixed with the yowling of the dogs, whom the earthquake had collectively dismayed, it was like the plaintive cry of an animal whose mate had just died.

We ventured over and found the Count on his knees, his lover knelt to his side trying to comfort him, sobbing uncontrollably. I wondered if he would rebuild this time! Matt told him he'd done a quick survey of the property and it didn't look too badly damaged, that the main structure was still intact. This was little consolation to the Count who wept in great emotional ebbs and surges that were difficult to be in the presence of.

Jack pulled me aside, "We should get out of here. I mean, if everyone's okay."

I nodded. "Man, how long was I under all those books? It felt like hours. I didn't know what had happened. I thought I was going to die, man!"

"Thank God Matt knew where he had left you. I would never have guessed you were there."

Jack and I hugged. "I'm glad you're okay, brother."

"Yeah, me, too."

Midnight came and there was no celebration in the fantastic fires. The collective yowling of the dogs from Hades was deafening. Everyone was still debating how big of a quake it must have been judging by the damage done to the Count's *estancia*.

Jack and I said goodbye to Matt and Andrea and threaded our way through the dogs and the dark and intuited the direction to the Qubo. The lights of vehicles sprayed everywhere and lit up the parking area. There was an exodus from the Count's of vehicles of all variety: four-wheel drives, SUV's, sedans, motorcycles. As if the *carabineros* were raiding his property.

Still shaken, I handed the keys over to Jack and we started off on a path lit only by our headlights. What few lights had been strung up to light the entrance were out. Soon we were on a dark dirt road. Neither of us said anything for the longest moment.

"I'm going to go back," Jack said.

I just nodded.

"That was insane. Scared the shit out of me. If it had been in L.A. I maybe could have handled it, but being in Chile, fuck, man, that was ... spiritual."

I managed a sardonic chuckle.

"And you under all those books. That was rich!"

"Thank God you found me. I wasn't looking forward to rereading the Collected Works of Jung again to claw my way out."

Jack laughed. "Did it hurt?"

"No. It was just the feeling of being buried alive. And not knowing what the fuck it was. For a moment I thought I was having some kind of catastrophic medical event, and this was it, here comes the blue light, all the ex-lovers' faces fleeting past me like a film that had come out of the gate in a broken film projector. It's as close to death as I've come, or thought I had come. It was just blackness, man, until you and Matt rescued me.

We finally turned onto an asphalt street and the relief was palpable in our voices. We debated our guilt about leaving the Count and his property, but we rationalized our choice by the realization that he had many friends and vast resources. The first village we came to was cast in darkness. Mostly, we glimpsed Chileans huddled close to fires burning in rusted petroleum barrels.

"Do you know where you're going?" I asked, fishing around in my pocket for my cell.

"Vaguely," Jack said.

I couldn't find my cell. I slapped all my pockets. "Fuck, I left my cell back there!"

"We're not going back," Jack declared. Adamantly.

"Fuck!" Panic started to set in.

Jack whipped out his cell, glanced at it, then shook his head disgustedly. "We're not getting a signal anyway. I'm sure all the cell towers are down. If they have any out here!" he said in a peevish, rising tone.

The dark, narrow two-lane road back to Lapostolle Winery had Jack and me both on edge. More than once Jack had to swerve to avoid another one of Chile's lost *perros* and each time he swore.

"Slow down," I urged.

"I just fucking want to get back," he groused.

As we raced through the string of villages it was as if we were in a Humvee moving through a war zone where we were embedded journalists or something. Occasionally we saw buildings that had pancaked, victims of the earthquake flailing their arms on the side of the road, trying to flag down rides to the nearest hospital, their faces and limbs bloodied. One woman, carrying an infant, ran bow-legged to a car, a look of anguish on her face that will haunt me until my dying day.

Jack's sense of direction was astonishing without GPS. I would have gotten lost for sure. In the dark you'd better have the tracking instincts of a Native American. Jack was that guy. Even on a bottle or two of wine he could always get us home.

Lapostolle Winery was an oasis of light in the desert of calamity. Obviously they had major back-up generators because the whole place was lit up like a spaceship that had landed in some science fiction movie. Our frayed nerves calmed a little.

When we stepped out of the car we bumped into employees scurrying about, checking for damage. We found our way to our *casitas*, but we both went to mine, to be together, not wanting, either of us, to be alone.

Sitting on the edge of the bed, Jack fiddled with his phone. "Still no service."

I had my laptop open. "And no Internet."

"Fuck," Jack said, collapsing on to the colossal bed. "Fuck!"

I slumped into a chair. Then, I got up, crossed the room to the mini-bar, found a bottle of Lapostolle's finest Cabernet and uncorked it. Poured two glasses, brought one to Jack who accepted it with alacrity. We clinked glasses. "Here's to Chile," I said sardonically.

"Here's to Chile," Jack echoed, just as sardonically. Then, we both degenerated into laughter.

We roared with laughter until suddenly we felt a trembling. We simultaneously leapt to our feet. I flung open the door and braced myself like Christ on the cross. Jack went to the ground, threw both hands over his head, and hoped that this wasn't the big one. The tremor quieted almost as quickly as it had begun.

"Aftershock," I said.

"Fuck, man, get me out of here!" Jack cried. "This whole country's like a dolly on ball bearings!"

That made me laugh. After we had decided the aftershock had passed and the earth had settled for the time being, we resumed our respective positions: he on the bed; me comfortably in an oversized lounge chair that swallowed me up in lavishment.

"I'm going to have you drop me off at the airport tomorrow," Jack announced. "I've got to get back to my kid."

"That's cool," I said.

"I mean, I'd like to stay and help you through this research trip of yours, but I'm just missing Jason, you know, and maybe this earthquake kind of put things into perspective for me. Or something, I don't know. Hey, do you have any of those Xanaxes of yours?"

I found my vial, fingered out one of my blue pills, then tossed it to him. It wasn't hard to retrieve on the stark white bed.

"Bite down on it, then let the powder seep down under your tongue, it'll take effect quicker."

Jack did as I instructed, then chased the pill with the marvelous Cabernet that I was also finding to be the perfect anodyne.

There were a few minutes of silence. "Maya said she was coming down."

"Really?"

"Yeah. But with this earthquake, I don't know. But she has a ticket."

Jack didn't say anything. He didn't know what to say. His brow was corrugated with worry and he had an absent expression on his face as if he were thinking of his son and his uncertain life back in L.A.

"I thought she was living with someone," Jack mused.

"I don't think it was going all that well," I said.

We sipped our wine. Suddenly, there was a loud explosion, as if a cherry bomb had been detonated by a teenage prankster. We were jolted to standing positions, ready to brace ourselves for another aftershock, but the earth didn't shake. Then, all the lights winked off, plunging us into pitch darkness.

"Generator must have gone out," Jack, a former gaffer, said calmly.

"I'm sure it'll be back on soon."

"Yeah," Jack said.

"I wonder how bad the damage from the quake is. Just so weird to be without news, TV, Internet, phone service ..."

Jack didn't say anything. We found our way to the bed and eased down onto it on opposite sides. We lay there in sepulchral silence waiting for the generators to come back on. It was just the two of us. No colored lights, no waiters, no ruddy-faced tasting room managers, no women hanging coquettishly on our arms, flirtatious badinage, no raucous laughter, just the two of us, total blackness, the cavernous emptiness of no sound, the air warm and immobile, as if we were in a sensory deprivation chamber, only our minds, and what was in those now depleted vessels. We were willy-nilly hurtled back to a kind of pure primitive analog time when there existed only the pure, unadulterated—and terrifying!—sense of just being. Thrown back on only the quivering marrow of our own ego-consciousnesses, we longed for the peace of sleep to claim us before our clamorous thoughts swamped us with fatalism.

"Pure nothingness," I said, stating the obvious, "no Internet, no TV, no radio, no lights. This is how it was for millennia when the sun went over the hill and there was no fire."

"I'm surprised whole civilizations didn't go mad," Jack said, in a rare moment of insight, as if he, too, were suddenly dredging deep for the meaning to this moment; as if he, too, were now grappling with the fact that we only had our minds and our perfervid imaginations and nothing else to quell or obliterate the rushing tide of just being in the moment with nothing to distract us. It was the pure heroin of being. And, in that moment, while we didn't voice it, or were too afraid to because it would have sounded mawkish, we realized that we needed each other, that to go alone in this way, without the comfort of some technological window to the world, virtual and impalpable as it might be, would indeed be the definition of a full-blown psychosis.

"Maybe," I suggested, "it was living like this that prevented societies from collectively going mad. That today civilization has walked so far out to the end of the pier with all this technology that if there's a massive energy crisis and the whole world goes dark, what's going to become of mankind? There would be total chaos. People would murder you for a pack of matches. We would degenerate into mass savagery. Only the brutish would survive. And when the sun came up there would be a new generation of monsters ruling over the desolated, plundered and desperate planet Earth."

There was a silence. Then, Jack said, "Could we talk about golf?"

I laughed. My laughter rolled like a wave to where Jack was and then he started laughing. In that moment, laughter prevented *us* from going insane. It opened up the floodgates of joy and lashed us together in our temporary predicament here in the faraway country of Chile and, in its liberating catharsis, helped ease the journey toward sleep.

Aeropuerto Internacional de Santiago

We had a makeshift breakfast at Lapostolle Winery, but Jack, his face still pinched in anxiety, was impatient to get back to Santiago, so we packed hurriedly and wordlessly, then rode down the hill along the viticulturists' trails through the verdant vineyards which towered next to us on both sides.

The cell sites were still down, so there was no Google maps, no email, nothing, on Jack's phone, as we intuited our way back to the main road, steered east toward *Ruta 5*, the main north-south artery. One of the concierges at Lapostolle had informed us that though it was a strong earthquake it was only a 7.5—*only a 7.5!!*—not even close to the 8.8 off the coast of Curanipe that wiped out that village and devastated Chile far and wide. Still, it was destructive enough that power lines were down, electricity was still out in much of the country and chaos had descended over much of Chile. We learned, however, that the airport was very much open, that they had a whole plethora of emergency back-up generators. Chile may have just come out of developing nation status, but the Chileans were a smart people. They knew they lived on an unstable landmass where massive tectonic plates were constantly moving, volcanoes raged just beneath their surfaces, that they were cut off on all four sides: the Andes to the east; Antarctica to the south; the Pacific to the west;

and the forbidding Atacama Desert, the driest desert in the world, to the north. And where I would be sojourning with Maya, assuming her flight wasn't canceled.

It was New Year's Day, and though the country had taken a serious jolt—we learned that the epicenter was off Concepción, some 500 miles south of Santiago—it didn't appear to be too destructive as we headed north. We saw armed *carabineros* everywhere—Chileans were always prepared for riot and civil unrest—but the freeway was surprisingly empty of cars.

"You want to go straight to the airport?" I asked. "You don't want to check into a hotel?"

"Yeah, I just want to get back."

"I hope there aren't a lot of people trying to get out of Chile because of the earthquake."

"I already have a ticket," Jack said. I looked at him. He stared straight through the windshield. "I missed my son, so I changed the flight back," he confided, somewhat shame-facedly. "I just didn't want you to go on a bummer. But," he changed his tone, "now that you have Maya coming, it's all worked out."

"That's cool, man. But, I wish you would tell me this shit. I'd be less panicky if you didn't spring this on me last minute."

"I'm sorry."

"Forget it. I'm glad you could come. You got me over that hurdle with Laura."

Jack handed over the wheel to me at the drop-off point for LAN Airlines. I waited outside for him to make sure that his flight wasn't canceled.

"Total bedlam in there!" he said, exasperated, as he came back out into the bright sunlight. "But, fortunately, my flight's only delayed an hour, so should be cool." He held out his hand for the peace shake and I took it. Then, we embraced. It seemed like we were always saying goodbye.

"I'm going to miss you, man."

"Yeah," I said.

"Got enough Xanax?" He patted my jeans pocket where he knew I kept them.

"Barely," I chuckled.

"Say hi to Maya."

"Have a safe flight."

He walked off and disappeared into the terminal. I got back into the car and drove to Hotel Rêve. I needed some *rêves!*

Maya: Goddess of Illusion

My favorite hotel, the Aubrey, was predictably booked, but my contact there, Kristina, got me into the Hotel Rêve in Providencia. Great little oasis for the panicky. It wasn't cheap, the rooms were small, but there was a beautiful courtyard where guests still read analog newspapers. And the staff was unbelievably courteous, solicitous to a fault. I was running low on Xanax. Without a cellphone I had no one I could call. Without an Internet connection—the sites were still down due to the earthquake—I had no way of getting in touch with anyone. And, laughably, even if I went to some emergency phone place, I couldn't tell you, for example, what Maya's phone number was. Everything was in my Contacts app on my phone. Indeed, what would happen to the world if all the power went out?

Fortunately, I had cash and that definitely worked. I went outside and ducked into the nearest restaurant. The streets were empty. There was a pretty strong military presence everywhere. Several years earlier, riots staged by student protest groups over rising tuition costs and social mobility and polarization of wealth issues brought students by the thousands streaming into the streets. Police in riot gear employed water cannons—and worse—in an attempt to quash it. Five universities were shut down for several months. The leader, Camilla Vallejo, a young woman of communist leanings, and a Botticellian beauty as someone described her, became the face of a new Chile that the aristocracy was desperate to suppress. An earthquake, I'm guessing, was the potential flashpoint for another series of mass riots protesting the inequalities that still plagued this great country, a country that was unstable both underground and above-ground.

After dinner, I slept fitfully. Dreams of desolation chased me like hungry, rapacious hyenas. My whole being was fixated on Maya coming, and that brought me some comfort. I could have called Silvio, and I'm sure he would have come to my rescue, but I wanted to be alone. I didn't want anyone's solicitude, not if I had to pay a price for it. I didn't want anyone to own me.

On the day that Maya was to fly in I felt almost paralyzed by fear and anxiety. Without any connection to the world for several days, my cellphone missing, all I had left was a plane ticket to the

Atacama Desert and a fateful meeting with Maya at *Aeropuerto Internacional de Santiago.*

Hotel Rêve arranged a limousine service to take me and all my luggage to the airport. I felt more dispossessed from myself than ever before. I had no home. I had few possessions. I wasn't even in possession of my own thoughts! I was down to my last two Xanax. It would be enough to get me on the plane. Then, hopefully, I could find a sympathetic doctor in San Pedro de Atacama who would refill my prescription. I was sleep-deprived and anxious to the point where I started remembering the time I had been hospitalized for a panic attack so paralyzing I thought I was having a heart attack. It was a time when my career was in the shitcan. Now, here I was in Chile—Chile!—all alone, feeling that same sense of dread rumbling in my psyche like the Pacific plates moving under Chile and causing volcanic and seismic activity on a ubiquitous scale so grand that it seemed almost unfathomable. All at once I was fatalistically imagining being swallowed up by the earth. I wanted to stop the limousine guy and implore him to take me back to the hotel. When panic rises in you like this you need to talk to someone, you can't be alone with these thoughts swirling like dust devils in your head. You need someone to bring you back to reality, to ground you.

Maya.

I got dropped off at the airport, my fragile psyche now cantilevering on pins and needles. I kept taking deep lungfuls of air, kept thinking as soon as I see Maya everything will be fine. She'll calm me. Hell, she knows me! She knows I suffer from panic anxiety. She knows I don't like to fly. Everything will calm. It'll be okay.

In the crowded terminal, my sleep-deprived brain in a veritable fog, I found my way to the LAN Airlines check-in. The lines were long and my anxiety was accelerating. Up on the electronic Arrivals and Departures board I found the flight information for Maya's flight and saw that it had landed on schedule. She would be going through Customs, then rerouted to the First Class waiting lounge for the flight to Calama Airport in San Pedro de Atacama, a two-hour breeze of a flight. I breathed a sigh of relief! I would have normally made a beeline for the bar and downed four glasses of wine, but I didn't want Maya to find me in bad shape. We had been there before, and I didn't want to begin again—if that's what we were going to do!—that way.

A general sense of euphoria suffused me as I checked my luggage, slogged my way through security—I felt like a great condor when I spread my arms in the X-ray machine for an assay of my body!—and then found my way to Gate 11 from where our flight to Calama would be embarking in less than two hours.

I looked all around, but couldn't find Maya. I went into the first class lounge and there was no sign of her there. No doubt she was being held up in Customs. Besides, I reminded myself, her plane had just landed, we had two hours before the flight to Calama and the driest desert on the planet, the Atacama. Relax.

I opened my MacBook, drove the din of the airport out of my ears with a pair of Bose earbuds and some music from iTunes. I tried to find a Wi-Fi connection, but nothing was coming up. A young Chilean woman carrying a tray bent over at the waist and said something I couldn't hear, as if I were in a bathysphere and she was a marine creature looking in from outside my porthole. I yanked out one of my earbuds and said,

"*Una copa de vino rioja, por favor.*"

She smiled at me and walked off. I put my earbud back in. The wine came and I sipped it slowly, my self-admonition keeping me to the straight and narrow. I was still on friable ground psychologically, but at any moment Maya would walk in, flash that sultry smile of hers, and we would collapse into each other's arms.

I turned my attention to a film I had downloaded that Felipe from Casa Marin had advised me to watch titled *Nostalgia for the Light.* It started out as a documentary about the Atacama Desert and the many observatories there with their great telescopes gazing up into the skies searching for the origins of life. But, then, hauntingly, it abruptly changed course and was about these weathered elderly Chilean women who were looking for the remains of their loved ones—known as "The Disappeared"—whom Pinochet and his regime had brutally tortured and murdered and buried in mass graves in the Atacama. The Chilean director skillfully and artfully made a profound, and poignant, connection between the search for life in the infinity of the heavens and the search for the remains of lives that had perished in the vast, arid desert of the Atacama. Most of the mass graves had been excavated and the bodies barbarously dumped into the cold Pacific in order to avert international crisis of crimes against humanity should they be disinterred by international war crimes organizations. But, regardless, knowing that their search was futile, it was anything but pointless. Just as the astronomers knew that no matter how far they penetrated into the universe almost for certain they would find new nebulae, nebulae behind nebulae, and that nothing was finite, nothing was permanent, and that death was a continuum and not really death at all.

I was so engrossed in the troubling, but moving, documentary I didn't notice that an hour had gone past. I looked up from where I was sitting. No Maya. My heart started to race a little. I asked the bewhiskered man sitting next to me if he would watch my computer. He smiled and nodded, then I straightened to my feet and walked out into the waiting lounge for the general public. I looked all around through the throngs of passengers coming and going, but I didn't see Maya. I glanced at my watch. There was still an hour to go before the flight to San Pedro de Atacama. But, they would be boarding soon! Where was she?

I stood underneath a LAN Arrivals and Departures flat-panel and, sure enough, her plane from LAX had landed over an hour and a half ago. Could Customs be taking that long? Did she ... get cold feet?! We hadn't been in touch since the earthquake, but I had a copy of her plane ticket in my email folder. I could have double-checked it to make sure, but there was no way I could get to my email. Anyway, I was positive that was the flight. It was the only nonstop from L.A.

I sucked in my breath and went back to the First Class lounge. The bewhiskered man smiled when I thanked him for keeping an eye on my laptop and carry-on. Against my will, I shook my head no when the waitress asked me if I wanted another *copa de viña*. I did, desperately, but soon I would be deep into my *copas* and I didn't want to end up like one of the loved ones of *The Disappeared* staggering through the driest desert on the planet, so arid that it didn't even support the lowest forms of microbial life. *The lowest forms of microbial life?* That's how I was starting to feel with every glance at the entrance to the First Class lounge and no sign of Maya.

I returned my attention to *Nostalgia for the Light.* The telescopes impressed me with their vastness. A young astronomer mesmerized me with his incantations about spatio-temporal unreality, the infinitude of the universe, that we were all once just calcium and one day we would all go back to being just calcium—how depressing! How fleeting life is, a blip on an air traffic controller's radar before plunging out of view into a cornfield.

My concentration kept getting broken. I jumped anxiously to my feet again and went to the LAN gate and inquired about messages for Miles Raymond. *Nada.* Anything from a Maya? No. Anxiety gripped me like her hand closing over my throat that night way back up in the Santa Ynez Valley. I didn't know if I'd be able to board the flight without her. Panic anxiety is a devilish affliction. You count on these little things to get you through it, to prevent you from going off the deep end and ending up in a hospital or being de-planed as you're taxiing down a runway. For me it was the Xanax in my left pocket, albeit only two left, and the calming, reassuring, sultry voice of Maya, holding my hand, as the engines revved and the jetliner angled back and we soared into the lowering afternoon sky.

I tried taking deep breaths, but it began to feel like I was hyperventilating. When you're in the throes of an oncoming panic attack the worst thing is to be alone. You tend to catastrophize everything. Worse is being alone in a foreign country, in an airport—my greatest fears having already been realized in one—your fragile psyche hanging on to just a few, what you thought were, guaranteed expectations. When those expectations are not met you start to view the earth as if it were tilting in the wrong direction, veering out of its orbit, plunging toward a galaxy where it'll either fry in the searing heat of a new, more powerful sun, or be shuttered in darkness and cold and eliminate all life forms.

A man across from me was playing with his cellphone. I got up and accosted him, no doubt my voice now in an excitable tone, and implored, "Could I check my email? I'm waiting for someone, my phone got lost in the earthquake ..."

He clutched his carry-on, twisted away from me and went and sat somewhere else, as if I were a crazy person. This thought made me feel even more like a crazy person.

I tried to breathe. I looked up every few seconds to see if Maya was there. Had she blown me off? Had she changed her plans, emailed me she couldn't make it for one reason or another, and I didn't get it? Had I gotten that email I would have surely been able to psychologically prepare myself for the flight to Atacama. Hell, I probably wouldn't be going to the Atacama Desert!

My head felt like it was detaching itself from my shoulders. My breathing grew more and more rapid and shallow: in through the nose; out through the nose. Again, I waved off a second glass of wine. I was saving the two Xanaxes I had left for the flight, and when the loudspeaker crackled with the announcement that they would begin boarding the first class passengers my heart started to palpably race. I had to get on that flight! Fuck, my luggage was on it, all my possessions, everything I owned in the world, everything I had to my name. I had nothing else. Laura had unceremoniously dumped me. Jack had jetted back to the U.S. to his young son, freaked out by the earthquake and me buried under a pyramid of books. And now Maya had bailed on me, abandoning me in this foreign airport. I had been stripped of everything and now was only a bundle of raw nerve endings.

Calm down, breathe, I kept intoning to myself. I fingered the vial of Xanax out of my pocket, popped the cap surreptitiously, shook one into my palm and looked at the blue pill as if looking at the microcosm of my life and what it had become: a tiny nothing of anxiety, the heart of an elephant in a flea. I slipped the pill into my mouth, crushed it with my front teeth, let the bitter granulations sink beneath my tongue, then got up and walked down the jetway, like a condemned man to the electric chair, to my waiting plane.

The seat next to me, of course, was empty. Though I was sure someone would soon upgrade, hopefully not some obese monster with a carry-on meal! I kept breathing in and out, trying to slow down the revving of anxiety in my now feverish brain. As I waited for the pill to take effect I put my earbuds in, opened my laptop and watched the last of *Nostalgia for the Light*.

The ending was haunting. A Chilean woman in her thirties, rocking a child on her knee, told about how Pinochet and his henchmen had taken her parents away from her when she was two years old, handed her over to the care of her grandparents, how she never saw her parents again, and how she saw a new life in her son, though a generation was ripped from her soul. Her absence of anger and her philosophical approach to life left an indelible impression.

The flight attendant caught my eye. "Would you like something to drink?" she asked in flawless English.

"Yes. *Un copa de viña roja, por favor.*" The Xanax was kicking in. I kept thinking about the woman, an astronomer, in the documentary, and what she had silently suffered her whole life, and how she had found a way to cope.

As the door to the plane closed I shut my eyes and breathed in as deeply as I could. For a moment I fantasized straightening to my feet and bolting. But, where? Santiago? Without my possessions? No car? I had nowhere else to go but the Atacama Desert! Even if it was without Maya. Surely I would find something at the end of the world! A piece of frangible gypsum to grasp onto, an ecosystem where nothing thrived, a mass grave with nothing but bones and the sorrowing women of The Disappeared raking over them with their raw and cracked bare hands. Pure nothingness. Bring it on, God! I came to the terrifying conclusion that I was clearly entering the realm of the unsound.

The plane taxied, then started down the runway, gathering speed. It started rumbling, vibrating, building up to something that, in my head, felt like an apotheosis of doom. Then, suddenly, its wheels had kicked free from the tarmac and we were airborne, lumbering into the sky with a tremendous power propelling us. A long-time sufferer of claustrophobia, as well as acrophobia, for the first time in an airplane I felt totally free. I did something I normally don't do: I gazed out the window. There were the Andes, majestic and cloud-shrouded, snow crowning their crests, framed by a sky so midnight blue it could have been the color of my heart at that moment because I really didn't care if I died.

The Atacama

The two-hour flight transited me from dusk to night. By the time the plane landed I was feeling so out of my body that I didn't know who I was anymore. I felt like I had been slipped some *ayahuasca* and had gone on a journey inside my head where Chile was nothing more than a ribbon of roads within the network of my brain.

We touched down at Calama, a small airport in San Pedro de Atacama. As I came down the jetway my panic started up again. I was all alone in the world, in a place where people came to be, and experience being, all alone in the universe, beneath the most magnificent canopy of stars visible anywhere in the world.

Suddenly, I stopped. I thought I was hallucinating. Seated in the lounge, facing the window and looking out over the tarmac was a strikingly beautiful woman. I stared, then started forward haltingly. The closer I neared to her the more positive I was that it was ...

"Maya?" I said.

She turned. It *was* her! "Miles."

I set my carry-on down. I almost wept openly. "When did you get in?"

"Yesterday."

"Yesterday?"

"Yes. Remember?"

"I thought you'd blown me off. Did I get my days wrong?" Tears blurred my vision. "It's been an insane trip. The earthquake. I lost my cellphone ..."

Maya rose and engulfed me in her arms. "It's all right, Miles," she whispered in my ear. "You're lucky because I was on the next flight out." She disengaged herself and looked me directly in the eyes. "I thought you had blown *me* off."

"Jesus Christ," I said. "This is so ridiculously incredible. I almost didn't get on that plane."

She gripped my head with both her hands and then our lips found each other's and it was as if we had fused into one. My hands sought purchase on her powerful back and athletic shoulders. The force of her hug nearly crushed me, and I willingly surrendered to it. I don't think I had ever willingly surrendered to anything in my life. It suddenly struck me that I don't think I had truly loved anyone in my life. Until this moment. And I didn't believe in fate. But there was something surreal here in the Atacama, how we had nearly missed each other and then re-found each other in this airport. In that lung-emptying embrace I glimpsed the palimpsest of a great love, and my heart deliquesced to water and flowed somewhere so peaceful I could finally breathe again.

"So, I hope you're not still planning to fly back to Santiago?" I asked rhetorically.

"No," she said. "I flew all the way here to be with you. And when you didn't show I thought maybe you had gone out, started drinking ..."

I shook my head. "I don't do that anymore, Maya. I stop at a glass or two now. Life is too precious to squander it in the gutter like that."

"I believe you," she said.

"What's our hotel like?"

"Un-fucking-be-liev-a-ble!"

I wrapped my arms around her again and drew her close to me, and held her as tightly as I could. I didn't want to let go this time.

"And you should see the stars," she whispered into my ear, "Oh, my God!"

"It's the driest desert on the planet," I said. "Nothing grows here. There's zero humidity. No ambient light. Stargazing is supposed to be surreal. For once I need to look at the stars," I said cryptically.

She held me by my shoulders. "Chile has changed you, hasn't it?"

"Chile has changed me. Yes."

Tierra (Firma) Atacama

Tierra Atacama is a luxury resort just outside San Pedro de Atacama, the main town that services the tourists who come from all over the world to see the desert's unique beauty.

Maya and I held hands on the limousine shuttle ride to the resort. We hardly spoke. There was a feeling that flowed through us like an endless loop, a uroboric stream. After the anxiety-riddled flight, a peace had come over me like a drug whose euphoria didn't seem laced with its evil opposite: dysphoria. After two months in Chile, Ping-Ponging around, in search of some semblance of a foundation to my life, I didn't find it necessarily in a place, or in a thing, or in a profession, but rather in a person. For once in my chaotic and depression-fueled life I was, or so I believed, glimpsing the restorative power of love. I was completely in the power of this woman who had traveled 7,000 miles across the equator and had leapt into my soul and rescued me from the abyss of despair.

Yes, Chile had transformed me.

"You're my eavesdropping angel," I said.

"Your what?"

"You're always hovering over my soul."

Maya tilted her head to one side, an affectation of hers, and smiled. We kissed in the limousine.

We checked into the hotel, freshened up in our room, and then went to dinner in the resort's restaurant. Maya had brought a bottle of her recent Chardonnay and Pinot Noir. I wanted to know all about her wines and her collapsed relationship with Cliff—she waved me off—and she wanted to know all about my trip. As humorously as I could I narrated my adventures. She laughed uproariously at the *yunta de bueyes* story and the Fiat 500, shook her head back and forth in dismay and incredulity at my vivid recreation of the earthquake at the Count's and how I was found buried alive under all his priceless and rare books. She reached for my hand across the table and squeezed it firmly when I described my near fatal panic attack at the airport. "And then when I saw you here in Calama I really did believe, for a fleeting second, that there was a God."

"Chile really has changed you," she reiterated. "I can hear it in your voice, Miles."

"I think getting out of L.A. has changed me more than anything else. I came here with only the clothes on my back. I gave up my apartment, my books, put everything into storage. I lived the writing life. And it hasn't always been easy. And, after much suffering, I found success. And I thought what I wanted was complete dispossession of all material everything. I wanted to be blown to the four corners of the world by a fickle wind. And what I learned, in the end, is that I longed for connection. That's all. The books, the movies, none of that matters if you don't have someone to share it with, someone who, when they hang the morphine, can look down at you and smile seraphically, and there's peace in knowing that they know; they know the life you've lived. And I want to be that person for you, too, Maya. We have so much to explore."

Maya smiled warmly, a kind of peace descending over her.

We left the restaurant, arms slung around each other, and returned to our stunning room, changed into our bathing suits, then went outside to the resort's pool, perched on the edge of the vast Atacama desert, a metaphor, if ever there was one, for the journey of my life. The air was nippy, but the water made us feel as if there were no atmosphere, only our bodies floating in a temperature-controlled equilibrium. We lolled our heads back and gazed up at the heavens. We were at nearly 8,000 feet, in the driest desert on the planet, with no ambient light, and the sky was luxuriant, literally encrusted, with stars, so luminous, so refulgent, so incandescent, it was almost as if we were in New York City at night during a snowstorm, or immured in one of those little glass globes depicting a yuletide scene that when you shake it it shows you a simulacrum of a wintry night on a farm in New England during Christmas. Yes, we were at 8,000 feet, but the nebulae were so fantastically lit up that it was as if they had been lowered down over us and were coruscating all around us, not just above. Meteors and shooting stars and comets and supernovas seemed to be zigzagging across the sky with manic regularity. So often the cosmos looks fixed, unmoving, even if one knows this astronomically not to be true. But, here in the Atacama Desert the empyrean was constantly alive, in flux. Maybe explosions we were witnessing had happened millions of years ago and their light was just now reaching our atmosphere, but it lent the impression that time no longer had any finite value, that we were just part of a vast continuum and that, in the end, death was not to be feared, but rather seen as that uroboric return to the beginning.

"And what I'm really thinking when I look up there," I said to Maya, "is how fleeting life is. This life. Our physical body on this planet. It just goes so quickly."

"I know," she said. "I wasn't sure I wanted to come. I didn't know what you would be like, Miles. But that last email you wrote me, where you practically begged me to come ..."

"No, I did not," I said.

"Yes, you did," she chided.

"Well, I was pretty panicked after that first earthquake."

"There was a lot of feeling in it that I hadn't seen in you before. You opened up to me in a way that you've never opened up before. You showed me your heart."

"In Santa Ynez, when you came into the room, and you closed your hand around my throat and just took charge of me, I didn't know if you did that in anger, or frustration, or in a demonstration of love. But I remember surrendering, just letting go, not fighting it. I think I almost wanted you to strangle me to death, then and there. I wanted to die looking into your eyes because I knew that those eyes were the ones I wanted to see on my death bed."

"Oh, look," she exclaimed, gesticulating to the sky. I looked up and saw yet another asteroid or whatever celestial body cross a section of the star-scintillated sky and then explode into nothingness. "Remember the comet?" she said. "That first time, a long time ago, when you came up to Santa Ynez?"

"Yeah. I do. But, here, it's so much more spectacular."

"So much more spectacular."

"I was thinking. You're such a fantastic winemaker, Maya. I've traveled all around Chile. The soils are amazing—alluvial, granite, volcanic, really mineral rich. The waters from the Andes are just mind-blowing in their purity. You can taste it in your mouth. Hell, see it in your hair."

"Yeah, I noticed," she said, ruffling the hair on my head, chuckling.

"It makes your hair thick and wavy. They call it Andean hair down here." She laughed. "No, seriously, the soils are unique here, the waters mysterious. And the land, compared to California, is relatively cheap. There's a community of winemakers down here who are on the precipice of something astonishing, revolutionary, trail-blazing. I can taste Chile's future in these wines. They're not there yet, but they're getting there. I'd love to do Pinot and cool weather Syrah and, my favorite down here, Sauvignon Blanc. In Casablanca Valley or Leyda, places I want to take you to. We could live in Valparaiso, this really cool, charmingly dilapidated city that was once considered the San Francisco of the south. And it, too, like their wine industry, is an emerging gem." I lowered my head from its view of the heavens and looked at another image of heaven: Maya. She was still staring up at the star-ablaze sky, but I knew she was taking in my every word by the thoughtful look of her expression. "And here's the beautiful part. We're on the other side of the equator. Their fall is our spring. We could live in both places ..." I trailed off when she dropped her head and turned to me.

"What are you saying, Miles?"

I blinked back tears. "Marry me."

The End

Epilogue

We spent a week in the Atacama Desert. We visited the Paranal Observatory and were vouchsafed a look that took us so deep into the heavens that it was difficult to come away from the massive eyepiece and still feel the same about planet Earth. We toured the Atacama Salt Flat and saw Salvador Dali-like pink flamingoes on the stilts of their fragile legs against incandescent white terrain and aquamarine waters that came bubbling up from the core of the earth where Chile was always rumbling away. On another excursion we stood agape in the shadow of the Andes at the Tatio Geysers, which spewed their scalding water into cobalt blue skies. At the Puritama Hot Springs we found transcendence in emollient waters.

We flew back to Santiago and I took Maya to Bocanáriz and she got to sample some of her first Chilean wines and pronounced them, as I had, extraordinarily rich and amazingly and surprisingly complex. From Santiago I drove her to Valparaiso where we stayed at the grand Hotel Astoreca in hip *Cerro Alegre*, dined on their huge marble patio that overlooked the harbor. From Valparaiso we tasted our way through the wineries of Casablanca and Leyda Valleys, and Maya started to see what I was talking about. We met winemakers who were passionate about what they were doing, and not just hobbyists like so many of them in the Napa/Sonoma area. Chile, with its daunting recent past, had a promising future.

Over an incredible home-cooked dinner at Amayna Winery, where we were feted in a family-style cottage situated on the property, I said to Maya:

"So, what's your answer?"

She swallowed hard, then looked at me and narrowed her eyes. She looked at me for the longest moment. I thought time had stopped. I didn't know if she was going to say something that would destroy all my dreams or not. Then, she reached a hand to my shirt and grabbed it like a kneading cat. She pulled me toward her and kissed me hard.